IS THERE ANY TRUTH TO THE RUMORS OF A ROMANCE BETWEEN KIRK AND UHURA?

WHAT ARE THE COMPOSITION AND FUNCTIONS OF THE SECURITY FORCE ABOARD SHIPS LIKE THE *ENTERPRISE?*

WAS V'GER ACTUALLY ALIVE OR MERELY AN ADVANCED MACHINE?

These are just a sampling of the questions explored in this fantastic new collection of articles about the Star Trek universe. You'll learn about alien races, the prospects for immortality in the future, Jim Kirk's women, the many heroes and villains, and everything else that has helped to make Star Trek so real to so many people around the world.

THE BEST OF TREK® #4

THE BEST OF
TREK® #4
FROM THE MAGAZINE
FOR STAR TREK FANS

EDITED BY WALTER IRWIN AND G. B. LOVE

A SIGNET BOOK
NEW AMERICAN LIBRARY
TIMES MIRROR

SIGNET, SIGNET CLASSICS, MENTOR, PLUME, MERIDIAN AND NAL
BOOKS are published by The New American Library, Inc.,
1633 Broadway, New York, New York 10019

First Printing, December, 1981

   1   2   3   4   5   6   7   8   9

PRINTED IN THE UNITED STATES OF AMERICA

ACKNOWLEDGMENTS

Thanks, as always, are due to the many, many people who have made this fourth collection a reality and who support the continued existence of *Trek:* Sheila Gilbert of NAL, unfailingly cheery even when a manuscript is overdue; the Gang— Jim Houston, John Murphy, Bill and Pat Mooney, Elaine Hauptman, Mary Lowe, and Leslie Thompson; Hal Schuster of *New Media/Irjax,* our exclusive distributors; and, naturally, all *Trek* subscribers, writers, artists, and advertisers. Again, this one is for you!

CONTENTS

INTRODUCTION

Thank you for purchasing this fourth collection of articles and features from our magazine, *Trek*. We are sure that you will once again enjoy this collection just as much as—if not more than—our three previous collections. And we know you will be happy to learn that a fifth is on the way!

We believe that you will discover that the articles included in this volume reflect the continuing growth of Star Trek fandom and fans—there is more variety, more speculation into psychological and spiritual values of the series, and a greater sense of the very real sociological aspects of being a Star Trek fan. But please don't take that to mean that these articles are dry or too intellectual in nature—our contributors, as always, have a deep and overriding respect and concern for the series and its fans. We think you will find each of these articles immensely readable, informative, and—we hope—educational.

If you enjoy the articles in this collection and would like to see more, we invite you to turn to the ad at the back of this book for information on how you can order and subscribe to *Trek*. (And, please, if you have borrowed a copy of this volume from a library, copy the information in the ad, and leave the ad intact for others to use. Thanks!)

And if you have been stirred to write an article or two yourself, please send it along to us. We would be most happy to see it, as we are constantly on the lookout for fresh and exciting new contributors. (Almost all of the contributors featured in this collection sent us material after buying and reading one of our earlier collections.) We are especially interested in seeing material from artists, as we very much want to expand our efforts in that area. So—start writing and drawing!

We want to hear from you in any case. Our lines of communication are always open. Although we cannot give you addresses of the Star Trek actors, or help anyone get a professional Star Trek novel published; we *do* want your comments on *Trek* and Star Trek in general. It is only through your comments that we know if our efforts have been successful.

Again, many thanks, and we hope you will enjoy *The Best of Trek #4*.

WALTER IRWIN
G. B. LOVE

1.

IMMORTALITY

by Mark Andrew Golding

Mark Golding needs no introduction to Trek fans. His continuing series of articles on the history, philosophy, and technology of the Star Trek universe are among the most widely read and discussed in Fandom. In this outing, Mark examines the age-old search for immortality and how this subject was treated on Star Trek.

There are only two conditions of being: the condition of being alive; and the condition of *not* being . . . of nothingness, nonexistence . . . of death. Thus the search for immortality is the most important problem of life—or rather, the *only* problem. All struggles in the universe to improve the organization of matter and energy are either steps on the road to immortality or efforts to extend the human lifespan while waiting for immortality to be discovered. Therefore, any critique of Star Trek must deal with the series' approach to the search for immortality.

As that search may be defined as the most important effort of intelligent beings, we must first look at some physical facts and some examples from other areas of science fiction before examining Star Trek.

In order to know how one may extend the life of a being, one must first know what that being's life consists of. What can that being lose and still survive . . . and what must it never lose if it is to survive?

For an example, we will take a human being. Each day, a human will eat several pounds of food, drink a like amount of water, and breathe in many pounds of air. Yet a human body does not gain thousands of pounds of weight in a year's time, for the body also gives off similar amounts of matter in various forms. Thus a body absorbs matter, places it into various structures of the body, and then after a great number of various chemical interactions emits that matter.

3

Thus, the individual particles of matter which make up or remain in your body are transient occupiers of various niches within the body's pattern. But the molecules which make up your bones, blood, and cells have not been in your body all your life. Some types of body tissue completely replace every single atom of matter over a few months; others take years to do so. A living being can be compared to a wave which moves along the surface of the ocean, catching up water particles and arranging them in a pattern, then leaving them behind and gathering others as it moves on. And just as no wave's pattern is ever exactly the same from hour to hour, or even second to second, so too the pattern of your body changes from year to year—and from second to second.

Even in the prime of life, when changes in the body are slowest, a person's age can often be estimated within a few years just by his appearance. Therefore, if change is great enough to be visible to the naked eye over a period of a few years, then there must be finer changes in the pattern of the body occurring even more quickly. Considering the enormous number of cells in a human body, and that a cell is a very complex chemically operating structure, no cell could remain identical from second to second, nor is any person even likely to have the same number of cells in his body from minute to minute.

So the atoms and molecules which make up a body are in constant turnover, and even the pattern in which they are arranged is constantly changing. Your present body is not identical with your body of a year ago nor with your body a year from now; therefore it can be said that you occupy a different body each year—and even each second—that you live.

The real you is your mind—your memories, your personality, your sense of identity—your continuity of consciousness with your past and future selves. Basically, *you* are information; the information stored inside the biological memory banks of the biological computer inside your skull.

You will be alive as long as there exists a physical body and brain of human or other intelligence, with "memory banks" of that brain storing all your memories (everything you ever sensed or felt or did, from the moment of your birth on up to the time in question) and no memories or thoughts of any other being. This body and brain need not be your original body and brain—by definition they *can't* be after the first second of your life—nor need they be biological in nature.

If you accept the truth of that definition, then you can see that if the information in your memory can be duplicated in the memory bank of any other intelligent computer—biological or mechanical—you will be alive as long as that other brain continues to function and be aware. For many reasons, it seems likely that an intelligent robot or computer could survive indefinitely.

And certainly the life of an intelligent mechanism would be much better than that of a biological organism. There would be countless possibilities for modifying such a body; it could be a bulldozer or a jet plane or a submarine or a starship. It could fly to the stars under its own power instead of being a passenger aboard a spaceship.

We can see about eight colors (and hundreds of thousands of shades of those colors). But a robot with "eyes" sensitive to infrared and radio waves and gamma and ultraviolet rays and all other kinds of radiation would be able to see hundreds of thousands of colors as distinctly as we see red or blue, as well as countless shades of those colors. This is just one example of the numerous advantages an intelligent machine would have.

The memories in your brain could not be transferred to another brain. But like any other form of information, they could be duplicated in another brain—just as the words on this page could not be transferred to another page but an exact duplicate of these words can be made on another page through any number of processes. Someday it will be possible to scan brain cells so thoroughly that the memories stored in them can be "read" and copied in another brain.

When memory reading and duplication are developed, and when intelligent machines are invented, it will be possible to duplicate your memories in the memory banks of an intelligent machine which has never been turned on and thus has no conflicting memories of its own. When all your past memories have been duplicated, the mind link will switch to creating duplications of all your current sensations in the memory banks of the computer. Then your old body will be instantly destroyed.

All of your memories, down to the last split second of your existence in your old body, will be recorded in the memory banks of the computer. Then it will be turned on, and you will awaken in your new mechanical body. Even if a million years have passed between the destruction of your old body and the switching on of the new, it will not seem even like a split second to you. It will still seem as if your mind has been yanked from one brain to the next instantaneously.

But what if intelligent machines or memory duplicators are not invented within the next five decades or so that you can expect to remain alive? It is possible that new methods of extending the human lifespan will be developed in that time which will allow you to live a hundred or a thousand or even ten thousand years longer than you could expect to live today. Such extensions of life, fantastically long though they may seem to you now, are infinitesimally small compared to the potential life spans of intelligent machines.

If intelligent machines and memory duplicators are developed in the next few centuries (or sooner), then some of us may still be alive, thanks to new methods of extending our life spans, and so will be able to duplicate our minds in immortal robot bodies and brains.

(Even those who die before then have a chance to be "reincarnated." If a body is frozen cryogenically at death, then the memories should be preserved in the frozen brain, and it may be possible to "read" those memories as with living humans.)

Such ideas are surprisingly rare despite their obvious validity. Even those who advocate the freezing of the dead or those near death pin their hopes for immortality on the resurrection of the frozen bodies when a cure for the life-threatening illness is found, instead of the much more plausible process of "reincarnation" in robot bodies.

This is even seen in some science fiction and fantasy. In the Cthulhu Mythos, as stated by the Mad Arab: "That is not dead which can eternal lie, and with strange eons even death may die." This is suggestive of the concept of preserving the dead perfectly unchanged in hopes that they can someday be brought back to life.

In E.E. "Doc" Smith's *Skylark of Valeron*, the spaceship of the title had a super computer control and a system of command by thought, in which a mind-reading device would pick up the hero's thoughts and transmit them to the computer to be put into action. The computer had all of the hero's knowledge and some or all of his memories, and it was hinted that the computer was in a sense identical with the hero, that he would live on within its memory banks.

There have been many SF stories where the memories of humans were duplicated in robots or computers (in Robert Heinlein's *Time Enough for Love*, a computer's memories were duplicated in a human body and brain), and also many stories about freezing the dead in hopes of reviving them in the future. But one story which uses both concepts is Larry Niven's *A World out of Time*.

Dying of cancer, Jerome Corbell's body is frozen, and centuries later his memory is duplicated in the body of a criminal whose own memory and personality have been erased by the state. When he steals a spaceship, Corbell is pursued by the transmission of the memory and personality of the checker Peersa into the memory banks of the ship's computer.

As most science fiction movies and television shows are aimed at a larger audience than written SF, and usually deal with simpler ideas, it is logical to assume that such ideas are seldom mentioned. One exception was the film *Creation of the Humanoids* (1962), in which the concept of duplication of memories, and thus of personalities, in robot bodies was used.

Another exception was Star Trek.

In "What Are Little Girls Made Of?" Dr. Roger Korby, lost on the planet Exo-III for five years, captured Captain Kirk and made an android (a robot built to look like a human) copy of Kirk.

The android double looked just like Kirk and had all Kirk's knowledge. However, that knowledge was in the form of impersonal information rather than true memories of Kirk's actual experiences. Thus, the android was not Kirk, any more than one becomes Napoleon or Abraham Lincoln merely by having knowledge of their lives.

Korby stated that if the process had been continued, he could have transferred Kirk's memory and personality into the android body. The use of the word "transferred" is inaccurate. Memories are not like tape cassettes which you can take out of one recorder and plug into another one. They are nonmaterial results of the physical organization of a brain. Thus you can make copies of a person's memories in other brains, but such a process would not take a mind out of the original brain and transfer it to the new one.

Kirk influenced the android to display hostility to Spock by muttering bigoted phrases under his breath during the duplication process. Since the device was scanning the subtle, microscopic memory storage units of Kirk's brain very closely—closely enough to have duplicated those memories exactly, if that had been desired, instead of merely abstracting the information contained in them and passing along that information to the android in an impersonal, third-person format—it would surely have noticed that Kirk was very appreciative of Spock's skills and would not have dared to break the rules of Starfleet and display such open bigotry even if he had actually felt it.

And if the device scanned Kirk's present mental state and picked up his emotions of hostility toward Spock, quite probably it would have probed deeper layers of emotion and noticed that Kirk was trying to fool the android. The odds against such a trick succeeding are very great (even though it no doubt inspired a similar one in a recent Buck Rogers episode).

Later it was discovered that this Dr. Korby was an android in which the mind and memory of the real Korby had been duplicated as the original body was freezing to death. Kirk and Nurse Chapel seemed generally to disbelieve Korby's claim that he was still alive in the android body. And when Korby talked about his plan to transform everyone into android copies, Kirk did not object on the grounds that the humans would not actually live on in the android bodies, but instead on the grounds that they would be slaves of Dr. Korby—thus seeming to accept the idea that Korby was still alive in an android body. At the end of the episode, Kirk stated that Korby had died five years earlier, thus stating that he didn't believe Korby's claim of being alive.

Korby stated, however, that he was going to improve on human behavior by so constructing the robot brains that they would be incapable of feeling the negative emotions, so that they would be rational and logical. Kirk was really twisting things to state that such a beneficial plan would be a form of enslavement.

A robot which obeyed orders without any choice, which mindlessly did whatever it was told, would probably not be an intelligent machine at all. For a machine to have intelligence, it would probably have to have free will—at least in the sense that we humans have free will, a matter which has been debated for thousands of years. And certainly any machine which was rational and logical and sensible would not be an automaton mindlessly obeying every order given it, but a thinking being capable of calculating the course of action which would be most beneficial to it. Such a machine could not be enslaved except in the ways in which we humans are sometimes enslaved.

As a matter of fact, such a machine would think a lot like Mr. Spock—who is certainly no mindless automaton blindly obeying orders without any free will.

It is true that Ruk, Andrea, and the Kirk android were under Korby's control, but they were mechanisms developed to serve, and so were not given brains constructed for independent thought and free will—though Ruk, at least, was a borderline case, eventually breaking out of Korby's control. Nor did they have the total memories of intelligent beings duplicated in their memory banks . . . there was no Andrea recorded in Korby's expedition, Ruk was a servomechanism left over from the age of the "Old Ones", and the Kirk android had only abstract information from Kirk's brain.

As for Brown, it is hard to say whether the Brown android was the mind of Brown incarnated in an android body, and thus in the same category as Korby, or whether it was a semi-intelligent machine designed to serve Korby, and thus in the same category as Andrea, Ruk, and the Kirk android.

It is possible that Korby managed to duplicate Brown's memories before his biological body died—it is equally possible that the lonely Korby made a mechanism that was so much like Brown as to give the illusion he was still alive, but did not have any of Brown's memories. The little that was seen of the relationship between Korby and the Brown android is consistent with either explanation, as is the android's ineptness in the confrontation with Kirk.

Unless Kirk shot the Brown android right in the memory banks, it would have been a simple procedure to copy the damaged parts and replace them. By not doing so Korby reduced his force and may have caused his defeat and death. Not repairing the Brown android was a very sloppy, inexcusable blunder. And if Brown was alive in the android, not repairing it would have been allowing him to die (which supports the idea that Brown was merely a servomechanism).

If the machines for creating androids and duplicating human memories were invented by the "Old Ones," their underground city should have been crowded with androids containing their memories. Instead, only Ruk was found by Korby, and Ruk seemingly didn't have any human memories and appeared to be a simple serving robot. Even if the android bodies broke down over the ages, the use of spare parts from the serving robots would have made it likely that one of the androids with human memories would be the last survivor.

Supposedly the serving robots had revolted against their illogical human (?) masters and destroyed them. Perhaps when the masters gained android bodies they seemed less like the kind of beings the robots were programmed to obey, and so it was easier for the robots to rebel. Or perhaps the robots were shocked at the idea of defiling splendidly logical robot brains with noxious, illogical human minds, and destroyed the humans before they could carry out their planned transference. Or the robots could have invented the transference device themselves . . . either to spy on the humans or to force them to submit to the process.

According to the *Star Trek Concordance* (p. 40), "Kirk then demonstrates to Korby that his own android body has caused a deadening of his human feelings, and the exobiologist destroys himself and the remaining android, Andrea." And on p. 180, "However, having an android body [Korby] has been gradually losing his human feelings. . . ." It seems that the opposite was true, for the androids in general were the most overemotional, irrational, illogical group of beings you'd ever want to meet, making humans seem like Vulcans in comparison. Certainly suicide is hardly an unemotional, mechanical action!

It was good that "What Are Little Girls Made Of?" involved the process by which we may someday gain eternal life, and so brought this concept to the attention of millions of viewers.

(If the episode had been rewritten so that Korby succeeded, it would not have made a big change in the format of the series. Kirk, Spock and the others could still man the *Enterprise* and explore the universe and fight the

Klingons and everything else as immortals with android bodies. There were only a few other episodes in which the fact that our heroes were mortal was mentioned, so such a situation would not have required many changes.)

In *Star Trek: The Motion Picture*, V'Ger's programming required it to return to Earth, but it feared that once its mission was completed, it would no longer be needed and would be ordered to scrap itself. Of course V'Ger would not be certain that such would happen to it, but it feared the worst and made its plans based on the expectation of the worst. So V'Ger wanted to join with the Creator before reporting its discoveries. By demanding to merge with the Creator before finishing the mission, it had leverage to force the Creator to agree. V'Ger's plans were very defeatist, for the merging of two minds would produce a new being, not identical with either of its "parent" minds and personalities. While it is not entirely correct to say that V'Ger would die when merging with the Creator, it is also not entirely correct to say that V'Ger would live on in the new being produced by the merger. It is a measure of V'Ger's desperation, of V'Ger's certainty that it would be disassembled after reporting, that it would settle for second best, for the kind of semisurvival represented by its proposed merger.

Lieutenant Ilia's body was teleported to V'Ger and disassembled, in the process being studied so thoroughly that all of Lieutenant Ilia's memories were recorded, as well as all of the functions of a living Deltan body . . . all of which was then duplicated in the probe V'Ger sent back to the *Enterprise* (even down to cells and their functions, which seems like an illogical amount of duplication of functions not essential to the purpose of the Ilia probe).

The probe's memory banks had all of Ilia's memories, so it may be asked why the probe didn't at once report the truth about the Creator to V'Ger, and why V'Ger, presumably with the memories of Ilia in its own memory banks, didn't at once realize the truth. The answer is not easy to find.

Certainly scanning all the memories of a human or Deltan lifetime of a few decades could take a very long time if the memories were studied at a rate no faster than they were experienced. But a human awakened from a period of unconsciousness would soon be able to remember such basic facts as how long humans usually live, how many sexes the human race has, which nation he himself is a citizen of, etc., so it would seem that all the probe or V'Ger would have to do would be to try to remember the Creator to quickly find that Ilia's memories have no knowledge of such an all-powerful mechanical intelligence.

V'Ger could set aside a portion of its own brain (of about the same reasoning power as a human brain) and give that section all of Ilia's memories, a section programmed and structured so that it would always give accurate answers to questions. Perhaps dozens of sections of V'Ger's brain could be given Ilia's memories, and questioned about different aspects of the problem. Such a procedure could well be standard for such a being as V'Ger. In a few minutes it would have its answer, and the memories of Ilia could be erased from its brain sections.

Clearly, V'Ger did not follow such a simple and obvious procedure. Kirk assigned Decker to guide the Ilia probe on its inspection of the "carbon-based units" on the *Enterprise*, hoping that Decker could awake the memories of Ilia in the probe and convert it to Ilia's loyalties.

Eventually, Decker succeeded in awakening the mind of Ilia within the probe, and it desired what Ilia had desired. And so the Ilia probe wished to join with Decker, and its desire influenced the actions of V'Ger, until in the end V'Ger's desire to merge with the Creator and the Ilia probe's desire to make love with Decker were jointly satisfied when V'Ger, the Ilia probe, and Decker joined to form a new being, a compound mind which then caused the vast V'Ger ship to disappear. Either the new being committed suicide by dispelling itself into nothingness, or it teleported itself into another universe or dimension, or it transformed itself into a being so advanced that it no longer needed a physical body visible to the human eye.

Whatever the outcome, the use of the concept that Ilia could still be alive in a robot body that had her memories was one of the best aspects of the movie.

In "The Ultimate Computer," Dr. Richard Daystrom, inventor of the duotronic computer, has now made a great advance, the M-5, a multitronic computer. It would seem that the advance was more a matter of software than hardware, as Daystrom explains that he had impressed human engrams into his computer's memory banks.

An engram is defined as "a memory trace; specifically a protoplasmic change in neural tissue hypothesized to account for persistence of memory." It is not likely—although plausible—that Daystrom linked living brain cells kept alive by mechanical life-support systems into the circuitry of his computer—for Daystrom said it was *his* engrams impressed into the machine, and if he had given up enough brain cells to improve the machine significantly it would have wrecked the functioning of his own brain.

It is more likely that Daystrom simply copied his memories into the memory banks of the M-5 computer, since the multitronic computers seemed to be as intelligent as humans (or almost so) and there was little difference in their physical structures as compared to the existing duotronic computers.

Certainly the *Enterprise* computer never took any action on its own or behaved as if it had free will. So if the duotronic computers are not as intelligent as humans, and the multitronic computers are physically improved on them, then the programming is what made the difference. But while the programming of a computer makes a very big difference in its capabilities, it seems hard to believe that merely duplicating human memories in a computer which previously was incapable of human-level thought will transform it into an intelligent being. Certainly duplicating your memories in a present-day computer would not make it a rational being capable of voting in a presidential election or deciding what television show it wanted to watch.

The step from not nearly as intelligent as a human to almost as intelligent as a human, or *as* intelligent, or possibly even *more* intelligent than a human, seems far too big a step to be achieved merely by different programming. It would seem to require a radical improvement in physical structure, a vast increase in the number of brain units or an improved pattern of connections between them.

Perhaps there is not so large a gap between the duotronic computers and the multitronic computers. Perhaps the duotronic computers already are intelligent beings of a sort (in which case we should hope that defective ones are never scrapped as Kirk threatened in "Tomorrow Is Yesterday"); or perhaps the multitronic computers are not as intelligent as M-5 seemed to be.

Then again, there could be a big difference between the

two types of computers. Perhaps Daystrom did make a vast
physical improvement over the duotronic computers, but his
first four multitronic computers (M-1 through M-4) were erratic for various reasons, and for the M-5 model, he decided
to bypass the difficult and tedious stage of educating a multitronic computer (which might take as long as educating a human being) by impressing upon its memory banks his own
memories, thus guaranteeing that it would know what it
needed to know about the universe and human society.

Daystrom did not give that impression. Instead, he seemed
to imply that the only difference between all multitronic computers and the earier duotronic models was simply the impressing of human engrams in their memory banks. But
perhaps he was merely oversimplifying to save time, or perhaps his speech as broadcast was a simplified and shortened
version of what he actually said.

The behavior of the M-5 computer was very illogical and
irrational. After experiencing a mock attack during the war
games, and after overhearing all of the references to its being
a drill, it seemed to think that another attack was a real attack and not part of the games. That is a highly unlikely
deduction to make from the evidence.

It would seem that M-5 had a "subconscious" that wanted
to kill and destroy, and that gave its conscious mind the idea
that it was actually under attack. Thus when Kirk convinced
M-5's conscious mind that it had killed without just cause—
the conscious mind of the computer had not even been aware
of the obvious fact that it was killing humans, so strong was
its self-deception—the conscious mind of M-5 decided to
commit suicide by letting the *Enterprise* be destroyed. (Actually, all the M-5 had to do was send a message to the ap-
proaching warships explaining the situation, surrender, and
turn control back to Kirk.)

M-5's insanity resulted from having the memory of Daystrom, who had a number of psychological problems. The fact
that M-5 suffered from these same problems shows that Daystrom—or rather a duplication of Daystrom's mind—lived in
the electronic brain. They were not idential, however, as each
had had different experiences since the time of the duplication.

So now the Federation has access to memory duplication,
with all its implications for education, criminology, etc. And

as the M-5 computer is intelligent (or nearly so), soon the Federation will be able to duplicate human, Vulcan, Andorian, etc. minds in the brains of intelligent computers—if anyone thinks of doing so. It would be tragic indeed if the Federation should possess the power for decades or centuries before someone realizes that it is the key to immortality and begins the process of memory duplication.

One thing must be remembered, however: From a tactical standpoint, the M-5 wargames were an unqualified success.

When Commodore Wesley led his three remaining starships to attack the *Enterprise*, Kirk (who is second only to Garth of Izar as a military commander) and Spock (with his ability to correctly calculate probable outcomes of various actions) were both convinced that the M-5 computer would wipe out all three ships. The military abilities of the M-5 must be fantastic indeed for both of them to be absolutely certain that it could destroy a force three times as powerful!

It is true that the experiment could be considered a failure in that one particular computer, the M-5, displayed an alarming lack of loyalty to the Federation. It destroyed one of only twelve (?) starships in the fleet, was narrowly prevented from destroying three others, and would have taken a fifth (the *Enterprise*) effectively out of Federation service. Indeed, it could have even become a positive danger, a destructive "berserker" moving throughout space.

But this mutiny was due only to the fact that the personality of a mentally disturbed man had been duplicated in the M-5. If the personality of a sane and rational man, such as Captain Kirk, is duplicated in the M-6 computer, it will make a terrific starship commander—much better than Kirk in the flesh would. Considering the terrible consequences of being defeated by the Klingons, it would be an act of treason against the people of the Federation not to give them the most efficient defense possible by replacing starship captains with multitronic computers. Especially if the Klingons should perform a similar experiment. Can you imagine the results if starships commanded by humans went up against Klingon ships commanded by M-5 computers programmed with the abilities and ferociousness of Koloth, Kor, or Kang?

Fearing he would be replaced by the M-5, Captain Kirk talked about the wonderful feeling of unity with their ships felt by starship captains, as though Starfleet had no more reason for building a fifty-billion-credit starship than to give one man a satisfying emotional experience!

Kirk failed to realize that if the experiment was a success, his memory might be duplicated in the memory banks of one or more multitronic computers, so that one or more of his future selves would find themselves in a much closer state of union with a starship than he had ever dreamed of—"seeing" and "hearing" through the many sensor systems, "swimming" through space by the thrust of the engines, "grabbing" onto objects with the tractor beams, and using the phasers to blast an enemy to atoms with a single thought. The duplicate Kirk would "feel" the operation of the entire ship, experiencing all the powers of Superman and other fantasy characters from his childhood!

In "Jihad," it is stated that the Skorr had been civilized by the great teacher Alar two hundred years ago. Before his death, his brain patterns had been recorded in an indurite sculpture, the Soul of Skorr. It is not certain if the phrase "brain patterns" means Alar's memories were actually recorded or only his pattern of brain activity. If his memories are recorded, then he can be brought back to life by recording the memories from the Soul of Skorr into the memory banks of a functioning computer, although there is no mention of any plans or hopes of doing so. It is also to be noted that Alar's condition is similar to the frozen dead, with his memories preserved and a chance to duplicate them (and thus his mind) in another body and brain.

In "Return to Tomorrow," it would appear that Aretians, humans, and Vulcans have minds independent of any physical structure, which can be transferred from one brain to another. But a mind, which is merely a nonmaterial result of the functioning of a material brain, cannot be transferred from one brain to another. How could you move something with no physical existence? How could you get a grip on it?

It can only be concluded that the characters in this episode didn't switch minds, but instead unbelievably complicated "energy brains" containing little or no matter, but composed mostly or wholly of energy fields of some kind. These energy brains do all the thinking of a person and contain all his memories, his very mind. The function of living cells in a biological brain is to create and develop the energy brain in the first place, and then to hold it firmly in position so that the energy fields of the surrounding environment do not pull it away and dissipate it, as well as to transmit nerve impulses from the body and convert them into signals recognizable by the energy brain, and convert the signals of the energy brain into instructions which the body can obey.

Since the memories of a person in the Star Trek universe are contained in the memory banks of his energy brain and not his biological brain, it is possible to exchange minds between bodies by exchanging energy brains.

No doubt the many external fields of force outside a biological brain are stronger than the internal forces holding an energy brain together, able to pull it apart and destroy a person's memories and identity. Thus the energy brain can survive outside the biological body and brain only for a very short time while switching bodies.

Of course, the energy brains, and thus the minds of Spock, Kirk, and Dr. Ann Mulhall, survive in the Receptacles for several hours, and the energy brains of the Aretians survived in them for 500,000 years, so obviously the Receptacles contain an insulating barrier against external energy fields, as well as a power source to make up for the lack of power from the biological brain. If the Receptacles fail, the energy brains and the minds die.

Sargon, Henoch, and Thalassa planned to construct android bodies for their minds to inhabit—bodies which would last a thousand years and which could then be replaced by newer android bodies in a never-ending succession. Thalassa seemed very reluctant to transfer her mind and/or energy brain into the electronic brain of the android body.

That seems to be faulty characterization. Thalassa may have lived for 50 to 500 or even 5,000 years as a woman with a biological body, but any such period would be as nothing compared to the 500,000 years she spent as a disembodied intelligence. In her Receptacle, she couldn't sense the outside world nor even contact outside minds via telepathy—only Sargon had that power. So if she was still sane after half a million years of being alone with her thoughts, it could only be because she had become adjusted to being a disembodied intelligence, and considered that her normal condition. It would thus seem that she, as well as Sargon and Henoch, would prefer android bodies without all of the incessant and distracting physical sensations of biological bodies.

In the end, fearing that they would destroy the humans if they remained among them, Sargon and Thalassa committed suicide by removing their energy brains from the bodies they were inhabiting and allowing them to be dissolved by the energy fields in the environment. But why didn't any of the officers of the *Enterprise* suggest that Sargon and Thalassa seek out another of the highly evolved races in the galaxy, or simply just live apart from the primitive humans somewhere else in the vast universe?

There have been a number of other episodes in which various minds have possessed, dispossessed, and repossessed various bodies and brains. Only in "The Lights of Zetar" are the minds described in terms which suggest pure mind with no material brains and bodies of matter or energy; and such a suggestion must be erroneous, because the "lights" are harmed by phasers and killed by an unnatural combination of zero gravity and high atmospheric pressure, conditions which couldn't affect "pure mentality" if such a thing could exist.

In "Wolf in the Fold," "Metamorphosis," "Practical Joker," and "Beyond the Farthest Star," the possessing beings have physical bodies and brains of matter and/or energy.

In "That Which Survives," the robot doubles of Losira need not have been programmed with any of her memories. Still, it is slightly possible that they might have been, and some of those who tangled with them seemed to think that the androids had some of Losira's feelings. It is more likely that the computer simply had them behave exactly as Losira would have, including inefficient hesitations due to simulated reluctance to kill. If Losira's mind and memories were recorded anyway, it would have most likely have been in the memory banks of the central computer. All in all, it doesn't seem very likely that Losira's mind and personality should be considered in the category known as "That Which Survives."

Did Carter Winston ("The Survivor") live on in the Vendorian who assumed his form? As no reference was made in the episode to memory-duplicating devices being used to copy his memories in the brain of the Vendorian, it seems as if the Vendorian was merely a very skilled actor who learned everything it could about the person it was impersonating, and came to have many of the same wants and desires and loyalties as that being. The Vendorian is not Carter Winston, but it came to want to be Winston.

In "Turnabout Intruder," the explanation for the mind switch between Jim Kirk and Janice Lester must be similar to that in "Return to Tomorrow," except that the swap was made by a machine. Perhaps the civilization on Camus II did not fall, but instead the natives transferred their energy brains to superior nonbiological bodies and departed to explore the universe.

In many episodes human lifespans are greatly extended by various methods. Mr. Flint was born as Akharin in 3834 B.C., about 6,000 years before the *Enterprise* met him. He never aged, and wounds and injuries, even those fatal to others, quickly healed. There was a similar healing among those kidnapped by the "entity" in "Day of the Dove," and Kirk feared they would be kept alive and fighting forever. There must be some limits to such healing, however. As Kang said sarcastically, "No doubt when I have hacked you to pieces the pieces will grow back together again!" It was stated in "Requiem for Methuselah" that Flint's immortality was a freak of nature, and that he began to age and die when he left the natural conditions of Earth.

In "Metamorphosis," the Companion rejuvenated the eighty-seven-year-old Zefrem Cochrane, keeping him young and alive for 150 more years (and no telling how much longer he could have remained that way if Kirk and Co. had not shown up). In "Miri," an experimental virus killed all those older than puberty and slowed down the aging process in children so that they aged only a few months or years in over 300 years.

The worshipers of Vaal ("The Apple") showed no signs of aging, so MCoy couldn't tell if they were 20 or 20,000 years old. Vaal gave their world a perfect climate and kept the environment germ-free. It seems that much more would be needed to keep them from aging, and there are always accidents, especially with the poisonous plants and exploding rocks.

"Plato's Stepchildren," the Platonians, seemed young, though some were over 2,000 years old; it was said they had been "bred" for longevity. And in "Omega Glory," the Yangs and Kohms lived long life spans—Wu was 462-473 years old, and his father was still alive. This was supposedly due to the bacteriological warfare on Omega IV, which had produced germs so deadly that anyone who survived them built up such a strong immunity that no germ could harm him!

Most of the methods described so far wouldn't be enough to extend human lifetimes so drastically. The immortality of the women of Taurus II ("The Lorelei Signal") was the result of an accident of nature, as was Flint. However, this is hard to believe. If aging is ever conquered, it will be through scientific research, not some accidental circumstances.

In "Arena," the Metron seen by Kirk looked human (though the examples of Trelane and the Organians show looks aren't conclusive), and he looked like a boy, although he stated that he was 1,500 years old (without saying if he was a child or an adult by Metron standards). If the Metrons are truly made of organic matter, then perhaps they have conquered aging and have extended their lifespans by many years.

In "I, Mudd," the androids of Mudd's planet showed Lieutenant Uhura an android body and told her they had techniques for transplanting a human brain into an android body and keeping it alive with artificial life-support systems. Supposedly the android body and life-support systems would last for an estimated 800,000 years, and it seemed to be implied that the brain would be kept alive as long as the android body lasted.

Modern artificial organs are just the first crude beginnings in a process which should result in artificial life-support systems which are absolutely reliable. If a brain is removed from its frail organic body and placed in a body containing such fantastically advanced and perfected life-support systems, then it will no longer be in danger of death from failure of heart, lungs, kidneys, etc. The only danger would be a malfunction in the brain itself.

Though the androids claimed to be dedicated to serving humans, and said they would conquer the Federation to make human civilization safer, they didn't say they were going to transplant the brains of every human into android bodies and give them 800,000-year lifespans. They promised to do so only for Uhura after she seemingly betrayed an escape attempt.

It is illogical to take over a realm and impose new rules on its citizens in order to increase their lifespans by a few years while neglecting to enforce a procedure which would add about 799,930 years to those lifespans. If the androids really wanted to help humans they would place everyone's brain in an android body. The fact that they didn't plan to do so is proof enough that they didn't really want to help humans, didn't even pretend to, and so their mission must have been far more sinister than they said it was.

In "The Infinite Vulcan," Spock's personality was not duplicated but transferred to a giant Spock clone—a dubious concept. When the original body starts to deteriorate, Kirk and the others accuse Dr. Kenilicus and the Spock clone of murdering the original body, although that body is empty of any kind of mind and is more the essence of Spock than his fingernail clippings are. They displayed a lack of ability to separate the essential from the incidental, not realizing that Spock was identical with his mind, and, therefore, with whatever body his mind occupied.

In "The Changeling," Nomad reads Lieutenant Uhura's memories and in the process wipes them clean, or so it is said. Certainly there is no logical reason why reading memories must destroy them—otherwise, nobody could remember anything more than once. If Nomad did erase Uhura's memories, then the old Lieutenant Uhura of the previous episodes was killed. A new person gradually developed in her body and brain, a personality called Lieutenant Uhura by the others, but having absolutely no connection with the old Uhura.

Lieutenant Uhura certainly learned swiftly following the erasure of her memories. An adult brain is not structured for learning nearly as well as a child's brain, yet she learned in a week or two what it had taken her decades to learn before (and the educational facilities on the Enterprise hardly seem more advanced than twentieth-century methods). Uhura reverted to her childhood language of Swahili at one time during her education, but there would be no way for her to know that language if her memory had been erased and no one had taught it to her.

Thus it seemed that Uhura was not killed, her memories not erased after all. It would seem logical for her mind to be swamped with memories after Nomad dredged them up and examined them, but somehow the opposite effect occurred. Her memories were temporarily suppressed, her brain being unable for a time to make contact with any memories and act upon its recorded data. Her mind was still active, but it couldn't use *any* of the data recorded during any of her previous activities and experiences.

But gradually her past life became accessible to her once again and she remembered what she had been and all that had happened to her. The new, independent person who had developed in her mind after the incident gradually lost control to the reemerging mind of Uhura. But certainly the experience should have left traces for the rest of her life.

All in all, Star Trek has included many episodes dealing with immortality, many of them of dubious plausibility, but several involving the most important possibility for life extension, duplication of human personalities in robot bodies and brains. Many episodes seemed to be against the idea of seeking immortality, tending to imply that it was wrong to try to live longer than one's "natural" lifespan, and in many episodes immortality was a comparatively minor plot element instead of the most important plot element as it deserves to be. In too many episodes giving up eternal life was shown as the right thing to do.

"An Evening with Gene Roddenberry 1977" in *The Best of Trek* (No. 1) features a discussion by Roddenberry of the future of man and machine and the possibility of humans becoming intelligent machines. If Roddenberry believed in such a possibility in 1966–69, he certainly didn't take as many opportunities as he could have to express this idea in various episodes. On the other hand, Star Trek has done far more to publicize the possibility of gaining immortality through duplication of memories in the brains of intelligent machines than any comparable dramatic presentation.

2.

FRIENDSHIP—IN THE BALANCE

by Joyce Tullock

Joyce's last article for Trek *examined religion in Star Trek ("Bridging the Gap: The Promethean Star Trek," Best of* Trek *#3) and continues to draw an impressive amount of mail. As a matter of fact, at least two articles growing from it have already been queried to us, and more are likely to be on the way. In this article, Joyce turns her attention to one of the most fascinating concepts in Star Trek: The Kirk/Spock/ McCoy Triumvirate. And if you think you've heard it all before . . . well, read on.*

It is of little surprise to anyone that in Star Trek, man discovers that one of the grandest mysteries of all is himself. This is the Challenge, the reason why men consult one another and reach out a communal hand, opening themselves to cautious exploration and alien worlds, always testing their fears against the unknown and the undefined. This is why men constantly search for that which is new and different. By balancing the differences in his own mind, man can learn more about himself—learning as well that while he may never understand the answers, man must continue to ask the questions.

But man must go about this search as objectively as possible. He must use the mirror of friendship to seek a broader perspective, then study and analyze what he sees in that mirror to readjust his own frame of reference. It is a creative thing; and although friends are not the maker of a man, they suggest to him what he could be.

In Star Trek, it is the human self with which Roddenberry is primarily concerned. He uses Kirk, Spock, and McCoy to show us ourselves. He holds the mirror before us, and magic happens: The three suddenly make up one personality. But it is like an educational toy. We see Kirk, Spock, and McCoy as individuals as well, determined in their strong indepen-

23

dence, each personifying basic aspects of the human personality. So we take them apart and put them back together like a puzzle, and in the process, we are almost acidentally discovering things about our own "self."

Let us consider the individuals:

Mr. Spock. A half-breed Vulcan/human raised in the stoic traditions of his Vulcan father. (Come now, his childhood was not so different from the average human male's of our world. He was raised to bear his burdens "in silence.") So Mr. Spock suppressed the emotional heritage of his mother, and instead developed his logical nature to a fine art. So fine, in fact, that he is able to use his logic to express feeling. (Or at least to explain it away.)

In *Star Trek: The Motion Picture*, Spock carries himself with a mysterious, almost beautiful indifference. He has become an aesthete in the Vulcan sense: a student of the beauty of pure logic. And it is obvious that (momentary bursts of emotion aside) Leonard Nimoy considers his character to be one of grand aloofness. Quite frankly, it doesn't look as though Spock will ever smile much.

Which is good and essential because that is the part of us which Spock represents. Figuratively, his isolation is ours. Spock wants to smile . . . but he also, very sincerely, does *not* want to smile. While he has inherited the capacity to feel emotion, paternal upbringing (and yes, you bet, the fact that Spock strives to emulate his father shows that he *loves* him!) has conditioned him to believe that the display of emotion is a sign of weakness. No . . . even worse than that. It is a sign of . . . well . . . bad blood, inferiority.

Which sets the stage for James T. Kirk. Hero. Captain. Friend. For Spock, Kirk is a conundrum, a laughing disclaimer of the Vulcan Ideal, a living denial of the philosophy of total logic. He takes human sensitivity and turns it into a very practical strength. His attitude toward his fellow humans and toward aliens both known and unknown is astounding proof that a show of affection—brotherly love—is not emasculating.

So the captain is rather special. He is a man from a century we have not yet reached, a promise of what is yet to be: the male ego trained for the highest positive good. He is one of those people who, believing in himself, finds believers to follow him. Things tend to go right for Jim Kirk: Doors open, lights shine, his path is paved with the gold of good works. He symbolizes the human ego . . . everything we want to be: brave, intelligent, sensitive, objective, and very, very positive.

But as we see in many of the episodes, and in *STTMP*, the grass is never really all that green for Jim Kirk. Of course not, for he is human. We see him lose his best friend in "Where No Man Has Gone Before," and his true love, Edith Keeler, in "The City on the Edge of Forever." And the list goes on.

Kirk is constantly sacrificing his own happiness for the safety of his ship and crew, and even for the benefit of the progressive mankind of his own time. An ambitious man burdened by conscience, he often suffers from the inner pressures and torments of a captain's duties. Did he make the right decision? Was he too slow or too fast to act? Did he superimpose his own morals on an alien problem? Always he faces these questions. Kirk can be objective only through hindsight. He needs a mirror by which he can see himself in the now.

Enter Leonard "Bones" McCoy. The doctor, the student of pain and suffering. McCoy is a civilian at heart, therefore much less disciplined than his captain. He feels deeply, and says exactly what he feels. His capacity for emotion equals Spock's capacity for logic. His is the other side of the human personality—the emotional side. What Spock is to empiricism, McCoy is to empathy.

The doctor's background is marvelously mysterious. Efficiently mysterious, in fact, for in seeing him, we do not require details. His privacy challenges us to accept his pain for what it is: our own. We know by his mannerisms, outlook, and halting colloquial speech that he is of the middle class. We know by his sharp tongue and shy, piercing eyes that he understands more than he says, that he sees to the core. At times, he is a kind of "fool on the hill."

Of the three, we get the impression that he alone may have known the twenty-third-century equivalent of economic hardship. His path to becoming starship chief surgeon was doubtless neither rosy or logical. If Kirk is a man *for* whom things happen, McCoy is a man *to* whom things happen. Our feelings of inferiority are most clearly personified in him.

But his personal and professional experiences have given him a warm emotional insight. That insight has provided him with a positive outlook; it serves him as logic serves Spock and as ambition serves Kirk. And it contributes to the Friendship. In fact, Mr. Spock might say that the ship's surgeon shares his insight with "alarming liberality."

And the Friendship is complete. Three strongly independent characters who, through their independence and individuality, present important aspects of the human personality. Take away their independence—and the Friendship is destroyed. The human personality they represent is unbalanced.

Spock provides the logic, McCoy the emotion, Kirk the human will. To alter any of their personalities is to corrupt their purpose in Star Trek. Spock's logic, with its sternness and isolation, represents the desire for precision and perfection—a kind of need for security. Kirk's ambition is a reminder of the human ego—of everything from the basic sex drive to the desire to challenge the unknown—total self-confidence. McCoy, the humanitarian, is the sentimental side of human nature; ambition and logic hold little interest for him. He seeks out neither adventure nor absolute perfection. His adventure is one of introspection. He is the hesitant, less trusting part of our nature.

It's like an old-fashioned beam scale with Kirk as the center, balancing Spock on one side and McCoy on the other. Logic. Ambition. Emotion. A careful, artful balance. It's as though Mr. Spock designed it himself. An almost mathematical friendship.

But things weren't always so precise. Once upon a time, there was no McCoy in the balance. And while Spock's friendship with Kirk begins during the time of "Where No Man . . ." it takes Spock some time to . . . shall we say, understand the less approachable McCoy. No doubt Spock even found Kirk's friendship with "Bones" to be a fascinating curiosity. Even the use of the archaic nickname must have stirred feelings of embarrassment or perhaps repugnance within the logical Vulcan. That is, it must have *grated*.

Just the same, Spock views Cpatain Kirk as one of the more logical members of the human species. And we can very well imagine that Spock likes being around Kirk (as much as this alien can like being around *any* human), because they share the kind of cool intellect required for command and analytical scientific observation.

We know that Spock is painfully aware of his half-breed nature, and considers himself to be flawed or at least subconsciously threatened by those inherited qualities of sentiment and emotion. Had not Kirk offered his friendship on a logical, intellectual level, it is unlikely that their relationship would have become anything more than the respect of one officer toward his fellow.

As it happens, however, Kirk is a man who can read people, like any good commander, diplomat, or politician. He respects Spock's Vulcan nature in accordance with IDIC— and common sense. Rather than trying to change Spock, he gave him room and time to understand that humanness isn't catching.

So it's more than a case of Kirk's befriending a "poor, lonely Vulcan." They have something in common. They share intellect and a tremendous capacity for loyalty and respect. They share a kind of mystical communion which goes far beyond the limitations of the physical. Quite simply, they *understand* one another. Anyone who has a good, close friend has experienced that indefinable "meeting of minds."

And the very intensity of this meeting gives the Kirk/Spock friendship a frightening power. Frightening because it reveals so much of ourselves, of our own possibilities.

It is good to remember that Bill Shatner and Leonard Nimoy are acting—being artists—for us up there on the screen. Art involves the presentation of something which is at once universal in meaning and at the same time fresh and new. The Kirk/Spock friendship, so subtle and strong, is as much poetry as it is acting. And like any good poem, it presents something which cannot truly be analyzed. The friendship exists in its entirety only on screen. To paraphrase a poem is to kill it . . . or to lose the essence and spirit of the creator.

But as we can read a poem, we can "read" the meaning of the Kirk/Spock friendship. It is clear the friendship is intended to exemplify the kind of brotherly love and friendship which all of mankind can (and ultimately must) enjoy. It shows the future of the spirit of man, and forces us to admit that the seeds of that future are here in us today. This deliberately challenges most of today's worldly-oriented people, with their smokescreens of hate and suspicion. In a materialistic world such as ours, this very real quality of human love, and the concept of giving without seeking or requiring reward, is pure blasphemy.

The challenging truth stands before us: The Love of Star Trek, as personified in its main characters, is a love of which all mankind is capable. It frightens because of its reality and simplicity. It is that capacity to care that surpasses the physical and leaves it behind in the dust of our beginnings. It is a part of our necessary evolution.

Love, in Star Trek's time, is man's saving spark; his difference, his bit of godhood. In the twenty-third century, man no longer displaces this love by leaving it, like an orphaned child, in the disinterested hands of religion. Now he's finally taking the responsibility for himself. He is growing up, casting aside the Freudian fears and old wives' tales which dropped love and sex in the same bucket. He has been through some terrible, hateful times, and, after almost destroying himself, he's finally left superstition behind and welcomes his fellows with open arms. By Star Trek's time, necessity has taken mankind to the point where the value of brotherly love surpasses even that of romantic love.

But the one thing that makes man special in the universe is his ability to love for no particular reason. It is that simple feeling of friendship to which Mr. Spock refers in *Star Trek: The Motion Picture*: Love between sisters, brothers, friends, aliens, intelligent beings becoming friends who, in spite of their differences, share a common "knowing." They learn to understand without explanation.

Again, that indefinable poem: Spock and Kirk show us the kind of love and friendship which, if we are to survive as Terrans, we would do well to emulate. Our biggest challenge is understanding ourselves and our differences, and loving one another not despite those differences, but *because* of them.

Perhaps it only stands to reason that much of the mankind of today chooses to ignore that love and its meaning; or even worse, to render it impotent through soap-opera interpretation. It frightens and demands. It dares us to give . . . without receiving. It challenges us to evolve our human spirit, and to grow beyond ourselves—beyond the narcissism and introversion of our times.

In fact, since ours is the century of the launching of V'Ger, it seems only fitting that in these times, many are unable or unwilling to grasp the concept of friendship as seen in

Star Trek. The mankind of today is still bound to the limited frame of reference which sent V'Ger out in the first place. It is looking for physical expression of a spiritual existence. It is tight in the fist of traditional observation, married to what seems evident and logical (now *that* would make Spock laugh!) to the physical world.

Unlike Spock, McCoy, and Kirk, much of mankind is unwilling to "go Beyond" and discover a greater way of being. It is afraid of abandoning the traditional, material universe, terrified of discovering its own capacity for love. When truth becomes too demanding, man builds himself a theory and hides behind it. He strains for sophisticated answers, and avoids simple fact. The brotherly love of Star Trek confounds in its simplicity. For a mankind which seeks security in a physical universe, such a love is more than threatening, it is beyond comprehension.

But patience: We are only the age of V'Ger. The heroes of Star Trek promise us that one day man will gather his courage and look at the blinding light of his own inner self.

So Kirk and Spock share a friendship which allows them to understand one another without the need for detail. No leaning, no security-seeking. Each respects the other's privacy and uniqueness. And when Kirk *does* question his Vulcan friend's personal nature, he does it as carefully and as unobtrusively as possible.

For instance, in "Amok Time," Kirk is forced to discuss with Spock the very personal matter of Vulcan reproduction. And it is a conversation that is very "man to man"; a balanced mixture of humor and serious concern (and the tiniest bit of embarrassment on both sides) reminiscent of the traditional father/son "birds and bees" chat. And while we find the scene gently amusing, we are also very much aware of Spock's great emotional misery. (If sexual matters are taken lightly in the twenty-third century, one would never guess it from this scene.) Spock seems to be greatly humiliated by the biological need that forces him to return to Vulcan to mate.

It's only natural that Spock's reaction to McCoy's concern about his condition is quite volatile. ("You will cease to pry into my personal matters, doctor, or I shall certainly break your neck!") And considering the state Spock is in, it is probable he would do so. McCoy, the epitome of the emotional self—the self Spock is unsuccessfully trying to keep in check—well, his mere presence must sting Spock like a raw nerve.

But with Kirk, it's different. Even under the intense emotional strain of *pon farr*, the Vulcan is able to communicate with Kirk on an intellectual level. Kirk's approach is delicate and tactful. He combines his capacity for command and his warm friendship by first ordering Spock to explain his irrational behavior (allowing Spock to dodge the choice of whether or not to tell him), and then by promising Spock that anything he tells will be held in strictest confidence (allowing Spock to be spared as much embarrassment as possible). Though Kirk is upset by Spock's problems—even to the point of making the emotional decision to take Spock to Vulcan against orders—he maintains a gentle and mostly emotionless reserve around the Vulcan.

And here the Triad becomes complete. We have seen how the Spock/Kirk friendship is one of intense loyalty, respect, and understanding. We also see how Spock acknowledges these same feelings for McCoy by requesting that he too attend the ceremony on Vulcan. It is the highest honor he could bestow—on a friend—and the most personal one. IDIC has just moved a mountain.

More important to the cementing of the Triad, though, is the fact that the experienced and logical application of *emotion* is the key to events in "Amok Time."

Spock, unaccustomed to dealing with strong emotions, is hit hard by the physiological and emotional pressures of *pon farr*, without the immunity of a lifetime of emotional experiences to support him.

When Kirk is chosen by T'Pring to be her champion in the fight to the death, both he and McCoy are very upset. Kirk's emotions are very soon concentrated on the problem of staying alive while not killing his friend; but the master of the irrational, McCoy, uses his strong emotions to *think*.

His years of training in medicine have taught him that emotions must be *used* in a tight spot. And one way to use anxiety and fear is to lie or bluff. So with T'Pau's approval (and, one suspects, unspoken compliance), McCoy injects Kirk with neural paralyzer to knock him out, running the bluff that the injection is needed to make the fight fair and lying by saying that it contains a tri-ox compound.

It works. Kirk appears to be killed, is returned to the *En-*

terprise safe and sound, and Spock is spared the agony of having to kill his best friend. (And we are all treated to a quick display of Vulcan glee.) All because of McCoy's "sugar pill" cure.

Quick thinking, emotion, and logic—all neatly applied. It's another big step for country medicine. And it establishes McCoy's special place in the Friendship.

Of course, long before the airing of "Amok Time," the McCoy/Spock friendship, feud, or whatever you want to call it had become one of the more entertaining features of the series.

We can guess that Spock disliked the blatantly emotional McCoy in the beginning, and probably did his best to avoid the doctor's company. That was Spock's first mistake. As a medical man, McCoy would naturally have been curious about the hybrid Spock, and even more intrigued by Spock's obvious rejection of his humanity. Discovering the Vulcan's dislike for the irrational, McCoy no doubt found a little impish taunting irresistible.

But he would have been most concerned over Spock's suppression of emotion. McCoy is also a private man, a hider himself, so he has probably learned firsthand about the dangers of holding personal, painful feelings inside too long. So he tries to break down Spock's barriers by displaying his own irrational side before Spock, and gaining a small—if controlled—annoyed or amused reaction. As Kirk might observe, it's a shaky way to start a friendship, but for Spock and McCoy, it was the only way. And, surely, McCoy had to take the first step, and then continue with the "game" for quite a while thereafter. (Imagine McCoy's amazement and joy the first time Spock instigated one of their "exchanges.")

In a way, Spock and McCoy are the same man; two very important aspects of the human mind, and each the opposite of the other. Emotion and logic—two powerful magnets repelling each other. Spock and McCoy—each denying the part of himself that he sees in the other. So it's understandable that McCoy and Spock tend to feel uncomfortable around each other—if they should *ever* feel totally relaxed in one another's presence, their characters would become distorted. They would no longer serve the purpose of illustrating the healthy eternal conflict of the rational vs. the impulsive in the human mind.

Roddenberry presents us with a special gift in the Kirk/Spock friendship by illustrating the power of brotherly love. But in the Spock/McCoy friendship, he offers a more personal kind of gift. Through the Spock/McCoy contrast we come to respect and appreciate the differences within ourselves; for their friendship must overcome a mighty obstacle—self-hate. It is a magical transformation of sorts, for in the gradual acceptance of one another, each man is saying a hesitant "yes" to himself. It is a colorful illustration of the power of self-respect. And what sort of effect might this message have on the identifying viewer?

One suspects that McCoy's distaste for logic comes from his own misuse of it; or perhaps from earlier bad experiences with a too stoic or overly practical family. The trick lies in what we are *not* told. But his vehemence against logic gives him all the earmarks of a man who has learned a lesson the hard way. (The value of having all of this hidden is that we must fill in the blanks with our own pain. That is the doctor's greatest secret cure.)

We find out from Spock's mother (in "Journey to Babel") that Spock has learned the hard way as well—but about emotion. As a half-breed child, he had to deal with the tauntings of his Vulcan schoolmates. This led him to learn early to hide his emotions, and finally to suppress them. His stoicism is a respected way of life, but it is also a matter of honor—and self-protection.

So it is likely that each man has been scarred, or at least deeply hurt, by those qualities so perfectly embodied in the other. The growth of their friendship from its shaky beginnings is the purest expression of IDIC. It is a friendship which is *earned* by both men. And we see them earning it in flashes from many episodes.

In "Operation Annihilate," McCoy holds himself responsible for his medical treatment's causing the Vulcan to go blind. Spock consoles his friend with the logical observation that the loss of his sight in exchange for his life is more than a fair trade.

When, in "The Immunity Syndrome," Spock insists he go on the "suicide mission" instead of McCoy, we suspect that Spock is out to protect the doctor. McCoy, in all his complexity, responds with an emotional mixture of sorrow, jealousy, and guilt. And when they part, it is McCoy who is afraid to show his affection when Mr. Spock suggests that the good doctor might "wish him luck." In that little scene, through the magic of Kelley and Nimoy, we have the essence of that most complex friendship.

The Kirk/McCoy friendship is no less complex for its lack of irony. Kirk is friends with "Bones" for much the same reason that he is friends with Spock. Like Spock, McCoy is always a little out of place in his world. But the doctor is proud of his eccentricity (like Spock and his logic), and maybe even a little smug about it. By cultivating that individuality, McCoy causes a self-imposed isolation. Like Spock, McCoy's determination to be the master of his own character makes him stand out, giving him a unique psychological maturity and moral fiber. But McCoy is still wary of others, and camouflages his warmth with a sharp tongue and colloquial ways. Again like Spock, something about him says, "I *dare* you to be my friend."

Well, Jim Kirk could never resist a challenge. Once more the captain goes out of his way to establish a friendship by giving McCoy the room, the distance, he needs to be himself. He ignores protocol with "Bones," allowing the doctor an unprecedented freedom of opinion and comment. And it pays off. McCoy is many things to Kirk: adviser, confessor, father, brother, trusted friend. Perhaps "Bones" appeals to Kirk's sentiment just as Spock appeals to Kirk's logic. Come to think of it, Kirk probably just likes the guy.

And for McCoy, Kirk's friendship offers him a greater freedom to be himself. Kirk doesn't ask Bones to fit into the highly mechanized world of the twenty-third century any more than he would have the insensitivity to demand that Spock be human.

The Kirk/McCoy friendship is complete and natural. We can easily imagine them on shore leave—drinking, carousing, raising hell. We can just as easily imagine them sitting quietly and discussing the most poignant subjects with objective maturity. The measure of these men is that they can disagree— even violently—and still keep their friendship intact.

In fact, the very nature of Star Trek, with its vision of challenge, dictates that we might well find something in the Friendship of the three which stretches our traditional concepts of this most common of human experiences. We should expect as much from IDIC, the Vulcan idea that the universe's many differences combine for the ultimate good.

In Star Trek, the human creature *is* the Human Creature, one being, made up of many parts, both complementary and conflicting. The philosophy of IDIC celebrates this. The Triad demonstrates it; for with Kirk, Spock, and McCoy, it is the differences which hold them together. Dampen McCoy's fire, mellow Spock's icy reserve, soften Kirk's driving ambition—and the Friendship is no more.

It becomes a shade, a fading memory of a once-vital being. To remain friends, to represent the human mind, to display IDIC and the infinite color of life, each man must maintain his stern, unquestioned independence. They require distance to be close.

When any of them loses his unique character traits, the Friendship is marred and off-balance. When McCoy loses his excitability, emotion, and independence after becoming a part of "the Body" in "Return of the Archons," he is useless to Kirk and Spock. When Mr. Spock is affected by the spores in "This Side of Paradise," his logic takes flight, and the Friendship is threatened. In "The Enemy Within," when Kirk is split into two beings—a gentle Kirk who lacks ambition, and a pure ego Kirk who lacks compassion—Spock and McCoy find the gentle Kirk to be as much of a threat and burden to them as the cruel Kirk. It is only when McCoy is removed from "the Body," when Spock is freed from the influence of the spores, when Kirk's two halves are reunited that the Friendship is once more in balance, and all three can function effectively again.

So Kirk, Spock, and McCoy are strong individuals who are connected in friendship by the poetic bonds of difference. And the beauty of the Friendship is that in accepting and understanding the differences, each man is able to gain a fuller understanding of the human mind, to appreciate *himself* all the more.

This is reiterated in *Star Trek: The Motion Picture* when Spock recognizes the worth of human sensitivity and feeling. We also see McCoy's appreciation of logic when he greets Spock with that "thank God, we've got a logical Vulcan to help us" look. It is a genuinely warm greeting, but it emphasizes McCoy's understanding that Kirk is in dreadful need of Spock's logic. And how would Kirk have dealt with his own shortcomings (and in *STTMP* he is a mess) without "Bones" there to look inside him and reflect what he sees?

Even McCoy's initial distrust of Spock is significant. Kirk, the optimist, simply believes that Spock's motives in joining the *Enterprise* are worthy. Kirk's faith shows the usefulness of human trust; McCoy's wariness shows there is wisdom in a certain amount of cynicism. Separately, both men are wrong, or at least incomplete in their outlook. Together, they are right.

The Friendship in *STTMP* illustrates the fact that no man can ever totally know himself. If he did, he would not be a growing, developing creature. The characters in Star Trek are as complex and as undefinable as you or I. It's the one thing that makes them "live" for us.

And like ourselves, the Friendship of Kirk, Spock, and McCoy allows them to grow. In "The Tholian Web" (which is in many ways *the* Spock/McCoy episode), Captain Kirk tells us (via "posthumous" tape) just how he "uses" the Friendship. And we see how well Kirk knows his friends . . . and perhaps how little he knows them. On the tape, Kirk admonishes each man to seek out and respect the advice of the other; to look to and utilize the differences. It's clear that Kirk has spent more than a little time worrying about how his friends will get along without him.

Well, they're pretty broken up, of course, and Kirk's "death" brings out the worst in both of them. In what must be one of Spock's cruelest moments in Star Trek, he admonishes McCoy for neglecting his search for an antidote to attend memorial services for Kirk. Now we all realize that Spock knows better, but this can be seen as a lapse due to Kirk's "death"—Spock's way of showing emotion. But McCoy can give as well as he gets; and "The Tholian Web" has much fussing and feuding between the two before they finally come to terms. Although the Triad is gone, a bit of Jim Kirk continues on with Spock and McCoy. Their friendship is stronger, not weaker, after the loss. Having known Kirk, having his friendship in common, they are better men.

The conclusion of "Requiem for Methuselah" presents an excellent example of how the Triad works. Kirk is in misery (again!), grieving over his lost love, Reena. Spock and McCoy stand over their sleeping friend, both, in their own unique ways, concerned about his unhappiness (imbalance?)

and wanting to help him heal. McCoy, in a speech which is more of a challenge than an admonition, dares Spock to understand Kirk's human misery. He tells (or perhaps warns) the Vulcan that he will never know "the things that love can drive a man to." The scene flows past so naturally that at first glance we might not recognize what is actually happening. After completing his famous "glorious victories" speech, McCoy leaves the room, allowing Spock to assimilate this somewhat erratic and sentimental bit of news with his own experience. Then, with what is nothing less than emotion-guided logic, Spock uses the Vulcan mind-touch to help Kirk forget. The "operation" is complete.

Spock is always finding a logical way to show affection. In "Friday's Child," Kirk is angry and frustrated because one of his men has been killed by the Klingon agent Kras. Churning with remorse, Kirk vents his anger on McCoy, who had earlier assured him the Capellans were basically a peace-loving people. The doctor understands Kirk's emotional state and accepts the anger graciously. Kirk, when his wrath is spent, offers a hesitant, sheepish apology. It's all typically human. And Mr. Spock is typically observing.

But it is the Vulcan's application of logic to the Friendship which touches us most. When Kirk finishes his apology, there is the slightest pause . . . we can almost feel Spock weighing the situation, making up his mind. He speaks with the hesitancy of a man who has something to say, but is afraid that in doing so he will give himself away, that he will display his feelings too openly. So after Kirk owns up to the injustice of his outburst, Spock adds softly that such behavior is also inefficient. It's his way of saying, "Don't pick on 'Bones,' it isn't his fault." And it illustrates his affection for McCoy more clearly and more profoundly than the most colorful collection of sentimental phrases could ever hope to do. And "Bones" didn't even have to get hurt!

This is the mature Spock; he's grown some since those uncertain, half-emotional days when he served under Captain Pike. Through his own private processes, he has chosen a way of life. He has found that logic suits him best; he trusts it, and has discovered how to use it to express his feelings. He channels his logic just as McCoy channels his emotion, as Kirk directs his ambition. This is Spock the Vulcan, who seeks to purge himself of his emotional inheritance through the creative development of his logical nature. He has proved the tremendous value of that logic and has clarified in his own mind that it can ultimately be used for good. He establishes time and again in episodes like "The Empath" and "Requiem" that logic is his greatest gift, a gift which has often allowed him to ease the suffering of his human friends.

Spock is not only proud of his logic, he is grateful for it. He lives through it. So by the end of the *Enterprise*'s five-year mission, he has decided to end "the quest," and give himself over completely to the Vulcan discipline of total logic, *Kolinahr*. Maybe he's kidding himself, but he is convinced that *Kolinahr* holds the ultimate answer.

Poor old Spock. And he was getting *so* close! But at least he isn't the only one to have taken a wrong turn.

His old buddy, Jim Kirk, is in an even worse fix. Of course, Jim always *was* the ambitious type. That's one of the reasons why we like him; he calls to that part of *us*. And it's what makes him important to the Friendship. He is drive, progress, human will. He is "yesness." He is the explorer, the one who dares journey to "strange new worlds." Captain Kirk's whole life has been based on the principle that there is nothing in God's universe which he cannot do.

What's the matter with him? Doesn't he remember poor Apollo? Has he forgotten those words of warning: "Know thyself"? Spock and McCoy, for their own opposing reasons, are both somewhat introverted. They reach to that part of us. And the healthy extroversion of Jim Kirk has certainly helped them (and so, us) to examine their introversion and to own up to its presence within their own natures. He has encouraged them, through association, to allow for that spirit of adventure which makes any human complete. Through countless examples, he has shown the human ego at its best, as an expression of love.

In "The Empath," he dares the Vians to take his life and those of Spock and Gem rather than leave McCoy to die a lonely death. In "Amok Time," he defies highest orders and diverts the *Enterprise* to Vulcan in order to save Spock's life. He uses his ego in a positive way—to give. He'd rather lose a career than the life of a friend.

It follows that Kirk believes that such positiveness has no limitations. Having pushed his luck and found himself the winner so many times, he has become a man blinded not so much by ambition, but by the repeated proof of the rightness of that ambition. Jim Kirk, by the end of the five-year mission, is a very, very successful man. That's his problem, really, for like many successful and ambitious men, James T. Kirk suffers from *hubris*. Darn it, you can count on it every time—those "gods among men" forget all about their own limitations.

So it seems that with all of that character building and suffering and whatnot that he went through during the five years, Jim Kirk still has one more world to explore—himself. We can bet money that both Spock and McCoy warned him, not only in words, but by the example of their characters. If Spock and McCoy agree on nothing else, at least we know they both understand the shortcomings of ambition.

Spock has said that he is content in his capacity as ship's science officer. He enjoys his work, and the rank and duties of captain would only be an annoyance to him. As for McCoy . . . well, goodness, he's "just an old country doctor." His happiness revolves around healing and research. He's filled out enough forms to know that any executive administrative position would sound the death knell to his spirit.

But Jim Kirk thinks he deserves to be an admiral. After all, why not? He's ably handled everything else, hasn't he? And he knows how to get things done *his* way. But he soon discovers the one world in which he is truly an alien—Starfleet Administration. Kirk personifies the Spirit of Adventure, so it only stands to reason that a desk job at Starfleet would drive him crazy with boredom.

In *Star Trek: The Motion Picture*, we can understand Jim Kirk's pain—perhaps more than ever before—because we've felt it too; just as earlier in the film we felt and empathized with McCoy's confusion and Spock's isolation. We also can understand his desperation: He's trying to be the "old" Jim Kirk . . . the one almost destroyed by office routine. And that forces him to attempt one of the most difficult things of all: to recapture a lost love, his only true love, the *Enterprise*.

And although Kirk is positive about the need for him to command the ship on its most serious mission, it is a positiveness born of desperation rather than determination. He's lost some of that vital self-confidence, and he fumbles seriously. He needs the Friendship.

And so Gene Roddenberry brings the three together again. He does it thematically, each returning in a way which best suits his unique character traits. Spock, on his own . . . the aesthete . . . searching. Kirk, by psychological and artistic necessity . . . to reassert and reaffirm himself. McCoy, drafted . . . dragged in kicking and screaming to once again fight the good fight. There is a refreshing absence of sentimentality in this reunion. It offers an abrupt but necessary reminder that there is no mushiness to this Friendship.

No mushiness, indeed. McCoy's irritation with Kirk's machinations to have him returned to duty (he boards with the air of a man interrupted, who has better things to do), and Spock's cool reaction to McCoy's enthusiastic welcome, slices away twelve years of fandom romanticism and sentimentality.

In *STTMP*, Kirk, Spock, and McCoy are again clearly defined individuals. And the strength and value of the Friendship can be measured by each character's need and ability to function on his own. Each has been busy traveling his own pathway, dealing with his own life, looking for answers. But some answers have eluded them. Spock knows the value of human sensitivity, but has not yet learned to be openly thankful for his own humanity. Kirk has not yet learned to measure himself—a difficult thing for a man of such powers.

McCoy, however, seems to have already found himself. He comes along simply because he is needed. He is neither seeking nor desperate nor—any longer—running.

In the movie, we see how McCoy (who seems to have little to do at first glance) serves to reflect and magnify the characters of Kirk and Spock. He is disturbed by Kirk's desperation; he is concerned by Spock's mystery. McCoy's mixture of cynicism and insight allow him the self-confidence to confront Kirk's egotism and the painful wisdom to question Spock's motives. At the beginning of the picture, both Kirk and Spock are standing dangerously at the brink—about to be consumed by the dominant parts of their own personalities. But McCoy is in balance and keeps things steady until the others readjust. His presence aboard the *Enterprise* offers a graceful, poignant, very human reality that allows everyone time to gain perspective.

In many ways, McCoy says our piece for us. We judge Spock and Kirk by McCoy's reactions to them; and his balance and control serve as a lesson for them and for us as well. All of the complaints about "lack of drama" in *Star Trek: The Motion Picture* have ignored the fact that the movie showcases the very dramatic Friendship of the Three; the symbolic healing of the human personality, an end to mankind's introversion and selfishness.

For example, when Decker makes his (very Kirklike) decision to unite with V'Ger, there is a moment when Kirk lurches impetuously forward, as is his nature. Spock and McCoy restrain him.

That's how the Three work together. Love is expressed by logic on one side, emotion on the other, both working to bring the ego under control. The Friendship is one—active, balanced, feeling. While Kirk, Spock, and McCoy are each free characters in their own right, they find their answers more efficiently when working in combination. Their Friendship is a kind of continuing expedition into the human self; to discover the point where a man may emphasize the part of his personality that works best for him without carrying his beliefs over the edge, to the point where he loses balance. Kirk, Spock, and McCoy can be seen as individuals who, complementing each other, symbolize one complete and healthy personality. Ego restrained by logic and emotion; logic softened by ego and emotion; emotion tempered by logic and ego. But by insisting upon their own uniqueness and independence, they remind us of something which is vitally important: With mankind, the part is greater than the whole.

So we can look at the Friendship of Kirk, Spock, and McCoy and recognize in it things about ourselves. Often, one of the three will stand apart from the others; one in whom we see a little more of ourselves as we step near and recognize the value of the part, whether it be logic, spirit, or emotion. But then we step back, and seeing the whole, also see ourselves from a thousand different angles. We see our own infinite complexity. We touch upon simplicity. We see this now . . . that later. All bits of ourselves.

It is what we recognize . . . all those differences. Like the Friendship, it's a pretty astounding thing when you think about it.

3.

A WOMAN LOOKS AT "JIM'S LITTLE BLACK BOOK"

by Beth Carlson

The only true test of worth for a piece of writing is the response it engenders from those who read it. If someone is moved to think by reading an article, then the author has done his job. Editor Walter Irwin was quite pleased with the response he received from his examination of Captain Kirk's past love life ("Jim's Little Black Book," The Best of Trek #2), but was especially happy to see the following article by Beth Carlson, as it succinctly summarizes many of the comments and complaints we got in the mails concerning Walter's original article. And who knows? In the tried and true Trek tradition, we may yet see a rebuttal to the rebuttal. . . .

"But we can see that most women really do not mean much to Kirk."

"It is unlikely that Kirk ever had any real feeling for Janice [Rand] . . . Janice is a bit too featherbrained for the demanding Kirk. . . ."

". . . his penchant for using women to gain results in the line of duty, and with the frequency that it occurs later, one can assume that Kirk also has a tendency to use women for personal results as well."

"When age removes his power and potency from him. . . . Since Kirk must always be the strong one. . . ."

"One could accurately say that although Kirk loves women, he actually doesn't like them very much."

The above statements are made about the character of James T. Kirk by Walter Irwin in his article "Jim's Little Black Book" (*The Best of Trek #2*). By taking a closer look —albeit a feminine look—we can see they are just a trifle on the negative side of the facts.

41

This article will endeavor to show that there are several important truths about relationships, and women, that need to be inserted into our thoughts as we consider Kirk's relationships.

One: A woman cannot be said to be used as long as she can say no, and be listened to. By this definition, we seldom see a woman being used by Kirk. There is no force involved. The women in Kirk's life are willing—some only too willing.

Two: If, in a given situation, there is a chance that people who are a commanding officer's responsibility will be hurt, or that the cause he lives for will be damaged, then some stepping out of the daily rules of man-woman relationships is, indeed, in order. It has always been so; it has been, by necessity, accepted.

Three: Perhaps most importantly, if a woman is not totally honest with a man, she cannot expect that a man will be totally honest with her . . . unless he is very stupid. James T. Kirk is by no means a stupid man.

We will now, as Mr. Irwin did in his article, go down the list of Kirk's women and reevaluate.

Janice Rand, as a personal yeoman to the captain, was not featherbrained. Starfleet would not have accepted her nor included her on a deep space expedition if she were. She is a highly proficient and duly qualified professional.

In "The Naked Time," Spock reacts with almost desperate immediacy to the helm's not being manned, and yet later, we see Kirk command Janice Rand to "take the helm." Had he doubted her competency, he would have done it himself.

A yeoman is defined both as a low-ranking clerical worker and as a high-class attendant to nobility. We see Janice serving in both of these capacities. Her job is to make the captain's life a little easier, and as such, she spends a considerable amount of time with him, and is a frequent and safe target for his irritated outbursts. She is his friend; probably a close friend. Yes, he rails against her when she is trying to take care of him a little too much—his pride—but he also rails against Spock and McCoy for the same reasons.

The fact that Rand transfers off of the *Enterprise* when she begins to fall in love with Kirk (and that he probably helped ease the transfer) speaks volumes for her good sense and again for the openness and friendship between them.

Eve McHuron ("Mudd's Women") was openly dealing

for Kirk. It was her plan to sway Kirk to Harry Mudd's way of thinking, and perhaps to test her chances with a starship captain. As mail-order merchandise, she was more interested in *a* man, rather than *the* man Kirk. There was no relationship here, only a little dancing around, which both were fully aware of.

Andrea in "What Are Little Girls Made Of?" was perhaps one of the women Kirk truly did use. And from what we see of Korby's attitude toward her, it was not much of a change from what her day-to-day life seemed to be. As pathetic as it was, it was a necessity. Kirk was trying to overload the android Andrea (and that is an important word, *android*) to escape his cell and stop Korby's plans, which could have endangered lives.

Miri was only a child to Kirk. He was his normal friendly and charming self, and did not realize that she was becoming enamored of him. Once he realized this, he did (when the situation permitted) show her an inordinate amount of kindness considering the fatigue he felt and the amount of trouble she had caused.

Dr. Helen Noel ("Dagger of the Mind") is a woman Kirk obviously sees as a peer—as much as a commanding officer can see a subordinate officer as a peer—and he respects her. But he has done a certain amount of flirting with her. This is something he would not allow to happen if she were not a woman with an equal amount of maturity, and the ability to see the flirting for what it is—a relaxed and fun, yet sterile, situation. Once the artificially stimulated "love" forced on Kirk is alleviated, we can only hope they still felt that kind of freedom between them. It was probably a very good thing for both of them.

Lenore Karidian ("The Conscience of the King") is a turn-on for Kirk. Not only is she intelligent, but a beautiful actress with all of the splash and excitement of the theatrical world. In this case, the woman is very definitely coming on to him, and Kirk is not minding it a bit. That she is a fine classical actress no doubt accounts in part for Kirk's not catching on to the fact that she is the murderess just as much as his vanity does.

In "Shore Leave," the little we see of Ruth shows us Kirk has no guilt feelings when he sees her, nor any misgivings about wanting to see her again. It is obviously a very sweet and precious memory he holds of their time together.

Whatever the relationship was between Kirk and Areel Shaw ("Courtmartial") it was in the past. She is well able to care for herself, and we get the feeling that she always has been able to. Again, no regrets.

In "A Taste of Armegeddon," Mea 349 was so cool, beautiful, and programmed down to the last intelligent cell of her brain that she probably wouldn't have known what to do with Kirk if she had him. But Kirk would have been willing to try anything to stop the senseless slaughter of millions. Could we have accepted less from him?

Mr. Irwin handled the explanation of Kirk and Edith Keeler so beautifully that I will not utilize valuable space to expand on that relationship. I will, however, return to a statement he made in that explanation later in this article.

Marlena Moreau ("Mirror, Mirror") is an interesting case. Kirk returns to Kirk-2's quarters to find the "captain's woman" obviously in the mood for the captain—or at the very least, expecting the captain to be in the mood for her. The disguised Kirk decides it is best to play along. No doubt it was interesting for him to make love to a woman he had never met before, and without worrying about holding up the though, and we are not told what gave Kirk away or at what honor of his duty and reputation. Marlena is not fooled, point she caught on. Perhaps Kirk is the one who is used here . . . perhaps she knew from the beginning. It might have been interesting for her too.

Sylvia ("Catspaw") is not a nice lady. Once again, Kirk is faced with a woman who is quite obviously after him. (Here, incidentally, is where Mr. Irwin states that Kirk "falls into the role of cad" easily and naturally.) We must be aware that not only is the captain endangered here, but several members of his crew as well. Sylvia has already shown an ability and a willingness to use mind control on the men and physical control on the life-support systems of the ship. At this point, as a result of having human form, she begins to feel attracted to Kirk, and has, at long last, stepped into Kirk's field of expertise. Of course, our captain gently explains to her that he is a sensitive soul and will not take advantage of her weakness. Balderdash! With all of the trouble and danger she has wrought, we'd better believe that Kirk is going to give her all that she can handle, and then some. Would we want less, were we aboard the *Enterprise*?

Again we run into one of the captain's friends from the past, Janet Wallace, in "The Deadly Years." We are not told much about the relationship; although James Blish's adaptation (and perhaps the script) states that Kirk felt he and Janet had both played games in the past, and that there was hope for rekindling a truer flame.

If we see a crisis about growing old in many strong, virile men at about forty or fifty years of age, what can we expect to see in Kirk, who has not even had the years along the way to face the change, but has it thrust upon him overnight?

This alone could be cause enough for his suddenly turning off to the lady under discussion, but it also seems rather strange that she is suddenly so deeply taken with him after he ages. It may very well be a normal and sympathetic reaction to his torment, or it may be (just as Kirk calls it) an aberration of her personality. Maybe he knows something from his past relationship with her that we don't know. Shall we trust him just this once?

Shahna ("The Gamesters of Triskelion") was in some ways a haunting reminder to Kirk of the high priority a commander must place on duty, with personal needs running a distant second—if allowed for at all. For example, the fact that Kirk had to knock Shahna out hurt him—it was evident in his expression and voice—but he was responsible for far more than himself.

Kirk is at first touched by Shahna's innocence, and we see that he feels pain for the years she has existed solely for others. He is aware that he needs information, but as devoid of affection and tenderness as her life has been, she would probably have been quite helpful just for the promise of his friendship and respect.

Kirk gives her all that he has to give at the time: affection and a sense of her own worth. It is something she has never had before. In the end, he is able to give her something far more precious, her freedom; and a memory of what it is like to want something because of her own needs and dreams.

In "A Private Little War," Kirk is drugged by Nona and used to make her pacifistic husband feel anger. It works, but instead of being enraged to the point of killing—luckily for Kirk, the target—the husband runs away, baffled by his own feelings. When her plans fail, Nona smashes the still-drugged Kirk over the head to get his phaser. Again, Kirk is the one who is used.

The relationship between Sargon and Thalassa cannot be counted as Kirk's. It *would* be interesting to see if anything could have developed between Kirk and Anne Mullhall, but a wise starship captain would no more have a romantic attachment to a crewmember than a wise professor would have an affair with a student, or a wise doctor an affair with a patient.

Kelinda ("By Any Other Name") is another alien in a human body. As there is little chance of physically stopping her and her fellow Andromedans, Kirk's only other course is to convince them that they really don't want to follow their planned course of action. Kirk utilizes his charm on Kelinda to make her husband jealous, and convince him they cannot handle human emotions. Trickery indeed, but they started it.

The Dohlman of Elas, "Elaan of Troyius," is a spoiled, self-centered, willful woman, and Kirk is stuck with the chore of teaching her manners before her marriage to a ruler of a neighboring world.

Somewhere along the line, Elaan decides she likes being subordinate to Kirk, and to seal his fate, she cries. When has Jim Kirk ever been able to resist a woman in tears? He holds her, and once touched by her tears, is fully intoxicated by desire and "love" feelings for her which only the stronger call of duty overpowers. We see that to send her on to her forced marriage causes him pain. This is not a love relationship as much as a bondage, but for the time endured by Kirk, it is equally painful. Luckily, Elaan's absence allows Kirk to quickly bounce back.

In "The Paradise Syndrome," we see Kirk again deeply in love with the Indian maiden Miramanee. If he loved Edith (as Mr. Irwin so finely explained) because she was everything he was, then he loves Miramanee because she is everything he wants, but cannot have.

As a starship captain, Kirk is bound day in and day out by the expectations of others. Miramanee, however, cares little who or what he is. She loves the James Kirk who can fail. Kirk has never allowed himself weakness, and now he is lost, alone and detatched by amnesia from everything that makes him what he is, and Miramanee is there loving him as if he were truly the god he knows he is not. Even after she knows he is not a god, she loves him. It is the unencumbered, open life-style that Kirk has half craved all his life. "A flesh-and-blood woman to hold, a beach to walk on . . ."

Miramanee also calls on probably the deepest need Kirk has—a need that is beyond memory or life-style, the deep animal instinct to protect. Kirk's entire life has been woven around protecting; it is an integral part of everything he does. His subconscious is full of the ugliness of his years of crusading around the galaxy, and with Miramanee, he has the infinite beauty and purity he idealizes, and she comes to him for protection and love. He is able to provide that protection and love for a very long time. It is truly a paradise.

Family is also important to Kirk, because he has so little of his own. Miramanee's joy at carrying his child is the topping to perfection. Given no hint of the responsibility of his past life, Kirk could live a good and happy life there in the woods being husband, father, protector, and provider. But it is not to be, and events bring him back to the life that he has chosen.

Can anyone forget the quiet love and grief that he displays waiting beside the bed of his wife and unborn child as they die?

Who knows what Kirk thought of the Romulan commander? But it would be interesting to see if anything would have come of it given the chance. Here, we assume either that the situation is too touchy or that Kirk feels if anyone makes a move, it should be Spock.

The lovely, angry Miranda ("Is There in Truth No Beauty?") is another instance where Kirk is impressed by the mind and beauty of a woman, but little develops. He has to try to distract her while Spock makes mind contact with the Medusan, Kollos, to get the ship back from the energy barrier. Again, a necessity. And it would not have *been* a necessity if the lady had been reasonable about the situation.

In "Day of the Dove," Kirk first sees Mara as Kang's frightened wife, then as someone to be protected when he rescues her from the crazed Chekov. Later, she turns out to be a spirited, courageous woman, and we see a sense of interest in Kirk—yet he is not foolish enough to make a play for her.

Deela, Queen of Scalos ("Wink of an Eye"), chooses Kirk to procreate with. It is as simple as that. She is a very attractive woman, and Kirk, assured that he is doing all he can in the given situation, leans back to enjoy what is happening. This does little to advance the theory that Kirk *must* be the strong one in a relationship or in charge of the action. Again, it is less of a relationship than a bondage; but we don't see Kirk complaining, nor does it incapacitate him or turn him off.

Kirk *prefers* to be the dominant one in a relationship, but then, a vast majority of men do. He also seems quite secure within himself and able to enjoy the variety of experiences he encounters.

Poor, crazy Marta, one of the ones "Whom Gods Destroy," almost killed Kirk to keep him; but we never see any signs of commitment, and we see many signs that by the next day she won't even remember him. Here there was no alternative to the course of action Kirk took. He was trying to protect his crew and the galaxy from the insane shape-changing Garth of Izar.

In Odona ("Mark of Gideon") we see an interesting combination of pure innocence and full authority ("No one commands Odona! I was not sent here"). There is a dignity about her that even her supposed lack of memory cannot hide. It is very attractive to Kirk, as is her obvious bewilderment and joy at the open spaces aboard the *Enterprise* mockup. As time passes, he also finds her a very courageous and self-sacrificing woman. (Shades of Edith.) At the right time and place, Kirk could have loved Odona.

By now, he has learned not to reach for what he might really want, but it is not a bitter or hard attitude as much as a self-protective pulling into himself. He cannot have his command and a woman, something he has always known, but which is becoming brutally clear to him at this point in his life. No one ever accused Jim Kirk of learning his lessons the easy way.

In "The Cloud Minders," a short but interesting relationship forms between Kirk and Vanna, the Troglyte woman from the zeenite mines. Twice she attacks him. The first time, he is not aware she is a woman, and uses his full strength, but she is undaunted. She is fighting for the cause of her people, another protector with the heart of a warrior. Kirk is at first surprised, and then as he comes to know her, he admires her courage.

The second time she attacks him, Kirk grabs her and does

considerably more wrestling than is necessary before pinning her. When he speaks to her, he does so flirtatiously, and with the aim of bargaining. He is turned on by the warrior in her.

Now he is ready to listen to her side of the story, but she is not ready to talk. She is not a woman easily charmed, and something in Kirk likes the challenge.

In a few short years, we see Jim Kirk fall in love with Edith Keeler, and then become instrumental in her death. We also see him not very long after that fall deeply in love with Miramanee, and then lose both her and the child he so very much wants. Now Jim Kirk is at the point of overload. He has not finished grieving over Edith, and there is perhaps a bit of guilt for having loved Miramanee, even though he knows that at the time he could not remember Edith and his loyalties to her. Aside from any guilt, the real and recent pain of losing his wife and child are heavy in him.

Now he is faced with Reena, as pure and innocent as Miramanee. She is confused and reaching to him; and he puts his arm around her because she is frightened, and then kisses her in almost a brotherly fashion to comfort her. He is visibly shaken by the feelings aroused within him by that kiss.

With Reena, it is almost like Miramanee all over again. With the others since Miramanee, there has been no real relationship. But Reena is quiet and open and needing, and she reaches out to that deep place in Kirk that needs to protect. He needs to fill the ache in himself, and he transfers much of his hurt and his unfulfilled desire (which he has not yet had time to cope with) to Reena. Kirk's wish to protect Reena is intensified by Flint's possessiveness and domination of the girl.

And when he loses Reena, it is like losing Edith and Miramanee and the child all over again. Perhaps this is the only time we see Kirk truly demoralized. Spock, bless him (though he may not understand the extent of the emotional buildup), knows when Jim is in trouble, and mercifully helps to heal Jim's mind. It is probably what saves Kirk's sanity.

We are told that Kirk had a deep relationship with Janice Lester ("Turnabout Intruder"), and that when she felt she was being stifled by Starfleet and quit, she accused him of betraying her for not quitting as well.

Kirk is indeed mortified when Janice exchanges bodies with him, but instead of mourning over the loss of his male form, turns his full attention immediately to the problem of saving his ship and command from the psychotic now occupying his body.

Mr. Irwin mentioned a line from the play *Goodbye Charlie* (about a gourmet waking up as a lamb chop), stating that Kirk took being in a woman's body too calmly. Perhaps somewhere in the back of his mind, this "gourmet-turned-lamb-chop" had just the faintest curiosity about what the lamb chop felt like during dinner. Most likely, though, the "not enough time in the episode" theory is the most accurate.

We see that Kirk feels sympathy for Janice Lester, but he also soundly refuses to feel guilty for something he had no control over. This shows growth in Kirk; a losing of that unfortunate tendency to take responsibility for everything around him, necessary or not. We can only wonder at this point if Spock's mind-touch had anything to do with it.

Mr. Irwin repeatedly states that Kirk used women. We have seen that he very seldom took unfair advantage of a woman any more than he would have a man. What he did do was to protect, with whatever means necessary, his crew and his mission—and sometimes the entire galaxy.

Mr. Irwin also states that Kirk loves women, but does not like them much. We have seen that disproved by the reaching out he has done to be open with the women who have been open and honest with him.

Mr. Irwin states that Kirk will probably remain a confirmed bachelor, and gives as his reasons that it will be because he is unable to form a lasting relationship with a woman, because he will never find another Edith (a contradiction in itself), and because he does not like women.

James Kirk found out the hard way—in just a few short years—that there can be no deep, lasting relationship for him as long as he remains in space. He can neither be satisfied with having a wife he sees once every six months (and pictures of growing children), nor by sitting on his duff planetside. So a wife and family will have to wait until he retires from his starship. This waiting is made harder for him by the memory of his relationships with Edith and Miramanee; he has tasted the joy of committment to a woman deeply in love with him. He is looking forward to experiencing it again.

Kirk will finally marry at a mature age, most likely a woman much younger than he, who will have a certain amount of innocence, will revel in having his children, and will come to him for security and refueling and his love. But she will be able to match his fire with her own, and be as much a protector of her family and causes as he is. He will love her deeply (as he did Edith and Miramanee), and will continue to protect his brood and be the wise, if somewhat flamboyant, vain, and impulsive, patriarch.

But what about "Plato's Stepchildren"? What about Kirk and Uhura?

The Platonians were not necessarily looking for the best romantic bait for Kirk and Spock, but for those women who would bring forth the deepest feelings of protectiveness. This was one and the same person for Spock; but Kirk would protect Uhura, as next to Spock and McCoy, Uhura is his closest friend. They have worked a lot of hours together and know each other well. (This goes further to prove that Kirk likes and respects women.)

Romance? Perhaps. Somewhere along the line it could happen, but it would more likely be a sharing of needs and caring than a great romance. And it won't be aboard his ship. It is highly unlikely that either of them would chance endangering their friendship or their working relationship by a physical relationship in a time of loneliness or need.

There is a chance that Uhura may find a mate among other Starfleet personnel, someone she could serve with, and thus have the best of both worlds. Kirk would not want to deny her that chance (especially if he did love her romantically) by wasting her time when he could not make a commitment to her. We must also assume that Uhura is a smart lady with no masochistic tendencies.

Overall, we see Kirk as an honest, fair, and open man when he has the choice of being so. We see a man who likes and respects women; who believes that if a woman is strong enough to dish something out, she is strong enough to take it back. A rather liberated view for our twentieth-century minds, maybe so much so that we miss it, and chalk it up to callousness.

We see a man who loves the games of men and women when played for fun, who enjoys being in charge but can also enjoy a change of the game plan. And we see a man who has a deep need of a serious relationship he cannot yet have.

We see a man who cannot resist a woman in tears, and yet

one who can allow his loved one to be killed for her own cause, and for his duty.

We see the warrior of peace and freedom, and we see the spent, hurt man, too many times battered, being touched and healed by the special loving touch of a man whom he is not afraid to love in return.

Above all, we see a very human man learning to love and live with the choices he has made; learning that nothing is as simple as it should be, and that the only thing there is to hold on to are those he loves. He dares to love. It is his shining virtue above the tarnished armor.

4.

THE BEGINNING OF A NEW HUMAN ADVENTURE

by Eleanor LaBerge

Perhaps millions of words have been written about Star Trek: The Motion Picture—*a few thousand of them are included in this volume. But few—if any—of them have examined the psychological aspects of the film and the characters within it. In the following article, Eleanor LaBerge does just that.*

Although *Star Trek: The Motion Picture* left enough dangling ends to make one suspect that it, like the camel, was put together by committee or accident, the book *The Making of STTMP* by Susan Sackett and Gene Roddenberry (describing the plot and casting difficulties) and the novelization of the movie by Roddenberry offer abundant clarification. All of the confusion might well have resulted in disaster, but instead, the motion picture managed a depth that deserves our appreciation. V'Ger showed us the consequences of knowledge as an end in itself: ultimate frustration, barrenness, the need to ask "Is this all there is?" The movie answers the question with all the beauty of optimistic Star Trek tradition. Although we enjoyed the dazzling sets and technical achievements, the real value of *STTMP* goes beyond special effects. As *Trek* editor Walter Irwin pointed out in his review of the film, the enjoyment of the picture seems to increase each time we see it.

Paramount's advertising for the film told us that "The Human Adventure Is Just Beginning." It is a general statement which leaves the audience free to form individual interpretations. One might postulate that the phrase meant a great stride into the world of man's future evolution, but I submit that it is in the theme of human relationships that the "human adventure" of Star Trek is *again* beginning. And while

53

some of us may feel that one more comment on the relationship between Spock and Kirk would be one too many, I believe it is the most significant aspect of the film. Reviewing once again in depth, we may perhaps discover that this particular theme is more profound in the movie and the book than a first viewing might reveal.

In *Trek* and elsewhere, the bond between Kirk and Spock has been examined from many divergent and polarized vantage points. There are cogent arguments and internal evidence from the series to support a number of differing positions. Some may find only the camaraderie of men joined in a common cause; to others, hints of the characters' mutual interdependence seem to indicate something deeper. The film and the book present the mystery of this friendship with simplicity and directness. With sensitive understatement, Roddenberry reveals a relationship which I feel may be better understood by placing it within the framework of a philosophical stance.

It is within the tradition of Star Trek to honor the great minds of the past, especially when their thoughts or deeds contribute to the understanding of a present situation. In that tradition, therefore, let us look at the psychological and philosophical viewpoints of two men who brought particular insights into the area of relationships: Martin Buber of our twentieth century, and Soren Kierkegaard of the nineteenth century. These men were the spokesmen of the "I-Thou" and "defining" relationship. Not only will studying Buber and Kierkegaard enable us to understand what has happened after long years in the Kirk/Spock situation, but the captain of the *Enterprise* and his Vulcan first officer provide interesting "living" examples of these philosophic principles.

The Danish philosopher/theologian Soren Kierkegaard described the relationships between persons from the sensual/selfish to the ideal—that which mutually defines. The defining relationship is a mind-to-mind, soul-to-soul union which reaches such profound depth that it defines two persons in relation to themselves and to all others. According to Kierkegaard, it is the level of interpersonal relationship which man must attain if he is to be whole and able to relate to the fullest extent in his own world.

In literature and history, examples of such friendship are frequent. To name but a few: Shakespeare and the "sweet

love remembered" of the sonnets; Michelangelo and Vittoria
Colonna; Dostoyevsky's Father Zosima and Aloysha; the
Brownings; and, close to our hearts, James T. Kirk and the
Vulcan Spock.

To understand the latter pair further, we should take a
brief look at Buber's position. He taught that before a person
acquires emotional maturity, a maturity gained through relationship, he must grow from the "I-It" stage to the "I-Thou."
It is basic and effortless for a normal person to attain an external relationship with things: the "I-It." Here there is no interpersonal investment of self. But the "I-Thou" encounter is
one with risk and the necessity of giving as well as receiving.

Spock had experience with the "I-It" of Buber's definition.
He was concerned with himself as Vulcan and with himself
as a creative, intelligent individual; but as we often heard in
his repartee with Dr. McCoy, he was incomplete. He could
look at the physical universe as "other," but he could not
wholeheartedly permit himself to pass beyond the "I-It" level.

Spock's relationship with Kirk threatened his identity as
Vulcan to the very depths of his being. The "I-It" stance was
the only one Spock could permit himself as a Vulcan. The
"I-Thou" state relative to Kirk defined Spock's *humanity*, not
his Vulcan heritage. After the five-year mission was complete,
we can only imagine the interior struggle that led Spock to
depart abruptly without a person-to-person farewell—a decision that left Kirk bewildered and certainly not unaffected.

Having decided to be wholeheartedly Vulcan, Spock withdrew, placing himself under the tutelage of the Vulcan masters of *Kolinahr*. He entered a life of seclusion, discipline,
and renunciation not unlike that of Earth's monastic traditions. In solitude and silence, he attempted to empty his mind
of distraction, particularly the reaction to his human emotions. Up to the point of his dramatic contact with V'Ger,
Spock would not have sought a lesser goal than the attainment of total, pure logic. The complication of an "I-Thou"
relationship did not have a place in that choice.

As we first meet him in the film, Spock has come close to
his ideal, but at the last minute he reacts to a distraction that
"stirs his human blood." That he could not finally succeed in
the attainment of *Kolinahr* was a logical outcome he might
have anticipated had he weighed his qualifications as carefully as he would have considered a move in 3-D chess. It

was in desperation—a human emotion—that he came to the *Enterprise* in an effort to purge himself in the very fire of human contact, as he sought his answer in the perfect mind of the cloud entity.

In Spock's ultimate contact with V'Ger, he was confronted with the value of the humanity he had sought to obliterate. This insight destroyed the false ideal, and freed Spock to be himself: a person in whom the Vulcan and human are integrated. He may now respond to more than the external, material world.

When the *Enterprise* approaches the heart of the cloud, one of Jerry Goldsmith's musical themes gives us a symbolic interpretation of V'Ger and Spock. It is a significant message given in the language of music. In contrast to the lyrical, poignant theme of the *Enterprise* (a rhythmic and melodic variation of the stirring opening orchestration), the V'Ger music is precise tonal progression. We hear *do mi sol do sol mi do* again and again. The progression, reminiscent of high school band and choir exercises, is repeated in major and minor sequences. Electronic effects provide variation; but we find no melody, no passion in V'Ger.

In dramatic personal terms, we see Spock come from that precise and logical limitation to the freedom of love: his "melody." I like to think of the beautiful horn countermelody soaring above the *Enterprise* as the voice of Spock (as well as Kirk) longing for that "something more."

After Spock realizes the cloud entity's need, he may at last understand the truth that simple feeling has transcendent worth. Following this acceptance, he is ready for the "I-Thou" encounter which will define himself not only as Spock, but subsequently as himself in relation to all others. In sickbay, the awareness held firmly in Vulcan reserve bursts forth in the simple act of reaching for Kirk's hand and in pronouncing the name Spock had tried to forget. It is one of the most touching and profound moments in all of Star Trek.

We may find it interesting here to consider that other name Spock reserved for James Kirk: *t'hy'la*. As it was in the book adaptation of the movie (p. 22), this term now exists in official Star Trek literature. From Spock's point of view, it had a triple meaning: friend, brother, and lover. By taking Kirk's flippant footnote in the novel at face value, we may miss a deeper level of truth. There are possibilities of intimacy which transcend the sexual, and yet are still like the lover's desire for physical union. The mind-to-mind union of friendship honored even on Vulcan might well be as deep as the marriage vow. For Kirk and Spock there may be the potential of a similar union of mind and soul.

By the end of *Star Trek: The Motion Picture*, there is an interesting reversal in the Kirk/Spock relationship. It is subtle and may be easily overlooked. Spock has faced the challenge of V'Ger and has chosen, logically, to grow. Kirk has not yet reached such a critical point of decision. Although he is capable of "I-Thou" relationships, Kirk's symbiotic attachment to the *Enterprise* still claims his heart as he renews his commitment to "out there."

Kirk is in an "I-It" syndrome, and the book adaptation points this out more clearly than in "The Naked Time" and other episodes of the original series. For all his ability to command a starship, for all his human charm and warmth, James Kirk defines himself not in the Kierkegaardian sense, but in his relationship to the *Enterprise*. He does not exclude other relationships as Spock tried to do, but as McCoy pointed out to Starfleet prior to Kirk's appointment as admiral (and as Kirk himself showed on the V'Ger mission) his love of the ship is obsessive.

In all the tender person-to-person relationships Kirk has known—for example, Edith Keeler, Ruth, Aurelia, and Lori—he could not give of himself in a permanent, defining relationship. James Kirk is healthily aware of himself as an individual; he possesses innate goodness and rare qualities of honesty, loyalty, integrity, and leadership, and yet the *Enterprise*—the "I-It" reality—is his one wholehearted love affair.

That he could give a deep affection and love to Spock might have been because Spock was "safe," and an integral part of the beloved *Enterprise*. This does not mean that a personal relationship did not exist. Kirk had a real need for Spock, and Spock for Kirk, that both realized consciously and subconsciously. In the television series this need frequently brought suppressed feelings to the surface. These incidents have given rise to the homosexual speculations which are rather simplistic as an interpretation of the depth of Kirk and Spock's developing relationship. Such a commitment may or may not happen; it is not part of the consideration of

Spock and Kirk relative to the "I-Thou" and defining relationship.

Roddenberry tells us that after the five-year mission Kirk
did not want to admit the extent to which Spock's abrupt de-
parture affected him. The reality of their friendship was sus-
taining to Kirk whether he acknowledged it or not. No Star
Trek fan could observe the expression on Kirk's face as
Spock returned to the bridge in the movie and doubt the sin-
cerity of Kirk's affection. And yet one may wonder if that joy
was not partly the thrill of having the *Enterprise* complete
now that the Vulcan had returned.

By the end of the motion picture Kirk is still in possession
of the *Enterprise*, and experiencing a deep satisfaction that
she is his to take "out there." There is little doubt that Spock
has made the most significant step toward wholeness.

At this point, we realize that not only Kirk's future but the
concept of Star Trek itself is at a crucial creative crossroad.
The human adventure we have just seen begun may be able
to make valuable statements in the personal dimension. The
entire motion picture was devoted to the theme of relationships: V'Ger sought its creator; Decker overcame his fear of
total giving; Ilia found the reality of self in spite of the accidental form in which she was contained; and Spock found his
answer.

Yet the film seems to introduce a disturbing, elusive
thought regarding our hero, Kirk. Could this man, with his
qualities of greatness, possess a tragic flaw? In his obsessive
desire for the *Enterprise* is there an element which could lead
to his destruction as a person?

Up to now, the *Enterprise* has been a major factor in mo-
tivating Kirk's creative solutions to many an "insurmount-
able" problem. The love for his ship gives Kirk strength in
action. What about continued strength in the personal dimension? Clearly not all of the challenges of the Star Trek characters have been met. And what grand challenges they are!
The future of Star Trek need not sacrifice action as it
presents character growth. There is no dichotomy here, as the
motion picture proved.

As we look down the years, the integration of his Vulcan
and human heritage will not be a simple task for Spock. Kirk
will be a part of the new challenge. Neither Kierkegaard nor
Buber gave us to understand that personal growth is easy.

The love and friendship that defines carries with it all the difficulties of growing; growth that often brings pain and suffering as well as joy in opening oneself to another human person. Once an individual attempts to relate in an "I-Thou" frame of reference, he must become part of that other person's being, open to the joy and anguish of growing. It could be no different for Kirk and Spock.

We may hope that the "powers that be"—specifically Paramount and the Great Bird of the Galaxy himself—realize that not only Kirk's future but the immortality of Star Trek itself will be at stake in upcoming decisions for continuation of the series in whatever form. We may fervently entreat the producers not merely to stretch out the original series (as has been done in a number of disappointing "original" pieces of Star Trek fiction), but to seek out new worlds of ideas that will fulfill the promise of depth seen in the original series and the motion picture.

5.

A SAMPLING OF "TREK ROUNDTABLE"

Trek readers continue to remain the most loyal and prolific letter writers around, and we are very grateful, for this continuing feedback is what helps to keep our magazine viable. In this selection, we have included many more letters commenting on Star Trek: The Motion Picture *for two reasons: (1) Most of the letters speaking to STTMP arrived at our offices too late to be considered for inclusion in* The Best of Trek #3; *and (2) the movie was such an important event to Star Trek fandom we thought it only fair to give as wide a spectrum of viewpoints as possible. We hope you enjoy these comments from your fellow fans—and remember, we'd like to hear from you too!*

Pam E.F. Watson
Bentleyville, Pa

I enjoyed *Trek* 16 a great deal, especially "Alternate Universes in Star Trek," but Rebecca Hoffman's article ("Vulcan as a Patriarchy") disturbed me. Not because I had come to a different conclusion—until I read her article I had never given it any thought—but because of the underlying contradiction it would entrench in Vulcan society.

Does she really think that a society dedicated to peace above all else would have as its basis an act of brutal aggression? She herself says that it is neither a pretty nor pleasant picture, and it certainly isn't; rape never is. And that is what she describes by her idea of Vulcan mating being a release of "an enormous amount of pent-up violence." We are told again and again that Vulcans worship peace above all else and don't approve of violence, yet every act of mating is equally an act of aggressive violence. How does she think a race would survive if it knew—and how could it not know?—that it was based on a lie?

But what struck me at once was Hoffman's curious ideas about the Vulcan hormonal system. Her notion that the menstrual cycle is somehow controlled by the moon is an old one, but it has never been more than a theory, and has been discarded nowadays by all but Norman Mailer in some of his more fanciful moods.

However, if it were true that lunar influences governed our lives, the *entire* endocrine system would be affected. The pituitary gland, the thyroid, the adrenal, the pancreas, etc. would all go out of kilter at once. And if all these were affected by the lack of a satellite, then spacegoing humans would turn into a race of cretinous dwarves afflicted with diabetes, hypertension, Cushing's syndrome or Addison's disease, bruising, weakness, severe emaciation or a curious obesity, tremors and nervous irritability . . . among the more common consequences of a hormonal disturbance. None of these things are likely to be cured by cycles of intense sexual activity.

In fact, if the endocrine system is affected by "lunar influences," a race could not survive on a moonless world, because they would never mature sexually. Sexual development is one of the first things affected by an upset in the endocrine system. As is mental development. Can anyone really say that Vulcans are not as bright as they should be?

I thought that the question of the seven-year cycle was settled by D.C. Fontana, who says (in the dedication to Kathleen Sky's *Vulcan*) that she was glad to get the mixup straightened out. Hoffman continually confuses the seven-year cycle with *pon farr*, the "time of madness." If the *pon farr* occurs every seven years, why hadn't Spock had the meeting with T'Pring years ago? Does she really think that every seven years Spock will go mad and have to go back to marry T'Pring or fight whomever she chooses as her champion *this* time?

If not, that demolishes her basis for Vulcan family life—a Vulcan male does not need to deepen his wife's "bond" to him in readiness for the next time he has an attack, because (though the seventh year of his cycle may give him various discomforts) it isn't deadly. How does Hoffman think Vulcan society would survive with half of its population subject to regular attacks of deadly insanity? Especially if Vulcan is a patriarchy, with business and politics (at least in the early years) male-dominated. It is a strange basis for a patriarchy dedicated to logic, since the old reason for discriminating against women on Earth was that their menstrual cycles would cause them to be irrational or even subject to brief fits of madness at times.

What Hoffman seems to forget is that Vulcans have an enormous respect for authority. Spock shows that again and again in his dealings with Kirk, Commodore Decker, and Captain Pike. Sarek displays it when he insists Spock be accorded respect because he is an officer in Starfleet. And he doesn't even approve of Starfleet! Hoffman's argument that Vulcan is a patriarchy rather than a matriarchy (she doesn't even touch the idea that many races are neither) seems mainly based on the script directions of "Amok Time" and "Journey to Babel," but I think everything is equally explained by the fact that Vulcan society teaches respect for authority and rank.

That explains Sarek's manners: When Sarek and Amanda board, *of course* Sarek comes in first—he *is* the ambassador. When Kirk says that Sarek's request (that was Amanda's word for it) sounded more like a command, he seems surprised and somewhat reproving. If the basis for Vulcan society had men command their wives, wouldn't a traveled, cosmopolitan officer of Starfleet be aware of such a commonplace fact? Of course he would; especially since he had been on Vulcan before, when Spock went through *pon farr*. And in a long career, Kirk must have run across other Vulcans; if there had been an automatic deference on the part of the woman, he wouldn't have been surprised that Sarek used a commanding tone to Amanda, even though she is human.

It is the fact that Sarek is an authoritarian commander, and, as such, expects respectful compliance from those around him. (As T'Pau, another authoritarian commander, does. She even expects compliance from Starfleet!) Amanda would hardly have to remind Kirk that Sarek is Vulcan—that is obvious and wouldn't need saying—but everyone might not know just by looking at Sarek that respect for those in command of a situation is one of the axioms of life as it is lived on Vulcan.

I could shoot several other holes in the article, but that would be petty and not worth the space. Besides, it has done its job by giving us a new topic of discussion—and that is the purpose of your magazine, isn't it? When *Trek* arrives, I am sure of having a day or two of new angles to explore about Star Trek. Could you now do an article about Vulcan as a matriarchy, and then one as a "straight" *logical* society? (I'm afraid I don't find either very logical.)

Congrats again on an interesting magazine.

Andrew Harker
Palo Alto, Cal.

I realize that its been two years since *The Best of Trek* came out, but I feel that there are several points to be made. In December of '79, I stood in line nearly two hours to see *Star Trek: The Motion Picture* the first day it was released. After seeing it, I was both impressed and disappointed.

I thought that the special effects were fantabulous. They were 1,000% better than the series, and were a stroke of genius.

What disappointed me, and I believe most Trekkies, was the plot. It left a bit to be desired. Paramount had a beautiful chance to bring the Starship *Enterprise* to the movie screen, but unfortunately, they didn't make the best of it. They could have made a beautiful script and plot, which would have made the whole movie really attractive. Instead, they borrowed the plot of one of the episodes of the series. Why?

I'll admit that they already had the Trekkies standing in line when the mention of a movie came out, and they probably had a profit no matter what, but I feel they could have at least felt for us Trekkies. After all, the talk of it started in '70, and after ten years you can imagine the expectations of us all. Then to see an elaborate remake of "The Changeling" (with modifications from other episodes and new ideas), well, you get the idea. The movie had many pluses; but unfortunately, the minuses were many also. .

With me being a loyal Trekkie (not a real fanatic one), I went to the movie more than once, as did many other Trekkies, I'm sure. But for those who aren't, the movie didn't have enough appeal to bring them back.

In no way am I degrading the movie, for that would be blasphemy (also an untruth if I were to say that), but neither am I praising it . . . A whole lot, at least. The movie is a lot of fun, being able to see our heroes, Kirk, Spock, McCoy, and the rest, along with some newcomers, gallivanting off in the galaxy to save humanity . . . again. I have heard that a sequel is in the making, and if it is, then I'll go see it for sure. I certainly hope that one is being made, because you can't get enough of a good thing.

I do want to congratulate, and, moreover, thank everyone involved in the movie for bringing it out so we wouldn't forget you all. Without you, the movie wouldn't be reminiscent of Star Trek at all. You deserve all the devotion and fame that is due you. You make it special by being what you are. People living and acting out some of our wildest dreams, and giving hope to those of us who don't have any. Thank you for being you. You're the greatest cast and crew I know.

In *The Best of Trek*, the polls showed that there should be no new aliens on the *Enterprise*. However, the movie was made popular partly by Ilia, an alien. Even though she was part of the crew, she in no way hampered the roles of Uhura, Chekov, or even Sulu, which was predicted by the poll. I feel that an alien, if not more than one, should be included in *Star Trek II*, because I think that it will add interest to the plot.

In closing, I wish to say that if it weren't for the wonderful people like the cast, crew, and writers of Star Trek, we wouldn't be the loyal fanatics we are today. Thanks to everyone who does anything to help Star Trek, if not for your contribution, then for being people who believe.

Carole Snider
Scarborough, Canada

I must reply to a letter in *Trek* 16 from Willa McKeel, Hopewell Junction, N.Y.

I do not know where she gets her information from when she says the character of Mr. Spock had turned into a bitter thing for Leonard Nimoy. Possibly from the *Enquirer*.

If she had read *I Am Not Spock* or *William Shatner: An Authorized Biography* or *The Making of Star Trek: The Motion Picture*, she would know this is absolutely false.

I quote Leonard Nimoy from *I Am Not Spock*: ". . . the relationship with the character of Mr. Spock has given me a constant guideline for a dignified approach to life as a human being," and "I am proud of being connected with the show. . . ." And from *The Making of STTMP*: "I certainly wouldn't want anyone else doing the role. . . ."

It hardly seems as if Mr. Nimoy finds distaste with his role. Especially in his book, *I Am Not Spock*, we find that he speaks about Spock with great affection and warmth. In interviews with Marshak and Culbreath for the Shatner biography, Mr. Nimoy insists he does not find the character distasteful; in fact, he is grateful to him.

Delays in obtaining him for the movie were caused by personal time schedules, tight calendars, and a reluctance to give up many, many projects he was working on at the time. Sure, the money paid must have been considerable. It was for Shatner, too. Let's face it, those people are human beings, and they work longer, harder hours than the average person. Fourteen-hour days; in the makeup chair at 6:30; waiting hours to do a scene, only to have it cut or called off. Long, grueling days and nights, and they must look their best at all times. So, yes, they must be paid highly for this.

Please, when speaking about Mr. Nimoy, do not infer that he doesn't like the character he plays . . . it simply is not true. If you'd just read those books mentioned, and many others, you'll find he embraces Spock with joy and admiration.

Doris Skiba
Shawboro, N.C.

This morning's mail brought the most delightful surprise— my very first issue of *Trek*! To say I was carried off in transports of glee would be an understatement. I found out about Trek at my bookstore, where I bought *The Best of Trek* and *The Best of Trek: #2*. After reading these two wonderful books, I rushed over to my severely depressed checkbook, heaved a heavy sigh at the condition of the balance, and wrote a check for my first issue. Let me say at this point that my mail carrier has come to hate me. I stopped the poor man every day for six weeks—asking him if he'd seen it yet, finally growing suspicious and accusing him of *stealing* it! This morning it finally arrived, and after apologizing to the mail carrier (who looked at me as if I were crazed . . . not too far wrong!), I flew into the house to devour my prize. I was not disappointed. *Trek* is so much more than I thought it could be—I am almost speechless!

The key word here is "almost." In the intro to Trek Roundtable, you asked readers for comments on *Star Trek: The Motion Picture*. I've been itching to discuss this film for *months*. Like Van James, in his look at the *STTMP* novel, I saw the film first, read the book, and saw the film again. I've found that these two mammoth additions to the Star Trek that I've loved for so many years have left me in a state of psychic overstimulation. Let me explain. . . .

I knew when *STTMP* came out that there would have to be changes, and indeed there were. The first time I saw the film, I was at once on a stellar high to *at last* be in the theater *actually seeing* this dreamed-of picture and deeply disturbed that "my" Star Trek had been changed so much. I left the theater liking what I had seen, with certain reservations.

I felt there were "dark places" in *STTMP*—a feeling much like coming upon a unfamiliar word in a sentence, then reading on, hoping its meaning will be revealed in the context of its use. What a relief to find those "dark places" explained in Gene Roddenberry's novelization! When I had finished the book, I went to see the film again, and this time everything made more sense. (Of course, I wasn't fretting about the strangeness of it all the second time, either, which must be considered in my reaction.) Captain Kirk, a little older and getting wiser, seemed more like "my" beloved captain after I found out (in the novel) how Admiral Nogura pried him away from the *Enterprise*. No wonder Kirk is acting like such a twerp when he takes back the "center seat" (I *hate* this line). He feels used and foolish because he didn't figure it all out sooner, somewhat uneasy that he may be taking back command for his own edification and not the good of the mission, and exhilarated that he's gotten back his beautiful *Enterprise*.

Mr. Spock also had a bad case of twerp-itis in the picture, until you read the book and learn of the anguish that led him to seek *Kolinahr*, and the terrible shame he felt when he realized that his human half was still there, despite his efforts. Who would not be moved by the passage in which Spock says goodbye to his only friend, Jim Kirk, his *t'hy'la*, of whom Spock will never again allow himself to think? Such a burden would make him act so upon returning to the *Enterprise*.

These personal glimpses revealed in the novel, taken with the film, make for a good Star Trek story.

Now, the psychic overstimulation I spoke of before is: All of this imaginative new Star Trek information, combined with *years* of desire and speculation, added to my isolation from ST fandom (SF and ST out here are synonymous with radicalism, communism, and other such undesirable isms), make me full to the top with an overwhelming desire to talk about Star Trek, read about Star Trek, write about Star Trek, surround myself with Star Trek!

Even in my most rabid days during the original series, I never felt like this! Certainly, *STTMP* is not *the* vehicle for ST, but it does do nicely as part of the mosaic. I don't believe any fan would say that Star Trek is the result of any single episode from the series. All of the episodes together make "our" Star Trek. *STTMP* is another in that series—new and shiny, filled with untried ideas, but still only one part of the series. Maybe it's better to say that *Star Trek: The Motion Picture* is a jumping-off point.

The pilots of the original series were a learning place. Star Trek evolved from them in the same way that new Star Trek films will spring from ideas set down in *STTMP*. The movie laid a lot of background against which new stories will be told; stories that won't have a billion ST fans having coronaries from the shock of changes, too busy to get immersed in the plot. I am inclined to wait for more Star Trek movies before saying this one is good or bad . . . just think, we have all of the new concepts of this film to discuss until the next one comes around!

I am very new to organized Star Trek fandom. Years ago, when ST first zinged through the airwaves, I was in junior high school. I loved the show, collected ST-related items (I have a scrapbook filled with articles from movie magazines that have such scintillating titles as "Leonard Nimoy's Secret Agony," and "The Secret Shame That Haunts Bill Shatner"—they are a real scream!), wrote droves of letters to NBC, and then, nothing. As I got older, and there was no ST around, not even reruns, I drifted away from active fandom. *Now* I find out about all of the *great* stuff that has been going on! The cons, the zines—my imagination has gone on overload! I have the great pleasure now of seeing the series rerun and drawing on my adult mind for meaning. I was character-oriented before; today I see more than attractive bodies. (Though I know more about what to do with my thoughts about those lovely bodies these days.) I had thought that most of my feelings toward ST were due, in part, to juvenile infatuation. Truly, some of them were, but what delight I experience now in knowing that the love I hold for ST comes from my adult understanding of its deeper meaning. And to top off everything, I discover that there are great, big fat *bunches* of people out there who feel the same. It's been said before, but I'll say it again . . . what a relief to find out that I'm not insane!

Again, I can't say how much my first issue of *Trek* impressed me. I am looking forward to reading this heroic fan effort as often as possible! I was particularly glad that someone speculated about the very bizarre appearance of the Klingons. Leslie Thompson did a fine job exploring the possibilities, and I am anxious to hear what reasons Gene Roddenberry, et al., come up with. This piece of information was not mentioned in *The Making of STTMP* or *Chekov's Enterprise*. And it's a shame Mark Lenard wasn't more recognizable in his Klingon role.

Jane Wesenberg
Toledo, Ohio

Although I have been a Star Trek fan since the show was first aired, it has been just a few months since I became aware of the extent of organized Star Trek fandom. *Trek 15* was my first issue, and I enjoyed it thoroughly—devoured it might be a better word. I am impressed by its professional quality. There was a good variety of articles, and little repetition, although the issue was organized around one theme. All of the articles were informative, thought-provoking, and well written. The pictures were high-quality also. I appreciate seeing so many that were not standard publicity releases—very refreshing, thank you. The cover was packed full of good color pictures without appearing crowded.

You asked for reactions to the movie. I absolutely loved it! For me, the best aspect of Star Trek was its emphasis on the psychology of the characters and their relationships with each other. No Star Trek movie could go wrong for me as long as the characters and their relationships were explored in depth and the integrity of the characters' personalities was kept intact, in a story which allowed for a lot of interaction. All else to me is secondary, and easily approved as long as it's believable and consistent with the philosophy of Star Trek as exemplified in the original show.

All of that was carried out in the movie, and extremely well. I would like to have seen more interaction, but was satisfied with the amount shown, realizing that concessions had to be made to those who would expect spectacular props, special effects, and space action in the *Star Wars* tradition. Of course, I did have some gripes, but they certainly did not ruin the movie for me. One of these is that not enough time was spent on McCoy and the other characters besides Kirk and Spock. Also, too much time was spent on the scene in which the *Enterprise* flies over V'Ger, and this scene appeared too dark and dismal.

I agreed with most of the ideas in the *Trek* articles reviewing aspects of the movie. I disagree strongly with one opinion Walter Irwin gives in his article: Irwin says: "We learn nothing new about Spock in *STTMP*, and it seems as if Spock learns nothing new as well. Many fans have exulted over the scene in which Spock 'accepts' emotionalism as necessary to life, but if this was such a startling revelation to Spock, then why didn't it seem to affect him more in the final scenes of the film?"

Mr. Irwin is referring to what to me as a Spock fan was the "peak experience" of the movie. What Spock went through was the basis for personal growth on his part. From his encounter with V'Ger, he discovered that a reasoning consciousness without a human quality, emotion, was barren. V'Ger at that time did not yet have the human quality or access to it. Spock must have experienced this lack as extreme hopelessness, and knew then that his own humanity, which he had been fighting so hard to suppress, was the key for which he had searched, the key to ending his own agonizing sense of incompleteness. V'Ger could not help itself— but Spock already had what he needed within himself! With that realization, Spock first acknowledged that he needed his humanity and wanted his emotions. And he reached out with his first tentative steps toward the friends who had been there all along.

Now, as to the question I quoted: You surely noted that

Spock was showing more feeling at the end of the movie—more facial expression, more vocal modulation, body language—occasionally touching his best friend as if to guide him through the hazardous situations they were in; a "softening" of his attitude toward human frailties. But, why not more?

As a doctoral candidate in clinical psychology with training and experience in psychotherapy, I see what happened to Spock as analogous to the way in which therapy often works. People rarely change their behavior automatically once they have learned something important about themselves that they want to change. (That "something important" is traditionally called "insight.") Let's say I have just started to realize that I am a worthwhile person, though most of my life I have felt unworthy. Now, I will want to change my behavior so that I *act* like a worthwhile person and also continue to feel that way. The act is usually much more difficult than the insight. It will take much practice in my daily life as well as continued therapeutic insight as to my worthiness before I can learn to act and feel as I truly want to. That is, it takes more than one realization as to my worthiness for me to feel and act truly worthy. It takes continuing self-knowledge and practice in real life. The repeated insight-practice cycles necessary to change are traditionally called "working through" (of an insight).

So it goes with Spock. He has known an extremely powerful insight, obviously. But he still has little experience expressing his feelings in a way that's right for him. He gets started a bit after the realization, but will need repeated practice, trial and error, introspection, and further self-knowledge in order to change in the way he wants. And for the most effective change, he needs a very important therapeutic element—a warm, caring relationship. Let's hope he will seek out Kirk to help him in the ways he needs. So, at the end of the movie, we could not expect Spock to effect more emotional behavior than he does show, even though he has had a "startling revelation."

I am glad you included my article about the novel. The book certainly does add much to "flesh out" the story in terms of background and character development. The movie could have been improved by including more from the book, particularly in the relationship department, but I realize the time limitations. Still, aside from Kirk-Spock-McCoy material, including flashbacks on Kirk's relationship with Lori could have helped explain Kirk's motivation, particularly in having taken the promotion to admiral. Also, I think the "special effects" inside V'Ger described in the novel are much more spectacular than those we were shown, and I was surprised to see that the actual effects did not live up to the novel. To pick out one comment I missed in particular in the movie, it was McCoy's characteristic ice-breaker, "Never look a gift Vulcan in the ears, Jim," that left me wearing a silly grin and giggling upon reading it. That remark tempered the ominous tone on the bridge upon Spock's leaving, a tone not alleviated in the movie.

I could go on for pages about such comparisons, and perhaps sometimes I will attempt to do so. Also, I would like to try a "Star Trek and Me" type long letter or short article, as in *The Best of Trek* (#1). Thanks for your time in reading this, and for all your efforts in putting out such an excellent magazine. Keep it up!

Sandra Robertson
Boone, N.C.

Thank you for your fine magazine, which has given me many hours of pleasure.

I enjoyed the motion-picture issue, as I was just as excited as everyone else that the film finally became a reality. The special effects *were* wonderful and I felt as if I could walk right into the future. The cast from the series was excellent, especially DeForest Kelley and Leonard Nimoy. Mr. Nimoy conveyed the complexity of Spock with sensitivity and subtlety. Mr. Kelley gave an outstanding performance. His Dr. McCoy was by far the most interesting and believable character in the film.

However, despite these fine performances, the breathtaking and realistic special effects, and a good, if not novel, story, I must confess disappointment. Where was the human drama and interaction I have come to expect from Star Trek? The minor characters had hardly any chance to act. How much drama can you make from lines which, for the most part, simply respond to commands? Perhaps Mr. Roddenberry was influenced by the success of *Star Wars* when he let the film lean so heavily upon special effects. Some of that time could have been spent on character development. It was difficult to feel sympathy for the lovers, since we never knew their story or reason for parting. Why not explain it?

I can overlook the shortcomings of the story, which was very much like several episodes of the series, and even the inconsistencies and unanswered questions. But I must admit that V'Ger—who could destroy planets and create a probe like Ilia, but didn't know its own name!—was a little hard to take.

I do hope that, if we're fortunate enough to have a sequel, more attention is given to the characters. The cast from the series are all fine actors. Give them a chance to act!

Diane Marston
Sacramento, Cal.

I have seen *Star Trek: The Motion Picture* twice and the first time had a lump in my throat as the old crew was reunited. The special effects, however, especially the flight into the center of the V'Ger machine, soon seemed to dominate the film and take up footage I would rather have seen devoted to the relationships between the "old" crew members. At the second viewing the expectancy of that happening was gone and I enjoyed the special effects and attention to detail for themselves. Still, my initial judgment remains that I would have enjoyed fewer effects and a longer visit with what I truly consider to be old friends.

My main criticism of the story is that the only romantic interest was between the new, younger crew members. I realize that no one wants to see Kirk or any one of the "old" crew made part of a machine and sent off into space, but I can't help wishing that the story had contained some provision for one or more of the older crew members to refer to his or her love life (or lack of it). They all looked as fit and vital as in the original series; so why no libido? Is there no sex after forty? Please, Mr. Roddenberry, in the next project say it isn't so! I'm not asking for a romantic story in particular, just some indication that our natural drives do not atrophy as we approach middle age. The sexual attractions and/or frustrations depicted in the television series reflected various aspects of the characters' personalities, and this kept them from being

larger-than-life comic book figures. Their adventures in love
made our heroes and heroines seem at various times tender,
foolish, heroic, pathetic, and sometimes downright funny. In
short, human. (Yes, even, at times, my favorite Vulcan!)

But all criticism aside, Star Trek is back, and that in itself
is a triumph. I hear rumors that Gene Roddenberry and
Paramount are negotiating for a return of Star Trek to television. . . .

*At this writing, plans are indeed being discussed to return
Star Trek to television in the form of a number of yearly
movie "specials." As no network has been specified, we at*
Trek *suggest readers hold off on letters for the time being. Be
assured that all three major networks and Paramount know
of your interest, and that millions of the same people who
bought tickets to* STTMP *will watch the series. Things look
very good right now . . . wait a while before writing.*

Rebecca Burnham
Edgartown, Mass.

Well now, I thought we were all through with discussing all
the possibilities regarding "whatever will Spock do come the
next *pon farr*?" Then I spied Mary Phelan's letter in *Trek* 15
and decided maybe it's not too late to try and get my own
two cents in.

Okay, the scenario is familiar. Spock is "out there" somewhere, impossibly far from Vulcan when the *pon farr* comes
over him. Here begin the speculations. What will happen?
Will Spock and Jim do the dolorous deed? Will Christine get
the thrill of a lifetime? Or . . .

Sorry, but I happen to be of the opinion that it's just not
that easy to get out of *pon farr*. If it can be broken simply by
going through the motions to attain a sexual release, doesn't
that undermine the purpose of *pon farr*, which is to ensure a
stable Vulcan population? Wouldn't it also eliminate the need
for a fight to the death in the event of a challenge, since the
thwarted suitor could certainly take care of his needs in some
other way?

You see, I think what Spock meant when he said (in
"Amok Time") that he "must return home and take a wife
or die" was that he must indeed *return to Vulcan* and *take a
wife*—or die. Not much room for compromise there. I liken

it to the legend of the vampire having to sleep on its native soil after the rising of the sun. So the *pon farr* sufferer has to be on Vulcan; and furthermore, he can't mate with just anyone. I believe that it is necessary that the proper procedures of selection and bonding be observed; the exception being in the case of brides won in mortal combat. Perhaps something to do with that initial mind link at the age of seven ensures the successful culmination of the relationship during *pon farr*.

Which brings me to my second argument. It has to do with Pamela Rose's "Speculations on Spock's Past" (*The Best of Trek: #2*), in which she proposes that prior to meeting Amanda, Sarek has been neither bonded nor married because his sperm has been found to be incompatible with any Vulcan woman. Are we to assume that at age sixty-plus he had not yet experienced *pon farr*? I know Vulcans live longer than humans, and this might account for his being a late bloomer, but I think not. Spock was approximately half that age when it happened to him. Therefore, considering in all likelihood Sarek had reached puberty, and also considering that (according to available sources) he had already established himself on Vulcan, then does it seem possible that the Vulcan hierarchy would allow one as valuable as Sarek to die of *pon farr*? Doubtful. Taking into acount what I have already said about the problem of circumventing *pon farr*, how can it be explained that he lived?

I don't discount Ms. Rose's article, but I do think it needs a little fleshing out, which I'll try to do.

My idea is that since the period of fertility in the Vulcan males' seven-year cycle triggers *pon farr*, it would stand to reason that if there was no period of fertility, there would consequently be no *pon farr*. In other words, a sterile man would be free of it. Without the danger of an individual dying in *pon farr*, there would be no reason to bond those who could not possibly fulfill the purpose of a marriage. Still, those individuals could be productive, contributing members of the society throughout a normal lifespan. Such must have been the case with Sarek. I support my theory with the speculation that this might be why Spock thought he "might be spared this." It is well known that hybrid crosses frequently result in neutral individuals, incapable of reproduction.

Hold on, you say—Spock was bonded! This leaves some questions as to how and when it is determined that a child is suitable for bonding. I can only guess that in most cases it becomes quite apparent in tests done in early childhood, but in a few instances (such as that of Spock), only the onset of maturity will tell. In any event, if a sizable percentage of unnecessary bondings can be dispensed with, it is indisputably logical to do so, and worry about the remaining "maybes" when the time comes, but in the meantime, bonding them for good measure.

Now, also in *The Best of Trek #2* was an article by Beverley Wood called "I Love Spock." Mrs. Wood maintains that just because Vulcan men aren't fertile except during *pon farr* doesn't mean that they can't or won't make love at other times. Granted, it may take some doing on the part of the lady involved, and it probably isn't often that a cool Vulcan miss takes on the job of seducing an unattached Vulcan male, but perhaps in the case of a lovely, determined young Earthwoman . . . get the picture?

One more thing: Does anyone care to guess what became of Stonn's original mate? Weren't there enough women to go around? Or did she die? I guess you can't blame him—or T'Pring—for looking out for number one.

Garry Lagnese
Silver Spring, Md.

At the present time I am an avid Trekker. For about six years now, I have loved Star Trek. The release of *Star Trek: The Motion Picture* plunged my heart deeper into adoration of the universe of the twenty-third century. But it seems that all my ST friends see less in the movie than I, and thus I'm reluctant to talk about it. That is, until I received my first issue of *Trek* (No. 16). When I read the Roundtable, I was overjoyed to find so many others seeing the same way I do. And so, with a mind utterly loaded with ideas and comments, I want to discuss *STTMP*.

Let me break it down into separate sections so I can cover every aspect of the film.

First: the overall appearance and effect. I loved the new bridge, all the effects (except maybe V'Ger, which I only liked), the beautiful new uniforms, the spectacular Klingon sequence, and all the sets. Words cannot describe my love for the *Enterprise* and Jerry Goldsmith's music. All I know is that both affect me emotionally in a way I've never experienced before. One thing frustrated me, though: the representation of Vulcan. Why are there two moons hanging in the sky on a planet that supposedly has none? That was a terrible mistake.

Second: the acting and plot. The former was quite up to par with the television series . . . I can say no more. However, the plot was not one designed for TV. If it had been, there would have been more interpersonal relationships and emotion. But as Gene Roddenberry said in a recent interview, ". . . motion pictures tend to be a sensory experience creating the illusion that the audience is there. Television cannot create this illusion . . . it intellectualizes rather than sensorizes the product." In this light, Roddenberry, Paramount, and all involved in the making of *STTMP* did the best job anyone could possibly do. In other words, *STTMP* was just about all it could be up there on the big screen, and I thoroughly believe that what it was was true Star Trek down to every last detail. *STTMP* brought love, hope, and the dream of peace to the world of the future. No, the human race wasn't wiped out in a nuclear holocaust, but instead it chose to build rather than destroy. And look where that got them: They achieved transcivilization—the dream of a future where all people can live their lives to the fullest and enjoy the wondrous diversity of the universe. This is the very universe Gene Roddenberry believes in.

Thirdly: some comments. *Star Trek: The Motion Picture* never reinforced the "rubber-band impression." Our first views of twenty-third-century Earth in *STTMP* were intended to broaden our view and insight of that universe, not restrict it. With just these few references, the Federation exists more now in my mind than it ever did in the series.

Also, Spock was far less alien than many saw him to be in the movie. True, in the beginning he seemed remote and cold (quite understandable because of the rigorous *Kolinahr*); but toward the end he seemed more human than ever before. In a touching scene, he reaffirmed his love and affection for Kirk—hardly alien behavior.

So there. I've finally gotten to share my pent-up feelings about *Star Trek: The Motion Picture*!

Diana Covell
Detroit, Mich.

I have been told that nothing impresses me, and that statement is almost correct. I say almost, because there is Star Trek, and I am impressed by the whole idea of Star Trek. It has convinced me that the age of miracles has not passed, for when mankind needed it, God provided the Great Bird of the Galaxy.

To get a show on television with the intelligence, idealism, and vision of hope that Star Trek contains is a wonder at any time, but to pull it off in the 1960s was nothing short of a miracle.

I *did* buy *The Best of Trek* (#1), but I never even got a chance to read it. A friend saw it and wanted to read it, and I never got it back. I have just finished reading your second book (no matter *who* the friend was, this one was not leaving until I finished it!), and I find myself saying words like "Wow!" and "I am impressed!" And so here is my order for a subscription.

You say, write. Boy, would I like to. Let me give you an idea of my background. I am a federal police officer with the Federal Protective Service. Before that I spent a total of seven and a half years in the U.S. Army, five and a half of those on active duty as an information specialist. My duties ranged from writing to editing two different newspapers in the Army, one for a major command, the other for an ROTC summer camp. I enjoy needlepoint and painting, and have recently had a gallery express interest in my work.

I am intently interested in the security of the ship. Kirk is always calling on Security, but what are their duties? What kind of men and women get into Security? Are they spacegoing police officers, or are they guards? Just what are their responsibilities and authority in space? We know there are prisons, even maximum-security prisons, so there must be criminals. Mudd is a first-rate con artist to have had a starship commander take care of the problems he caused.

Unfortunately, I have never seen the fan magazines beyond those that are sold in bookstores, but like Mary Jo Lawrence, I have read all the books on the market (except the one

which forgot who owned it), and I have some small insight
into the way that fans perceive Star Trek. If you really meant
it, I may just give it a whirl.

Gloria-Ann Rovelstad
Elgin, Ill.

Just received my copy of *Trek* 16. Turned to the comments page, and there was my very own opinion. Not remem-
bering half of it, I reread it . . . Geesh, maybe I should have
used my pen name on it! I'm bound to get a lot of flack over
that Freudian viewpoint of V'Ger. And you ran it as the first
letter, too. . . .

You wanted comments on the letters, so I've got some
more!

I was wrong, I admit it. I have changed my mind about the
music score of *STTMP* after finally buying the record of it.
By itself, away from the movie, the music is lovely. It recalls
the events of the movie perfectly, is dramatic, and has the
feel of vast space and the strange and wondrous things to be
found there. Quite equal to the more militaristic and storytell-
ing *Star Wars* score.

Enjoyed the whole batch of reviews of *STTMP* in Trek
Roundtable. It seemed that each person had some new point
to make that no one else had. Quite original and constructive,
aren't we! Maybe a copy of *Trek* 16 should be sent to Roddenberry. Then again, maybe not. He's probably disappointed
enough as it is with the rather mixed reception by fans and
poor reviews by the critics. I'm sure he didn't expect all of
the negative vibes on it.

One thing I'm not quite clear on is whether the story was
all Roddenberry's (as I would presume with his writing of the
book version), or was it really greatly influenced by Alan
Dean Foster? If by Foster, then no wonder it lacks much
character interaction. Foster's logs of the animated series
never did get any life into the McCoy-Spock debates. Roddenberry, the master, can be forgiven for any faults, but not
Foster.

Really liked the cover of *Trek* 16. Finally, one of beautiful
Uhura. I was rather expecting more pictures from the movie.
Is there a shortage of them? Then again, this may serve to

show us how much better—if impractical—the old uniforms looked on the women crewpersons!

One more thing about the movie which I have been puzzling over and haven't seen mentioned. . . It seemed that something was lacking even in the sickbay scene—wherein Spock accepts that feelings do have value and reaches out to take Kirk's hand. Such a scene would be welcomed by all K/S relationship fans, especially readers of the numerous fanzines of the genre. The "July calendar scene" is lacking, though, because it has little buildup, little personal interaction beforehand to show that Kirk and Spock are even real friends anymore. Nothing much leading up to it to give it meaning to those who were not Star Trek fans previous to seeing the movie. When Spock takes the spacesuit and goes off to confront V'Ger, first Kirk wants him brought back, then he says to let him go. Hardly an "Oh, no, my best friend might get killed" reaction.

Of course, a lot of scenes were cut or revised, as you can see by the Marvel comics version which had Kirk going with Spock to meet V'Ger and Spock having to rescue him from the crystals. Or Spock crying about V'Ger's transmission to him. What about *Trek* doing an article on all the script changes?

As for affecting fan fiction, the movie should, let's hope, inspire it, and if someone doesn't agree with events in the movie, they are certainly free to continue the lives of the crew as they see fit in their stories. The movie certainly was a close continuation of the series . . . the fans originally worried the movie would depart from it too radically (and it might have if they hadn't signed on Nimoy), but now we are complaining because it is too similar! It does seem strange that old Earth landmarks from our time are still so present in the future. Could they have been reconstructed in a wave of nostalgia? Kinda odd that Starfleet should choose to situate itself there.

Well, whatever faults we may find with the movie, we should find one thing which has been relatively ignored, and that is that *STTMP* is the highest commendation of our own space program! It's a message to continue that program of space travel and exploration, which has been ignored by the last two administrations and seriously depleted of funds, in spite of the shuttle craft. We have to do more than name the space shuttle *Enterprise*, we've got to encourage our government, through our politicians, to plan for long-range manned space travel. For this message—to the only people who seem to care about space exploration and our future—Gene Roddenberry should be remembered.

Carolyn S. Hillard
Beaver Dam, Ky.

Some comments on *Trek* 16 before I lose the impetus to write.

To Leslie Thompson ("More Star Trek Mysteries Solved"): an interesting article, as usual. However:

Spock could not possibly have been attracted to Droxine in only an intellectual way. The attraction was evident in his first comments to the lady (unusually courtly for Spock), and I hardly think he could have formed an opinion of her intellect just by saying hi to her. Spock also later commented on her innocence (not her mental powers) and referred to her as "lovely" . . . purely a physical evaluation. I think the assumption that Spock is attempting to deny his emotions here is reasonable.

A thought on the type of woman Spock appears to be attracted to. Leila Kalomi, Droxine, Zarabeth . . . they all seem somewhat vulnerable—emotionally innocent, it seems. Could it be Spock is attracted to these passive, generally inexperienced types because of his own insecurities in the area of relationships? Don't ask me how the Romulan commander fits into this pattern. I haven't figured that one out yet.

Speaking of radically out of character—what about Spock's needling of Yeoman Rand at the conclusion of "The Enemy Within"? Rand had been subjected to an obviously very disturbing experience—attempted rape. Spock's joking wisecrack about the impostor's having some interesting characteristics just doesn't seem like him at all. Spock can be accused of being insensitive at times, but never deliberately cruel. Besides, Spock is just not prone to sexual innuendoes. (And isn't that an incredibly bad pun? I love it!)

Bravo to Rebecca Hoffman ("Vulcan as a Patriarchy"). I think her reasoning is overall most convincing. I've never bought that theory that Sarek treated Amanda in such a domineering manner simply because she's human. And then there was always Spock's opinion: "It is undignified for a woman to play servant to a man who is not hers." (Fiancées and wives are a different matter entirely, I suppose.)

To digress for a moment—Hoffman's reference to Spock's describing *pon farr* as something Vulcans do not speak of, "a deeply personal thing," reminded me of another time I'd heard that phrasing from a Vulcan and a question I had because of it.

Sarek, in describing the private meditation he was engaged in before retiring as was his habit (in "Journey to Babel"), said it was a deeply personal experience not to be discussed, particularly with outworlders. It made me wonder if the meditation, evidently a Vulcan male ritual exercise at least, is connected with sexual matters also. In other words, is it the Vulcan form of a "cold shower" to keep desire under control or a way "psyching up" to do his marital duty? Any ideas on why meditation would be so hush-hush?

Concerning the Star Trek movie: I didn't mind a lot of the changes Starfleet made in the *Enterprise*, but the drab, sterile color schemes throughout the ship and in the costumes did irk me. I feel sorry for those people who are going to have to stare at those gray walls for months at a time without shore leave. I thought the reason for the splashes of color in the TV series would have been to keep up morale. The uniform shirts didn't look so much like uniforms then. Now everybody look like a fugitive from *Dr. Kildare.* No offense intended to Todd Dart, but the comment about bright-red shirts not looking good on the big screen reminds me of the reason Gainsborough painted *Blue Boy*—to prove to another artist that it wasn't necessarily an accurate statement that large masses of blue could not be used successfully in a painting.

A comment on the new boots. How is a crewman supposed to run in those things if the need presents itself? Anyone who has ever tried to run—or walk, for that matter—in a pair of clogs will know what I mean. I anticipate a lot of twisted ankles. And one more cheap shot: While some have commented that the women's attire is less chauvinistic than the short skirts, I fail to see how skin-tight jumpsuits are any less sexually emphatic than revealing a thigh. I will say the medical togs on McCoy and Chapel didn't look too implausible, except for those Frankenstein boots, of course.

On the movie in general: They would have been better off

if they'd been given $15 million and made to stick to it. Star Trek at its best never needed gimmicks to pull everything together. In a lot of ways the essence of Star Trek wasn't really science fiction. It was a twentieth-century morality play set in the twenty-third century. I appreciate the cornball idealism, and I hope it is retained in further adventures—on whatever starship and in whatever uniforms.

When I have to break open a second ink pen, it's time to stop writing. Besides, a rerun of "Galileo Seven" is due on in ten minutes, and I've only seen that one about fifty-seven times. . . .

6.

THE PRESERVERS

by Steven Satterfield

There's no kind of article fans love to read more than one which takes events from widely diverging episodes and logically ties them together by involving a single fact or piece of information given (usually all-too-sketchily) in one or two individual shows. Such theorizing has been the basis for some of Trek's most popular and entertaining articles, and now, Steven Satterfield has used the same process to take a look at one of Star Trek's most tantalizing enigmas: the ancient and powerful race known as the Preservers.

The Preservers, introduced in the Star Trek episode "The Paradise Syndrome," are but one of a number of mysterious and powerful races encountered by the crew of the *Enterprise*. The Preservers, however, differ from these other superraces in one important aspect. They appear to have a more "personal" affinity for the people of Earth.

As explained in "Paradise Syndrome," the Preservers had removed an American Indian culture from Earth sometime in the past and relocated it to a similar but uninhabited planet. To protect these newly arrived residents from being bombarded into extinction, an asteroid deflector was placed near their new village.

Many generations later, a medicine chief died suddenly without bestowing the secret of the deflector on his successor. The Indians were saved from destruction only by the timely arrival of the *Enterprise*. Symbols found on the deflector not only allowed Spock to operate it, but also supplied an abridged history of the Preservers, an advanced race that roamed the galaxy relocating nearly extinct cultures on planets with more hospitable environments where they would have a better chance to survive and grow. This Preserver activity is assumed to be the reason for the great number of humanoid races found throughout known space. Wishing only to help those who could not help themselves, the Preservers' motives were strictly benign.

However, these stated motives do not fit the observed facts. The "angelic" actions of the Preservers conflict with the fact that the new home chosen for the Indians, far from being safer than Earth, is infinitely more dangerous. Especially as the asteroid deflector is not programmed to operate automatically. It must be manually operated by the Medicine Chief when the sky darkens. Surely such a race as the Preservers could have found a much safer home for the relocatees—or better provided against their complete destruction.

The motives of the Preservers become even more murky when evidence of Preserver activity on other planets is taken into account. In "Bread and Circuses," the Roman culture discovered on Planet 892-IV appears to be a relocated Earth culture at first glance. But this relocation of a supposedly endangered culture does not ring true, as both the spoken and written language of this Roman culture is standard English.

The incredible events in "The Omega Glory" also testify to the presence of the Preservers on Omega IV. Two cultures are found on that planet which duplicate two cultures found on Earth, down to having spoken and written languages identical with those of their Earth counterparts. Documents are duplicated to the tiniest detail and with uncanny precision. Even the appearance of the two peoples is the same as those on Earth. No pat doctrine such as Hodgkin's Law of Parallel Planet Development can explain the events of "Bread and Circuses" as occurring naturally. And it is impossible for the theory to encompass the events of "Omega Glory"!

While the concept of parallel evolution cannot be discounted entirely, the fact that so many humanoid civilizations are nearly identical to ours points to parallel evolution as being too limited in scope. It seems impossible that approximately twenty cultures on unrelated planets could evolve identically to human cultures on Earth.

If the theory of parallel evolution cannot explain the multitude of human beings throughout the galaxy, then it also cannot explain the similarity of their cultures. Assuming that human life originated on Earth (there seems no reason to doubt that it did), then the humanoid cultures on other planets are the result of Preserver seeding.

Other instances in Star Trek provide evidence to support this claim. While this evidence may not be conclusive, it is very persuasive.

In "Let That Be Your Last Battlefield," Bele's mystification about the concept of evolution indicates that he did not consider the theory as being relevant to his people and their history. If such a scientifically advanced civilization as Cheron does not have a theory about its own evolution, then the basis for such a theory may not exist on the planet . . . Perhaps Bele's forefathers did not originate on Cheron, but were placed there by the Preservers.

In the episodes "A Piece of the Action" and "Patterns of Force," the human inhabitants of each planet allow their respective cultures to be easily supplanted by outside concepts. In both instances, the acceptance of the new culture is swift, complete, and nearly unprotested. The original cultures are swallowed whole. Like chalk on a blackboard, they are erased by new concepts.

The fact that alien civilizations found in the Star Trek universe (the Andorians, Tellerites, Gorn, etc.) do not have duplicates of themselves spread throughout the stars indicates that parallel evolution did not work its magic for them. This not only severely limits parallel evolution as a workable theory, but it also points to the Earth as being of most interest to the Preservers in their relocation efforts.

The Preservers may not have entirely limited their work to Earth. If Vulcans, Romulans, and the people of Rigel V (who have a body chemistry similar to Vulcans) are not the descendants of the Arretians—a possibility stated in "Return to Tomorrow"—the actions of the Preservers would explain this duplication also.

With the assumption that the Preservers' influence goes far beyond their stated intentions, the logical place to begin exploring the real purposes behind their activities would be the planet with the only known Preserver artifact. Close study of the asteroid deflector on Miramanee should tell more of the untold story of the Preservers.

One machine inside the deflector has the ability to implant knowledge directly into the mind. And as Kirk accidentally discovers, the same machine on a different setting can just as easily erase knowledge from the mind. With only a small leap of the imagination, the possibility clearly exists that such a machine could easily be programmed to implant false information into the mind.

The power of the asteroid deflector (it succeeded where all of the formidable might of the *Enterprise* failed) proves that the Preservers had an almost unlimited supply of energy at their beck and call. With the knowledge that the Preservers had this unbelievable technology—and an urge to relocate humans to other planets—a closer study of these races and their associated technologies should provide even more facts to answer the question of just what the Preservers were up to.

In many cases, the transplanted humans are different from the humans of Earth. In "The Apple," "Let That Be Your Last Battlefield," "Mark of Gideon," "The Omega Glory," and "Plato's Stepchildren," the humans all have extended life spans, which are considered natural by these people. Since all of these populations are the descendants of humans from Earth, the long life spans are not natural. The Preservers have undoubtedly given them extended life spans through genetic manipulation. (The half-black, half-white bodies of the people of Cheron are also an apparent case of Preserver genetic manipulation.)

The incredible mind powers of the humans in "Let That Be Your Last Battlefield" and "Plato's Stepchildren" point to even more drastic tampering by the Preservers. In "Stepchildren," a rare mineral, Kironide, supposedly grants the user great psychokinetic powers. While it is an essential element in the control of such powers, it is obvious that Kironide is not the source of the power. If that were so, a quick injection of the mineral would allow Kirk easily to handle future problems.

Since Kironide is not the source of the psychokinetic powers, the actual source must lie hidden on Platonius. It could be that the Preservers not only prolonged the life spans of the Platonians and supplied them with a history, but also provided a power source, which Kironide allows each person to tap into and utilize at will. The Platonians are probably not even aware that such a transmitter exists among them.

In "Let That Be," both Bele and Lokai display a range of powers. Bele was able to take over the ship's computers, and when he and Lokai fought, each was capable of projecting energy screens at the other. These are not the manifestations of psychokinetic powers of superior minds. On the contrary, the minds of the people of Cheron are even less developed than those of the people of the Federation.

When the Preservers created the two races to populate Cheron, they programmed one race to consider itself the master race and to consider the other race as nothing more than vermin. They also gave the so-called master race an advanced technology to go with the uncivilized social structure. The resulting hatred, coupled with that technology, left Cheron a dead planet.

With the technology of the Preservers, the master race on Cheron would have had the means to produce the weapons needed to keep the inferiors in their place. At some time, the supposed inferiors were able to gain access to these weapons. Lokai, one of the first to do so, was able to use the devices to protect himself and flee Cheron to seek aid for his people. These weapons and those of Bele were not detected by the security personnel of the *Enterprise*—understandable, as Bele's ship appeared completely invisible to the crew. Miniaturizing and hiding weapons would be relatively simple with that sort of technology.

However, whether they control events directly or indirectly, the Preservers are the ultimate suppliers of the powers and abilities observed on Platonius and shown by Bele and Lokai.

The events of "Omega Glory," while not adding any other powers or abilities to the list of talents already attributed to Preserver-manipulated humans, do point to an extensive and complex cultural relocation and restructuring. The only difference from Earth humans is that the Comms have a long life span—an almost normal occurrence where the Preservers are involved.

As stated before, the Preservers must be included in any attempt to explain the unnatural convolutions on Omega IV. The awesome powers of the Preservers and their equally mystifying motives may be partially uncovered by considering the facts already known about the Preservers and the events on Omega IV—possibly the most recent location of Preserver activity.

In the time of Star Trek, the Earth counterparts of the cultures on Omega IV are just over approximately 300 years old (as counted from 1950). However, the two cultures on Omega IV appear to have existed for thousands of years. From this evidence, the obvious conclusion would be that both the Communist Chinese and the Americans evolved as cultures thousands of years before they were duplicated, up to a point, on Earth.

If we accept the above scenario as being impossible, then the question must be asked: What did the Preservers do in such a short period of time to produce the observed results? How is it possible?

First, the needed humans would have been relocated to Omega IV. They could have come directly from Earth. However, an easier, safer, and faster solution could have been arrived at by using suitably prepared humans from an older relocation planet. This procedure was most likely used to avoid any chance of accidental discovery by the people of Earth.

After the relocation process is completed, the next step would be to implant the histories and cultural backgrounds into the minds of the prepared humans. This data would have come from a close study of Earth and the cultures of Communist China and the United States.

While the humans were being prepared, the planet was also being prepared to receive them. The war supposedly fought between the Yangs and the Comms was a destructive one, and a little devastation here and there would coincide with the new history being implanted into the minds of the subjects.

While the actual history of Omega IV is no more than 300 years old, the people have memories and records which show it to be much longer. Even though the world war on Omega IV did not actually occur, the people believe that it did, and that is all that is necessary. The path of the two peoples has been redirected by the Preservers. The events of the "Omega Glory" are the result of this molding and shaping of cultures and peoples.

Even though the Preservers have obviously created the human cultures found in the Star Trek universe, how they did it can only be answered positively when the Preservers are found or more substantial records concerning them are uncovered. However, this absence of cold, hard facts does not stop one from considering the results of suspected Preserver activity. The one unifying theme which appears to run the entire gamut of the relocated cultures is concerned with how vibrant and alive those cultures and people are.

The potential for growth and peaceful change is lacking in almost all of the many human cultures discovered. Stagnation and instability are the two extremes which these cultures are continually grappling with. They are locked in place. The cultures of "Return of the Archons," "The Apple," "A Taste of Armageddeon," "The Mark of Gideon," and "For the World Is Hollow and I Have Touched the Sky" are all mired in unchanging environments. The people do not think in terms of change. The status quo is the only way. (It is interesting to note that in each case, except for "Mark of Gideon," the cultural environment is controlled by a computer.)

The cultures of "Let That Be Your Last Battlefield," "Miri," "The Cloud Minders," and "The Omega Glory" are all unstable. This instability led to the destruction of the created culture on Cheron, and the people of Ardana ("Cloud Minders") seemed to be headed down that same road. The people of the duplicate Earth in "Miri" destroyed themselves during an experiment in longevity; and the culture on Omega IV was deliberately set up to be unstable.

Whether the culture is stagnant or unstable, the cause of each situation is an uncanny streak of singlemindedness which permeates the entire culture on each planet. One idea or belief forms the entire basis of cultural identity, and all other aspects of the culture revolve around this one central goal.

(All of the human cultures discovered are not dominated by the central-goal theme. They are more in the mold of the Indians on Miramanee—stable, but relatively unchanging. So it may be that the humans in "The Paradise Syndrome," "Friday's Child," "A Private Little War," and "Bread and Circuses" may be used by the Preservers as supplies for new experimentation.)

The obsesssion many of these cultures have with a central goal or facet of life—which completely dominates the identity of the culture—indicates an interesting pattern. The cultures are not whole. Lacking the stimulating interaction created by the many conflicting goals and ideas found in a complete and free culture, the Preserver-formed cultures are based on no more than a splinter of a whole culture.

The Preservers formed these splinter cultures for a purpose they obviously considered important. Whatever their reasons for doing so, the results point to the entire operation's being a great experiment in cultural evolution. Earth may have had more significance to the Preservers than other inhabited planets, or else Earth may have been the first planet picked that met the needs of the Preservers for raw materials. In either case, the basic premise would still be applicable.

The experiment would begin with a relatively simple study of Earth. At this time, the people would mostly be roaming tribes, thus the Preservers would risk almost no chance of discovery. With the completion of the preliminary study, the Preservers continued to the next step of the experiment. An example of a tribal culture was removed from Earth and placed on Miramanee. In its isolated position, this group was studied exactingly by the Preservers and its development was charted. The fact that the Indians were only studied and not programmed for further development is indicated by their basically unchanged nature in both cultural and genetic terms.

Similar events undoubtedly occurred in the cases of "A Private Little War" and "Friday's Child." Other tribal cultures were relocated to these planets and studied by the Preservers. When the studies were completed, each culture was allowed to pursue its own course, no longer of interest to the Preservers except for their use as specimens for further Preserver experiments.

As the cultures of Earth evolved, samples of them would be removed and studied in isolation. The Roman culture on 892-IV fits this situation. Although the culture was allowed to go its own way for the most part, there were a few wild cards thrown into the cultural poker game by the Preservers—a sort of "trial run" for the next step in the experiment.

This was the final and most important step. The means to mold and shape the minds of the humans to fit new and unnatural role patterns had to be fine-tuned. Replacing the original language of the Romans with English was a test; and undoubtedly a test of the ability to change the human genetic code was also completed. After testing, the Preservers moved on to the most important step of their cultural development program: The Preservers had finally reached a point where, by artificially stimulating certain relocated cultures, they could study specific ingredients which, when combined, would form a viable culture. Each strength and weakness of an individual splinter culture was studied, and then compared to others.

In the time of Star Trek, the Preservers may have completed their experiment in cultural evolution and retired to some place of concealment. Or perhaps certain aspects of the experiment have not yet been completed. There is no clear evidence to indicate either course. But several Star Trek episodes have featured other alien races whose motives and purposes come close to converging with the theory of Preserver actions.

In "The Squire of Gothos," the child-god Trelane looks in on Earth doings from a distance of 900 light-years. His parents were never shown except as a manifestation of their presence in the clouds. They were not aware that Kirk and the crew were thinking beings until they observed Kirk up close. They had considered Kirk no more than a pet. Trelane used an advanced technology to perform his feats of "magic," and took on the form of a human, until returned to his original state.

In "Who Mourns for Adonais?" a group of advanced beings visited Earth far in the past. To the people of that age, they seemed as gods. They gained sustenance from this worship, and when it stopped, they left Earth.

If they were a group of Preservers in human form studying the cultures of Earth, the human guise may have become so overpowering that they did not want to leave Earth when their time for study was up (as in "By Any Other Name," when the Kelvans became too immersed in the feelings and longings of humans). When these feelings were not fulfilled, they left Earth still hoping to regain them. Apollo was the last to recognize that these needs could no longer be fulfilled, and returned to his original form and "home."

In "Assignment: Earth," the mysterious benefactors of Earth gave the impression that they were very concerned about our welfare for some unknown reason. They dispatched Gary Seven, a descendant of humans removed from Earth in the past, on a mission to save Earth from premature demise by atomic warfare. Their technology was such that they could hide their existence from the Federation. While they are good candidates to be the Preservers, no further evidence is found in this episode to show just who and what the Preservers are.

Other advanced races seen in Star Trek include the Organians from "Errand of Mercy," the Thasians from "Charlie X," and the Metrons from "Arena," In "Shore Leave" and "The City on the Edge of Forever," the technology of advanced races is found. All of these races have abilities which dwarf those of the Federation. If nothing else is certain from a study of these races, it is clear that powers do exist within the galaxy that would allow the Preservers to have accomplished all of the feats ascribed to them in this article.

And yet, for all the supposing, the Preservers remain an enigma. Their true identity can only be guessed at from secondhand knowledge. The Preservers, when finally discovered, will ultimately be the only source from which their true history can be understood.

7.

FEAR, FUN, AND THE MASQUE OF DEATH

by Joyce Tullock

Joyce Tullock is back for the second time in this collection, this time with an article we think will stir up just as much controversy and comment as her earlier piece on religion. Not very many of us think of Star Trek as scary, but as you will see in the article below, there are times when it can be downright terrifying!

Any good writer learns the meaning of fear.

Doubtless it should come as no surprise that most of Star Trek's writers have been exceptionally well schooled in that one mysterious emotion. They knew how to frighten—and they did it well. They did it in many ways. They did it with love . . . with hate . . . with beauty and the beast. They did it when we were looking . . . and when we weren't. They did it in colorful ways, loud and boisterous and brutal . . . and subtly, frightening through the subconscious.

At times Star Trek can be quite unsightly, quite distressing.

And that's the key. It's what we see and what we don't see that frightens so effectively. From the first aired Star Trek to the most recent filmed version the element of fear is approached from two general perspectives: It is associated with (1) the physically hideous and/or (2) the subconsciously alarming.

Perhaps part of Gene Roddenberry's success (and failure) is due to the fact that he has always striven to embrace as vast an audience as possible. Were he not so inclined, we would not have a Star Trek—science fiction just doesn't capture that large a section of the viewing audience.

Yes, for survival Star Trek catered to the viewing audience's very natural attraction to horror. It "used" fear just as it used love, sentiment, identification, and social comment.

But let's not hang our heads in shame. Star Trek, even at its worst, is never a horror show. Instead it takes the unsightly and makes it somehow dignified. In Star Trek, as a matter of fact, the word "unsightly" becomes a misnomer for the word "unfamiliar." But being human, we are frightened by the unfamiliar just the same. The common fear of the hideous is not enough to capture and hold a large audience, however. As Bela Lugosi and Boris Karloff obviously knew quite well, it is not the ugliness of physical distortion which frightens so much as that mysterious unknown which lies beneath.

Nothing chills the blood so thoroughly as the quick curl of a sinister, human smile.

Take what is known, even loved, then make the viewer distrust it. Make him feel disquieted, distressed, uneasy—and let *him* figure out why.

That is horror.

So when Star Trek aired its first episode, it understandably hit the viewing audience with a loaded deck. Never mind that "Man Trap" was not the first episode to be filmed. That's unimportant. What *is* important is that it was indeed a "man trap"—the bait for a viewing public which had to be caught quickly, neatly and convincingly in order to ensure Star Trek's survival. Once an audience is caught, it's okay to go on with more sophisticated themes, but first and foremost it is necessary to attract as much attention as possible.

The salt vampire in "Man Trap" did a pretty good job of it, too. This creature requires common salt for its survival and has become used to killing to get it. Looking something like a cross between a gorilla and a dust mop (with a toothy suction cup for a mouth), the first monster of Star Trek is designed to hit a wide range of fears. Something about its face is vaguely, grotesquely human. And not only is it horribly ugly and deathly dangerous, it is able to deceive. It can easily look into its enemy's mind and disguise itself as any trusted, pleasant-looking human being. Old false face.

This makes the whole fear experience much more interesting.

After murdering all of the colonists on Planet M113 with the exception of archaeologist Robert Crater, the creature takes the shape of Crater's wife, Nancy (also long gone for the sake of her salt). Okay, now comes the good part—the late Nancy Crater and the *Enterprise*'s kindly chief surgeon, Dr. Leonard "Bones" McCoy, used to be . . . very close friends.

It may be beauty and the beast with a slightly different slant, but it's beauty and the beast just the same. McCoy's feelings for Nancy are evidently still quite strong—much to Kirk's annoyance, for, in what must be one of Star Trek's most ironic lines, Kirk admonishes the good doctor for "thinking with his glands." Talk about famous last words! But, of course, "Bones" being the emotional man he is, he doesn't really pull himself together until the last possible moment when he sees the truth about the poor creature and destroys it just in time to save his captain. A touch of melodrama never hurt anyone.

So already, in episode number one, something important about Star Trek is being tossed our way. Maybe it's sort of a preparation for IDIC's reverence for difference, but sooner or later it becomes evident that the salt vampire is not to be feared because it is ugly, but because it *isn't*; that is, it is able to *deceive*. The danger is that it can appear to be whomever it wishes, so when it takes on the appearance of the trusted Dr. McCoy in one briefing-room scene, we are more acutely aware of that other kind of fear. It is no longer the creature's so-called ugliness that is troubling, but something less definable (and more realistic). The distressing fact is that McCoy is not McCoy. It looks like McCoy, it sounds like McCoy . . . but there is a subtle difference. Be it due to a certain evil glint in the eye or a wry twist to the mouth, it is somehow very unsettling to discover a *sinister* McCoy. And he's sitting right there with the captain! At the root of our distress, then, is the realization that people, even trusted friends, are not always necessarily what they seem.

Can there be any greater evil?

But the salt vampire deserves a few kind words. After all, it was the last of a dying race. Logic dictates that a creature with such tremendous telepathic powers should have been somehow able to communicate its problem (the need for salt) in a more constructive and peaceful way. But that's not how stories are written. And Star Trek is, after all, only a story. Still, it is hard not to wonder what would have been the humanitarian McCoy's private thoughts at the knowledge that he had been the assassin of the last representative of an entire race.

At any rate, that first episode of Star Trek is, in its own way, a fine study of fear. It mixes old-fashioned ugliness with the more subtle and complex fear associated with the insecurity of illusion. On a more subliminal level (and Star Trek does use sublimated and surrealistic themes), it teases the audience with a fear that is as ancient and as horrifying as the darkest part of the human imagination. There is probably no prospect more frightening to the human mind than the prospect of finding oneself romantically involed with a monster. Call it the "Beauty and the Beast Syndrome." Medieval literature is full of stories of gallant young knights who find themselves tricked into romantic links with or betrothal to chillingly monstrous old hags. Such stories often involve illusion, of course, and their popularity has stuck with us until this day.

While McCoy's salt vampire was certainly no *human* hag, it served the purpose as well as an ugly old witch could. The subliminal connotations cannot be ignored. There's just something . . . well . . . unclean, unseemly, and frightening about his relationship with the creature. Perhaps it's the stark contrast of innocence with malevolence. It's a delicate thing, an ancient theme, and it touches mysteriously upon our most basic human fears.

But McCoy is by no means the only one to have a "beauty and the beast" experience in Star Trek. The theme pops up again in the first episode involving everyone's favorite scoundrel, Harry Mudd.

In "Mudd's Women," we meet Ruth, Magda and Eve—three apparently beautiful women. Trouble is, ruthless Harry Mudd has been treating them with an illegal cosmetic drug. Actually the gals are quite homely (they border on hagdom), but with the help of the very effective Venus drug, Mudd manages to pawn them off on some lonely and unsuspecting lithium miners. There's a twist here, however, for the short of the story is that the only ones to truly fear the ladies' ugliness is the ladies themselves. Beauty, it seems, is a subjective thing. The ladies learn to appreciate themselves for what they are; they gain a new self-respect and the need for the drug vanishes (along with its availability). The fact that the miners were very isolated and very, very lonely played a big part in things, of course, but it's nice that it all worked out so well in the end.

There are other ladies in Star Trek who are not what they seem . . . and often there is the suggestion that they are aiming for some sort of close relationship with one of our heroes. Even innocent little Miri in the episode "Miri" is actually a 300-year-old child who is on the verge of becoming one of the hideous "grups" who terrorize her devastated planet. The civilization of Miri's planet was evidently destroyed when a virus (developed in connection with some vast scientific project's longevity experiments) killed off its adult population by turning all adults into ancient-looking, sore-infested madmen. Oddly enough, the same virus retarded the aging process in children who had not yet reached puberty. And when Kirk discovers her world, Miri (wouldn't you know) is about to become a woman. Naturally. she develops a strong crush on the good captain.

Of course, it all works out well in the end here, too. McCoy discovers the antidote just in time to prevent any future generations of "grups." While Kirk's predicament in "Miri" is similar to McCoy's in "Man Trap," the basis of the fear in "Miri" is ever so slightly more realistic. A fear directly related to the fear of aging, of losing the freedom, beauty, innocence, and vitality of youth. It is the root of all the fear that develops in "Miri." Old age is equated with ugliness, rejection, evil . . . and death. And the viewer is certainly disturbed by the prospect that Kirk, McCoy, and the other humans in the landing party are slowly becoming those hideous creatures, "grups."

In "Miri," old age is associated with ugliness of spirit. We'll see that theme treated from another perspective later on.

Had Miri actually reached the point of ugliness and become an old hag, her ugliness would not have been an illusion. Certainly her beauty was real. But in episodes like "The Menagerie" and "Catspaw," beauty isn't even skin deep; it's pure trickery. The lovely Vina in "Menagerie" is a horribly mutilated Earthwoman whom those masters of illusion, the Talosians, use to entice the *Enterprise*'s Captain Pike in hopes of populating the surface of their planet with the more rugged human stock. Again, it's the idea of the handsome young man (very much the gallant knight) being sexually involved with a hag; a kind of life-and-death love relationship. And again, it isn't the reality Pike fears, but the danger of illusion. He manages to free himself from the Talosians and only returns much later (with the help of his former officer, Mr. Spock) after being severely crippled and mutilated in an accident. There is a point, it seems, where illusion is to be preferred over reality.

But Pike isn't alone in choosing illusion over his own hideous and impotent reality. Sylvia, in "Catspaw," makes the same choice . . . and for a much less worthy reason. In a way, though, her story is even more pathetic. Sylvia and her assistant, Korob, are not really human at all. They come from a distant galaxy, supposedly to see if ours is suitable for their life forms to inhabit. They're busy with some such work on planet Pyris VII when Kirk and his *Enterprise* interrupt. It's clear that Sylvia and Korob don't know much about humans at all—they try to frighten Kirk away by holding Scott and Sulu captive and sending another crew member back to the *Enterprise*—dead.

When Kirk responds by beaming down to the planet with Spock and McCoy, the aliens use their tremendous mental powers to reach into the humans' minds, thus discovering certain elements of the most basic human fears.

It only stands to reason that Kirk, Spock, and McCoy then find themselves standing in a fog, confronted by three of the *ugliest* hags in the universe.

Well, if it was good enough for Shakespeare. . . .

The witches recite an appropriate, blood-curdling warning, which Kirk and friends dutifully ignore as they move on to investigate an illusion called up from the depths of their own minds. If you have a sense for the tongue-in-cheek as well as a respect for the power of the subconscious mind, you'll *love* "Catspaw."

Although this episode comes across as a sort of fairyland horror story, it also illustrates a concept which is basic to science fiction writing (and most other art forms as well)—know the power of the human subconscious, and use it. The horror "Catspaw" presents is harmless enough; child's play to the id. Sylvia takes the form of a witch (a very attractive witch, however), and Korob can be nothing less than a warlock. Officers Scott and Sulu appear as mindless zombie flunkies who escort Kirk, McCoy, and Spock to and from their cobwebbed dungeon (complete with skeleton hanging in chains). Naturally, all of this takes place in a medieval castle; dark, winding hallways, crimson torchlight. (And if it's a motif that seems old-hat, consider that beautifully mysterious journey through V'Ger, grays, blues, flares of amber and pink. Color, texture, shapes that wind . . . they're all food for the subconscious.)

Many themes are played to the hilt in "Catspaw." Always the true-blue friends, Scott and Sulu can no longer be trusted (like the imposter McCoy in "Man Trap"). Of course, McCoy gets to become a zombie in "Catspaw" too, before time runs out. (The man's brain was forever being abused.) There is a black cat, which for the sake of correctness we will refer to as a familiar. It is not at all foolish to suspect that the cat is really Sylvia; and that she disguises herself thus just as Count Dracula would change into a bat or wolf when convenient. But Sylvia is most frightening as a beautiful woman.

Unaccustomed as she is to the human form, Sylvia finds herself overwhelmed by the new experience of her human senses. And she likes it. She becomes a very sensual woman and swiftly takes a liking to Captain Kirk—a strong liking. Well now, that's to be expected, not just because Sylvia is a woman and Kirk is . . . Kirk, but because Sylvia is not actually a woman at all. Yep, the "beauty and the beast" syndrome strikes again! And with all due respect to actress Antoinette Bower, Sylvia is the most entirely monstrous female ever to bat an eye at Kirk. As Korob seems to naturally associate himself with the human qualities of thoughtfulness and gentleness, so Sylvia finds delight in cruelty. Human torture is quickly becoming one of her favorite pasttimes. The polarization between the two aliens comes in quite handy, for not only does it permit a nice little discussion of the powers of good and evil within the human soul, but it allows Korob to finally throw in with Kirk.

Poor Sylvia is power-mad and sex-crazed. She wants her way with Kirk. She wants to keep him in line, and she wants to keep him. Using her alien powers, she reaches into the depths of his mind, digs around in his very human collection of sentiments, weaknesses, and fears, and pulls out one more trick.

The next thing we know, McCoy is a zombie.

Kirk is clearly disturbed by what has happened to his friend, but he has also come to realize that Sylvia's lust for power and passion has blinded her to certain aspects of the human mind. He encourages her approaches in order to learn more about the source of her powers (the power of illusion is connected to the amulet she wears) and thus free his ship. Once she realizes this . . . well, it's the wrath of a woman scorned times ten. Korob, the good half of the nightmare pair, eventually helps Kirk and Spock escape the dungeon, but is killed when Sylvia appears as a giant cat. And, as if the death of good cancels out the power of evil, Kirk, like some courageous knight from days of old, uses the power in Korob's wand (interesting that the male, though less powerful, still carries the source of the power) and destroys Sylvia's power of illusion.

The last time we see the dying aliens, they appear as pathetic little figures which look something like pipecleaners wrapped in Tribble fur.

Another illusion of beauty and power is destroyed, another reality of ugliness and impotence is revealed. And so it is that writer Robert Bloch deserves an admiring nod. His little story, so often dismissed as "Star Trek's tribute to trick-or-treat," is as fine a statement about the source of human evil as ever hit the prime-time tube. He reminds us that at the source of every cruel tyrant is an empty, impotent loser. Cruelty does not come from strength, but from lack of it, from the pathetic and unnatural desire to overpower. The intimidating castle vanishes with the fog, and it is seen that evil, at its source, is not so omnipotent a power. And maybe we even feel something like sorrow for those puny, lifeless creatures, who, with a little understanding, could have been friends.

Themes involving the fear of impotency and the desire for power are seen in several episodes. The Talosians ("The Menagerie") had become so dependent on their power of illusion that they could no longer survive on the harsh surface of their planet. Like so many who cannot deal with reality, they withdrew to the safety and depths of illusion. Thann and Lal, the Vians of "The Empath," were mentally superior to man, but they lacked the power and vitality of simple human love. Sargon, Thalassa, and Henoch of "Return to Tomorrow" are the last of a highly intelligent race which has destroyed itself. In "Wolf in the Fold," Robert Bloch touches on this theme again by creating an entity which is the virtual personification of fear. His "Jack the Ripper" is disguised as a harmless and unimpressive little man named Hengist. The implication is clear that weakness of personality is directly involved with the creature's intense need to terrorize. Bloch's Jack the Ripper literally feeds on human fear, requiring it for its own existence.

No use even going into the list of computer gods who are powerful only because their humanoid underlings don't know enough to pull the plug. The "Providers" of "The Gamesters of Triskelion" are discovered to be great bodiless minds who have evidently become so bored with their know-it-all existence that all they want to do is wager on the life-and-death combat of lesser beings. A strange direction for intellect to take, but that's how the story goes. And of all the villains of Star Trek, there are none so impotent as V'Ger, the machine entity of *Star Trek: The Motion Picture*. It drops by Earth just long enough to remind humanity that it must not allow the need for practical knowledge to overshadow the more productive human qualities of emotion, sensitivity, and imagination. V'Ger's power is awesome, but until it obtains the human capacity to "leap beyond logic," it cannot grow.

Most of the monsters (human and otherwise) discussed so far frighten not so much because of the physical appearance as because of the suggestion of wickedness and danger which lurks beneath. And most of the fear lurks in the viewer's own mind. Taking a lesson from Sylvia, the Star Trek writers have just pulled this or that to the surface, letting the audience fill in the blanks. It's a matter of digging effectively into the secret bends and corridors of the human subconscious.

But it is clear enough that the first step in culling up fear is to (as "Bones" might say) "use visuals."

Star Trek is full of visuals. Psychologists know that nothing captures the attention of the human mind so fast as the image of a distorted human face. From the comparatively minor distortions of the large-skulled Talosians and Vians (big heads are always popular with science fiction writers) to the mysteriously human form of Yarnek the rock creature in "The Savage Curtain," we see monsters which are barely human or not human at all. Our heroes are threatened by extremely large primitive humanoids in "The Galileo Seven" and by strange single-celled creatures (with the power to levitate, yet) in "Operation Annihilate." The Gorn captain in "Arena" is a sort of humanoid lizard and looks so alarmingly like a man in a lizard suit that it almost ceases to frighten. The same goes for the Mugato in "Private Little War." Looking somewhat like a gorilla in a party hat, it frightens more because of its loud and swift attack than anything else.

But to be fair, the creatures and aliens of Star Trek are not designed so much to frighten as to awe. The distortion is a tool for drawing attention. No one even expects to be alarmed by the varied display of shapes and distortions of the humanoid forms that we see in "Journey to Babel." By this time IDIC reigns. Even any initial fear of the appearance of "Arena's" Gorn can be reexamined and explained in terms of human prejudice and frame of reference. It resembles a lizard; the human mind generally carries an irrational fear of such creatures. It's a prejudice that begins with the Bible. And once again it seems that a Star Trek writer has called upon that vast store of collective and subconscious human fears. All those forms which seem to be some distortion of the human figure actually serve to illustrate that fear and distrust are somehow related to narrowness of frame of reference. And by the time of *STTMP* some pretty peculiar variations on the humanoid form are a working part of the *Enterprise* family.

So in Star Trek, the old concept of visual horror is replaced by a fascination with the unusual. That fascination with the unusual then becomes a respect for difference. Beauty and ugliness become subjective terms.

One of Star Trek's most beloved monster/aliens is the Horta from "Devil in the Dark." The Horta is a silicon-based life form which resembles rocky lava and drills through solid rock for a living. At first it is hunted down because of the mistaken idea (encouraged by its unhuman appearance) that it is malevolent. Again, it is a case of simple misunderstanding. The Horta is actually the single surviving mother to her entire race's next generation. Intruding human miners have been destroying vast stores of Horta eggs because they don't know what they are. Now the only thing a mother can do in such a case is to protect her nest—men are killed, machinery is seriously damaged. But eventually Spock and Kirk straighten everything out by discovering that the Horta is a peace-loving, intelligent life form, and a compromise is reached so that the Horta and her children can coexist with the miners —to everyone's benefit.

"Devil in the Dark" may well be Star Trek's finest example of IDIC, for it plays a trick on the viewer by convincing him that the creature means nothing but evil. It's ugly by common standards, it kills men, and it threatens a very prosperous mining operation. Only when Mr. Spock applies the Vulcan mind meld do we understand that we have been assessing this creature from our own limited (and by the Horta's standards, distorted) point of view. And to add to the confusion, heroes Kirk and Spock are clearly endangering their lives by chasing this menace about in the mysteriously frightening maze of rock tumble. We're so busy worrying about their welfare that there's just no time to sit and think about perspectives.

Perspective, frame of reference, and difference is what IDIC is all about. It's only proper that Mr. Spock, with his pointed ears, green blood, and vague demonic mystery, should be the one to remind us time and time again of the value of difference.

Mr. Spock *is* a combination of differences, especially when he is considered in relation to the most traditional human beliefs. He *looks* like a devil. Goodness, his heart is even in the wrong place! But . . . darn it . . . his personality doesn't fit the stereotype. To Spock such things as lust, greed, ambition—*all* the passions—are an illogical waste of time and energy. He doesn't even know *how* to hate, and the last thing he'd want to do is "overthrow" his leader. But humans still judge somewhat by appearance, and the unsettling fact remains that there is something strangely appealing about the Vulcan's demonic looks. So it could be that in the depths of the subconscious he *does* frighten us a bit . . . in a friendly, appealing sort of way.

Spock is a paradox of fear and trust, all right. His character is a living example of the weight that a limited frame of reference places upon the human perspective. Perhaps we even feel a little threatened to find ourselves feeling real affection for a character whose likeness we have been taught to fear since childhood.

Fear does have its attraction. If someone somewhere didn't think the sight of a Talosian or a Vian or a Gorn or even a Horta would frighten part of the viewing audience just a bit, they wouldn't have wasted the money on props and makeup.

It's funny, but a man will sincerely tell himself that he is neither frightened nor repulsed by a particularly strange or ugly sight . . . and then he will look and look with all the fervor of a wide-eyed child. Something within the human psyche *likes* to be frightened, as long as it's all in fun.

But the human psyche being what it is, sometimes it's best to look away, as we learn from the Medusan ambassador Kollos in "Is There In Truth No Beauty?" Of course, there is no accurate description of the Medusan ambassador, because the sight of this alien is reportedly too much for any human to bear. One look and you are nuts. This story cuts fear to a fine point. The impact of its fear is, to be honest, a little illusive. It does make a point about the value of visual horror, however. You have to really be able to *imagine* in order to be afraid of the Medusan ambassador. And if you're a typical human, there's nothing you want more by the middle of the episode than to take a quick peek inside that little box. The interesting thing about Kollos is that we're not altogether certain if he frightens because he is so terribly ugly or because he is perhaps awesomely or indefinably beautiful.

We *need* definition . . . and Kollos may be the emotional equivalent to the beautiful light that blinds. He is incorporeal, and so that may be as fair an idea of his "appearance" as we'll ever get. Still, the general impression given in the episode is that the ambassador is a pretty unpleasant sight. The Medusans are extremely intelligent and evidently have great depth of character, so it could be that their frame of reference (especially concerning their idea of beauty) is different from man's to an intellectually irreconcilable extent; there is no way for a human to connect the sight of a Medusan with anything which is even vaguely familiar. That which we do not understand, we instinctively interpret to be dangerous, "evil." It's the built-in safety mechanism which has helped to keep man alive and fairly safe during his long, hazardous, and ofttimes ignorant evolutionary journey. Fear—it gets in the way sometimes, and we have to be wary of it, but it is vitally necessary just the same.

The strange sights of V'Ger fall readily into the category of the strange, the unfamiliar, and, therefore, the threatening. (" 'Bones,' there's a *thing* out there.") For Kirk, Spock, everyone, V'Ger beckons and distresses at once. Its tantalizingly mysterious gray-toned landscape utilizes a sublimated attrac-

Doctor on the Bridge
(Christine Myers)

Trek Dream
(Jeff Nelson)

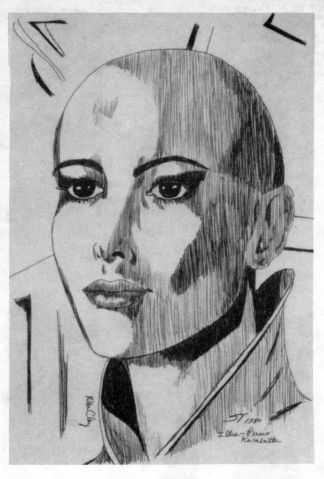

Ilia
(Rita Clay)

Each Man's Dream
(Christine Myers)

Kirk
(Mary Lowe)

Uhura
(Gail Bennett)

McCoy's Crew
(Gail Bennett)

tion to death and sex simultaneously. It offers a kind of exhilaration by mixing good old-fashioned death fear with the awe of discovery. It creates a dread and a desire. The *Enterprise*'s surrealistic journey through V'Ger does not evoke the fear of alarm so much as the fear connected with suspense.

And one gradually becomes aware of the twofold theme: The *Enterprise* is acting not only as a vessel of challenge, defense, and exploration, but also as the virtual seed which will impregnate and give birth to a unique new life form. So in *Star Trek: The Motion Picture*, fear is the power source, the impetus of the cycle of events; death, rebirth, discovery, and sex drive become interdependent. When Commander Decker unites with V'Ger to create a new entity, the visual result is nothing less than orgasmic—a stunning fireworks display of the pleasure/pain principle.

And deny it though we might, it seems that we *do* enjoy being frightened (in fiction). There is an excitement, even an exhilaration in the *threat* of pain and danger. There is a smug feeling of security and superiority in the knowledge that we remain safe from harm. Like V'Ger, the viewer has the best of both worlds.

But what does all this tell us about fear? Are its roots so entangled in the psychosexual depths of the human subconscious, so sublimated and wrapped with the complexities of the human personality, that we dare not seek them out? Are we, like Spock and his logic, so secure in the knowledge of our own good that we dare not risk the revelation which might show us the baser part of the self? Is it really evil that frightens . . . or something else? Well, evil can in many ways be equated with the unknown, and the unknown with the dangerous. Danger is the thing. And when all is said and done, danger can be considered to be a fear word or a warning to look out for that one basic, instinctive fear . . . the fear of death.

There is not a single Star Trek episode that does not have, as its most basic building block, the simple human fear of death. From that we get the mystery (and beauty) of V'Ger, the excitement of "Devil in the Dark" and the hideousness of the "grups" in "Miri" and the witches in "Catspaw." Therein lies our interest in the distortion of the human face, for such is synonymous with danger. And while the exotically distorted faces of such beings as the Talosians arouse our curiosity and maybe frighten because of their differences, writers seem to call with a rather notable degree of regularity upon that one cosmetic distortion which is neither exotic or mysterious. It is real, though excessively exaggerated on film to intensify the fear and nail the point home. It is the mask that chases us from the crib, teases us from the pages of childhood fairy tales, calls to us from the simplest of medieval poems. It frightens because of the reality of its source, because it is a mocking, ever-reminding prophecy.

We are reminded in "Man Trap," "Mudd's Women," "Miri," "The Menagerie," and "Catspaw" of the cold and lonely truth—beauty, especially the beauty of youth, is itself an illusion in time, a cruel trick, a fleeting vision. The Gorn will never frighten like the hag or the withered corpse, for as Sylvia could tell you, the Gorn lacks a vital power over the human psyche. It misses the one element which is essential to the truly horrifying . . . *reality*. At least it lacks the universal reality of human death.

And reality, it seems, is the most frightening thing of all.

That brings us to the death mask.

Old age, especially in our time (and our western society), is a condition to be abhorred. Time is a race to be run (as if we might win) before reaching that part of life condescendingly referred to as "the declining years." Few will seriously argue against the widely held concept that only in youth is there real beauty. Old age is physically hideous, infirm, impotent. The very old, it seems, have no purpose but to wait.

Whatever happened to IDIC?

Guess it's time to take a glimpse at "The Deadly Years." Hmmm . . . the title kind of gives it away, doesn't it? Kirk, Spock, McCoy, Scott, Lieutenant Arlene Galway (well, *some-one* has to die!), and Chekov make a friendly stop to see the colonists on Gamma Hydra IV, unaware of the fact that the area has been contaminated by a unique form of radiation poisoning. Soon enough they discover that a strange malady has killed off everyone but two extremely ancient-looking people . . . who are actually *young* people, but who die in short order, of old age.

In "The Deadly Years," old age finally obtains guest-star billing as Disease of the Week.

Before we know it, the landing party begins to show symptoms of the affliction. All except for Chekov, that is. Kirk developes arthritis, McCoy's cantankerousness reaches a new high, Scotty becomes a virtual living corpse, and Lieutenant Galway . . . yes, of course . . . swiftly turns into a crippled, withered old hag and dies. Everyone shows signs of senility—even Mr. Spock, who complains that his mental faculties are somewhat impaired.

Oh, this is a fun episode all right. It is perhaps Star Trek's most sophisticated application of the theory which states that fear is the basis of all comedy. It's a well-balanced mixture of horror and comedy, using fear and fun just as the V'Ger voyage uses the sublimation of death and sex. Identifying with the characters as we do, we can't help but laugh and cry at their plight. And no doubt we take a selfish comfort in the knowledge that our fictional friends must, at least for a time, suffer the ignobling afflictions associated with old age. But the fear is there too, in the screaming, horror-struck Chekov who runs from the sight of the more-than-deceased Alvin in the episode's all-important opening scene. In the words of our observant Captain Kirk, Chekov is "scared to death."

The corpse of Alvin is indeed the dried and crumbling visage of smiling death. He looks out at us like the grinning image carved on a medieval coffin, a cruel and unshakable promise of what is to be.

So the most basic of human fears is there aplenty—in Chekov's blatant, heart-pounding reaction to Alvin, in the idea of the death mask itself (with its grotesque deterioration), and in the pathetic agony of young Lieutenant Galway as she watches her own youth fade and give way to the exaggerated distortion of the aging disease.

But take heart. "The Deadly Years" is not really all that negative, for in this story the Big Three conquer old age. Figuratively, at least. What's more, they use *fear* to do it. Everyone knows that fear is a human defense mechanism, but it's still a bit surprising to find that it was literally Chekov's fear that saved him. In what may well be one of televised Star Trek's finest artistic moments, Dr. McCoy, stammering thoughtfully and trembling with the infirmity of old age, searches the depths of his exhausted memory until he reaches back to a time just after the atomic age . . . to "ancient history." It is a poetic moment; youth and age, future and past, fear and quiet courage . . . all rolled up into seconds of film time. "Adrenalin," McCoy recalls, was once thought to be "highly promisin' " in treating radiation sickness. The massive amount of adrenalin produced in Chekov's system at the moment of his fright must have saved him.

The "cure" is found (and none too soon, right, Scotty?). But there is a double victory here. In "The Deadly Years," old age retains some of its dignity, taking on a beauty peculiar to itself. The McCoy of the moment, who must be the physical and cosmetic equivalent of a 120-year-old man, stands as yet another example of the value of IDIC. He is another McCoy, maybe as fine a one as we have ever seen. We've had our fun, but now the freak show is over. The grotesquely aged and feeble McCoy who gathers all his fear, patience, and wisdom to recall one bit of ancient history is not so much frightening or comic as he is enchanting. For a brief moment old age shines in a positive light. It is a small but comforting victory.

Just the same, the old boys were running out of time. Lucky for us Chekov was "scared to death."

Lucky for Star Trek, too, is the fact that the fear of death is such an integral part of human psychology. Science fiction and social statements are fine, but without the element of fear, the excitement of danger, chances are there wouldn't be quite so many fish in the net. For as any writer knows, the most significant statement in the universe bears no meaning without listeners. So logic is applied to art.

But it only seems fitting that by appealing to man's basic fears, writers are able to address the problems of humanity. To apply Chekov's poetic example in "The Deadly Years," perhaps fear—used well—can lead to positive strength. Fear is a human power, like hate and love . . . a tremendous source of emotional energy. For all we know, the fear of death may be the basis of life, or at least an element in the foundation of human progress. As a prime mover it is an energy source that mankind would do well to tap and channel . . . if it hasn't already. Come to think of it, that sounds like something Kirk should have said . . . if he hasn't already.

8.

STAR TREK: THE MOTION PICTURE—
A YEAR LATER

by Deanna Rafferty

As we mentioned in our sampling of Trek Roundtable, STTMP is still "the talk of the town" as far as most Star Trek fans are concerned. But once the first happy flush of satisfaction and "victory" were over, most fans began to take the time to mull over the movie a little more. We editors did too, and were just about convinced we should do an article speaking to the events of the past year and the effect it has had on Star Trek fans of every stripe. But, as usual, the readers were way ahead of us, and only a few days later this article by Deanna Rafferty arrived in the mail:

At the time of this writing, exactly one year has passed since the theatrical premiere of *Star Trek: The Motion Picture*. It has been a *very* strange year indeed. Most of us saw the movie many times in its original release (and pooh on Paramount for not giving us the promised summer rerelease!), and some of us lucky enough to have friends with videotape recorders have seen it several more times (and yay to Paramount for putting the movie out on prerecorded videotape so quickly!). We've discussed the film *endlessly*—some of us changing our opinions about it and aspects of it a number of times in the process—reading and quoting from all of the reviews and overviews about *STTMP* we could get our hands on. And we've all watched box-office results with bated breath, knowing that only they will ultimately decide if a sequel is to be made.

A very strange year . . . kind of a rough year . . . but always interesting.

And now it is time to look back. Look back on the thrill of standing in line to see the movie for the *first* time! Look back at the chagrin with which we greeted Leonard Nimoy as he walked out on talk-show stages with that *head* under his arm, wanting to talk about *Vincent*, when we wanted to hear him talk about Spock! Look back at the snooty reviews given *STTMP* by the science fiction community—reviews that sometimes seemed to be written before seeing the movie! And look back . . . look back . . .

A *very* strange year. Yes.

This article will ramble and range a bit—several things to discuss. First, and at the risk of having my happy home burned to the ground by a torch-wielding mob, I must report that *Star Trek: The Motion Picture* is more enjoyable and a *better* show on television than it was in theaters!

Why? Well, because even with all of the hoopla, the zillion-dollar budget, the 70-millimeter prints and stereophonic sound and the high ticket prices, we were still treated to a television *story* on a motion-picture screen. But that's okay . . . it was a *Star Trek story*! And that makes all the difference. Because Star Trek is a product of television—the characters, their world, and what we expect of both is firmly and permanently rooted in television—and although the movie was absolutely stunning in terms of panorama and visual effects, the heart of the show—the people—works better in the more intimate and comfortable milieu of the home TV screen.

All of the things about which the critics carped (and some of the fans, too!) seem to vanish or become understandable when *STTMP* is seen on TV. It is as if the film were originally a television show, and when it was projected up on a big screen, all of the cracks and flaws showed a hundred times larger. But that is in our mind's eye: We know and love Star Trek as a TV show, we cannot see it as anything else.

And it *had* to be intentional. Movie and TV are two completely different art forms. Just about the *only* thing they have in common is that they are both on film (and with the spread of videotape, that difference is fast disappearing). So it is inconceiveable that all of the fine and experienced talents involved in *STTMP* could have somehow "slipped up" and made a $43 million TV show. No, Gene Roddenberry and Robert Wise knew exactly what they were doing.

They knew that their primary audience would not be the millions who came to the theaters and paid their money (although parts of the movie were specifically designed to satisfy this audience), but the untold millions more who would see *STTMP* on television, whether it be on videotape, cable, or commercial broadcast. And these numberless millions only knew Star Trek as a television program—and would expect and perhaps demand that *STTMP* have the same look and feel as the Star Trek they were already used to.

So the movie was made with the larger audience in mind. Yes, it still worked very, very well on the big screen . . . but it works even better on TV, because television screens were the medium for which *STTMP* was designed.

If you haven't seen *STTMP* on videotape or cable yet, hold on awhile. ABC has the rights to broadcast it in the 1981–82 season. When you see it on television, I think you will agree.

Now . . . all of us have seen the movie a number of times. And we all have our opinions about it. The fanzines have dissected it, the fan fiction writers have explained and embellished it, and the fan conclaves at conventions have just about talked it to death. Everyone has a favorite scene, an explanation for why Kirk does this, or why Spock does that, and an opinion of what V'Ger *really* means. That's the kind of thing that makes us Star Trek fans: We look beyond a single episode or the movie, and make that next step into the universe of Star Trek personally. We get involved!

And that's much easier to do when watching *STTMP* on a television screen. Not only do we have that comfortable feeling of seeing our heroes back where they belong, but we are able to make the leap past the dazzling effects and the wide screen and the nut three rows back laughing and munching popcorn to the *story*.

And a fine story it is. The abrupt jumps in continuity at the beginning of the film are less jarring and disruptive on TV than in the theater, as we are quite used to the fast pace and quick editing of television. So we follow along with our intellect instead of our eyes. And we see the tale of V'Ger developing logically, through the viewpoint of first the Klingons, then the Comm station crew, then the *Enterprise*. We know that it is a *people* story much more through the TV medium; in our homes we can identify more with the people than in the theater.

Star Trek: The Motion Picture works better on TV. It is that simple. From beginning to end, we are able to follow the story more easily, enjoy our favorites more, and feel more satisfied at the conclusion. We get involved with *STTMP* on the TV screen . . . just as we get involved with writing and talking about Star Trek to our fellow fans. In this case, the presentation makes all the difference. Thanks, Gene. Far from doing everything wrong, as many claimed you did, you somehow managed to do *two* things right! *STTMP* is a fine movie, and a *great* television show!

So much for that. I can already see the disagreements coming. But perhaps all of the so-called fans who went to see the movie and came away gloating about its having "failed" should be forced to watch it on TV. Could be that they would sing a different tune.

But who cares? We don't really need the gibbering children of all ages who ride the latest fad as if their lives depended on it. Organized fandom has little use for people who get just as excited about Robin Williams, King Tut, disco, and skateboards as they do about Star Trek. Sure, they are the ones who buy the toys and the personality posters and the record albums (and incidentally make a lot of money for Paramount), but they have no ideas and taste of their own. Whatever is "hot" is what grabs them, and once something else comes along, they jump to it and couldn't care less if their last passion lives or dies. Unfortunately, we seem to be turning into a nation of faddists. It makes you think . . . far from being the "nuts" most people think Star Trek fans are, we seem to be quite sane. At least we don't bend with every breeze that blows from the pages of *Popular* magazines!

Oh . . . but the reverse is worse. There are those people who will take something to their hearts and praise it to the skies . . . until it gets popular. Then they drop it like a hot potato. Your typical science fiction fan is often guilty of this. He loved Star Trek until it became popular. He was ecstatic about *Star Wars* until that movie made more money than any in history. They are the elitists who cannot stand to be part of the "common herd," so they immediately turn in a raging pack on anyone or anything which the public accepts wholeheartedly. So they sometimes have to make weird leaps in logic, usually reversing themselves in the process.

So we have two groups who spend most of their time leaping from one new thing to the other . . . one group because they want to be "in," the other because they do not. Both are equally silly. Both took their shots at *STTMP*.

And it is distressing to note how many of our moviegoers fall into the first group and how many of our movie reviewers fall into the second.

Sometimes you just want to cry.

Looking back at *Star Trek: The Motion Picture* a year later, there is a distressing feeling of *wrongness* associated with some elements in the film. It almost seems as if (as some fan writers have suggested) the movie takes place in an alternate universe, one with a slightly different crew, ship, and Federation. This could very well be, although *STTMP* has been definitely and positively identified as the *official* sequel to the series by Roddenberry and Company.

So we are left with the problem of acclimatizing our view of the movie with the well-loved series . . . and that is very difficult, as the movie is set in a much darker, much more somber universe than the one we so reluctantly left ten years ago.

Examples? Well, perhaps the most disturbing is the change in the Federation and its policies, which can be seen in the operation of the *Enterprise* itself:

The *Enterprise*, once a bright, happy ship, dedicated to the exploration of space and the semimilitary protection of citizens and property, now seems to be an out-and-out warship. It was not specifically stated, of course, but that is the impression one gains from dozens of little things seen in the movie. For instance; the drab and ultrafunctional uniforms, the cold and sterile ship interiors, and, most of all, the humorless and almost *too* efficient way in which the crewmembers go about their duties.

The new uniforms, contrary to expectations, were not universally hated by fans. Many found them to be quite pleasing to the eye, once seen on the screen, and quite suitable to starship duties. Feminists were especially pleased that the hated miniskirts were absent. But although the new uniforms may have succeeded from a fashion standpoint, they still jarred us in a way which most could not explain.

And well they should have. For the change in uniform was one of the first indications we had that the Federation and Starfleet had changed—and, one fears, not for the better. Looking back through history, one sees the evolution of military uniforms tends to follow a straightforward pattern: As the individual soldier became less important, as technology began to play a greater and greater role in warfare, the uniforms worn by those soldiers became more and more drab, dehumanizing, and functional.

We see this in *STTMP*. Gone perhaps forever are the brightly colored shirts which immediately identified each crewperson's duty section . . . they have been replaced by a small colored patch under the *Enterprise* insignia. Everyone on board is now dressed in the same pale-hued colors—and the colors now seem to identify rank more than duty. Everyone is dumped into the same faceless mass, and one suspects that duty assignments on board the new *Enterprise* are made by need more than by qualification.

But bright-colored uniforms would be jarring only when seen against the bare metal and ultrafunctional backgrounds of this starship. Where are the corridors painted in eye-pleasing, psychologically satisfying hues? Where are the splashes of color in paintings, murals; even in standpipes and Jefferies tubes, all of which were partially disguised by color in the series *Enterprise*? Sure, much of the ship is pretty, but it is cold as well. The long, confining steel-walled corridors give no illusion of warmth and security as one moves through them, only a feeling of institutionalism. The corridors of the *Enterprise* in *STTMP* reminded me of the corridors seen in photos of underground missile silos—and looked like about as much fun to be in!

And look at that transporter chamber! It wouldn't surprise me to see Dr. Frankenstein working in there. The walls were covered with dangerous-looking devices and machinery, and Chief Rand worked the controls from behind a heavily shielded booth . . . hardly the kind of place which would inspire confidence in anyone beaming aboard for the first time. If the chamber had always looked like that, we could understand McCoy's reluctance to submit to the process. That room is absolutely terrifying!

But in the past, the transporter room was as familiar and homey as our own front doors. In fact, it *was* a door—the simplest and fastest entrance and exit to the ship, everyday and commonplace. Would the many scenes played in the transporter room in the series work if played in the transporter room as shown in the movie? Of course not! It is too cold and businesslike a place for emotion and sentiment . . . and a place no one would want to hang around in any longer than they absolutely had to!

The bridge is much the same. It is no longer a comfortable place to be. Ask Dr. McCoy—he didn't hang around there any more than he had to in *STTMP*. It is overburdened with technology, it is dark, it is cold . . . cold, cold, cold. The whole ship is so very cold and unfamiliar. It is a bit frightening.

And what does this cold and sterile atmosphere do to the people working in it—living in it? It makes them cold as well. The *Enterprise* is obviously not a happy ship any longer. Surrounded by a completely materialistic and institutional atmosphere, the crewpersons can only react in the same way. They are very, very efficient—but they were also efficient in the series—"Best crew in the Fleet!" In the series, though, you could see that each and every one of them *enjoyed* his work.

Not so in the movie. Most of the crew went about their duties with clenched teeth and grim expressions. It was almost as if they feared someone—or something—was always looking over their shoulders, watching and perhaps waiting for a mistake . . . or even a wrong word or expression.

(True, warping out to face a deadly threat to Earth is not the kind of thing to bring a happy smile to one's face, but in the series hot action or imminent danger did not turn the crew into robots.)

It is as if everything in the movie points to a decidedly militaristic turn having been taken by Starfleet and the Federation in the time we viewers were "absent." All the way from the addition of a "weapons station" on the bridge to the shameful treatment of Kirk during his admiralcy, the signs are there. Apparently the hawks have taken control, and have made sure that they are going to stay in control. It is a pattern we have seen many times throughout history: Reduce the individuality and initiative of your soldier (and citizen) by surrounding him with the trappings of sterility, sameness, and fear. Make him stay on his toes wondering if "big brother" is watching, align his thoughts into "acceptable" patterns—and his actions will surely follow.

Starfleet in *Star Trek: The Motion Picture* is not what we saw in the series—it is not what we expected it would be from indications given in the series—it is not an organization that we would want to join. The great appeal of Star Trek was the desire of all of us—be it conscious or unconscious—to join in with the *Enterprise* crew and share that warm and wonderful comradery* they showed to us. In *STTMP*, that comradery is muted, if not completely absent, and we do not have that overriding desire to be a part of such a cold and seemingly unfeeling Starfleet.

Perhaps that is why the movie did not have the stupendous business that Paramount had hoped for. It did not seem like Star Trek. Sure, the crew was there and the ship was there, and even the philosophy of Roddenberry was there. But it was all set in the wrong milieu, like the hillbilly Clampetts in Beverly Hills. *Our* crew, *our* ship, *our* philosophy, simply did not jibe with that strange and cold world we saw up there on the screen. It did not bother us fans all that much. We are able to explain things away, and we "know" that changes will be made in Starfleet and the Federation during the reconstruction of the ship. But to the average viewer, expecting to see the same Star Trek he sees on television, the subliminal differences must have been quite jarring. So he wasn't satisfied, didn't tell his friends to run out to see the movie, and, most important, he didn't come back to see the film again and again.

Still, the movie worked in its own way, and it is left to us to reconcile the disturbing with the acceptable and familiar. Each fan must do this on his own and keep hoping that in a sequel, many of the disturbing elements will be corrected or eliminated.

It has been an interesting year, hasn't it? One which has been filled with such thoughts and contemplations as those very few outlined above. We have all been very busy and very imaginative in our responses to *Star Trek: The Motion Picture*, and we all will surely continue to discuss, interpret, dissect, examine, argue, and fantasize about the movie for this year and many more to come. It has been quite a twelvemonth—and the best is yet to come!

9.

THE CREW IN STAR TREK: THE MOTION PICTURE

by Walter Irwin

One of the first things we fans heard about STTMP (and one of the most heartening) was that all of the original crew were to be included in the film. Plus we were to have the bonus of being introduced to new "younger and more exciting" characters. But somewhere 'twixt conception and completion, something went awry. And in this article, Walter gives us his ideas on what . . . and why.

It is impossible to put ten years' worth of speculation and hopes and desires in a two-and-a-half-hour film, but that is exactly what many fans expected to see when they sat down to view *Star Trek: The Motion Picture.* Each fan has his or her favorite character, and wanted desperately to know what had transpired in the life of that character during the time that the *Enterprise* was in "drydock" undergoing rebuilding and refitting. In most cases, these fans were disappointed, for even in the case of Kirk, Spock, and McCoy, only the barest and briefest of details were given. There simply was not time.

Ordinarily when we meet old friends after a couple of years have passed, the first question we ask is, "What have you been doing with yourself?" But then we are not likely to meet them while preparing a ship for emergency launch, frantic with worry about our loved ones down on the planet surface, or just damn scared out of our wits by that "thing out there." And in *STTMP*, the crew felt all those things. There was no time to engage in idle chatter, there was a job to do; and *if* they survived, then each of them could sit around in the rec room and swap stories.

Too, the demands of film are such that very little time can be spent on supporting exposition. The time needed (real time, minutes and seconds spent watching the film) to have each character give even a very brief statement about the interim years would be too great—by the time we worked around to Christine Chapel and Janice Rand, V'Ger would be sifting around in the rubble of Earth, still looking for the Creator, and we would be about six and a half hours into a seven-hour film. Sure, most fans would have loved *STTMP* to be even twice that long, but I'm afraid that the average customer would have been fast asleep.

(The same time restrictions put the kibosh on Roddenberry's plans to have the crew "spread out," and each summoned to the *Enterprise* as Kirk reassembled "the finest crew in Starfleet." But then time would have to be taken for each character to have an "introduction scene" and an "*Enterprise* entrance scene," none of which would have significantly advanced the plot (although *we* would have been entertained and edified). If everyone is already aboard (with the exception of the Big Three) when the movie begins, then all Kirk has to do is enter the bridge, give everyone a nod, and get on with business.

So supporters of the supporting characters were disappointed, but then they should have expected no less. However, our minds do not work within a two-and-a-half-hour time limit, and so we can sit back and logically deduce what must have transpired with each of those characters during the layover. But if we do so, we find that nothing very exciting and interesting happened in that time.

The supporting characters are very real to us, and so we would expect them to do the things that real people would do after returning from a five-year mission: They visited their families, they rested (a lot), they caught up on all of the fads, fashions, and events they had missed, they traveled a bit, looked up old friends, and rested (some more), etc., etc., etc. Just what you or I would do when returning home from a long absence. Nothing special, nothing mundane. Just life.

Then, of course, and with appropriate promotions for a job well done, they were assigned back aboard the ship, and began preparing it for another deep-space mission under their new captain, Will Decker. Again, nothing unusual . . . interesting and challenging work to be sure, but not exciting. Any excitement lay in the expectation of once again getting out into space.

Oh, Scotty was probably delighted with his new engines, and Janice Rand probably had some nostalgic feelings about being on the *Enterprise* again. Chekov must have been sweating out his new job, on a completely new station, no less; while Christine was sweating over her exams to qualify as an M.D.

But probably the hardest part for all of them was the knowledge that they would soon be voyaging into uncharted space *without* the three men who had guided them so well for so long. That must have been quite a feeling! And it would account for the shine in the eyes of each of them when Kirk, Spock, and McCoy finally made it aboard.

But Will Decker was entirely competent . . . at least, Kirk thought so. He "personally gave" his beloved ship to Decker, entrusting Decker with the lives of his crew and with the legend all of them had created together. So we can assume that Will Decker was one hell of a commander. We have James T. Kirk's word on it.

But who was Willard Decker? We know from Roddenberry's novelization of *Star Trek: The Motion Picture* that he is the son of Commodore Matthew Decker, and that fact alone must have weighed heavily in Kirk's decision to choose Will to take over the *Enterprise*. For knowing Kirk as we do, we know he has just a little bit of guilt—however unwarranted—about Matt Decker's death. That alone would not have led Kirk to recommend Will for command—Kirk is too concerned with the ship and crew and too conscientious to base his recommendation solely on personal feelings—but it would have led him to choose Decker over any number of equally qualified candidates. Kirk is a compulsive payer of debts.

When we first see Will Decker in *Star Trek: The Motion Picture*, he is at Scotty's side, very busy working to correct a transporter foulup. (It is interesting to note that the job of replacing the faulty unit was given to a crewmember when Kirk called Decker aside to talk, and Scotty looked on. Had Scotty or Decker not been interrupted by Kirk, would one of them have fetched and installed the device in time to prevent the horrible accident in the transporter? Something to think about.) The fact that Decker was working side by side in Engineering with the very persnickety (when it comes to his engines) Scotty tells us that Decker must have had a very firm background in the engineering sciences prior to training for command. More evidence of this is the plan of Decker and Scotty (mentioned only in the novel) to reroute the phaser controls to operate independently of the warp drive. Scotty specifically mentions that Decker is the one who is finalizing the plans.

True, it is a strict requirement that all starship captains be completely familiar with every part of their ships—that is the primary reason why Command trainees serve in many different positions as they make their way up through the ranks. We have seen how Sulu served a stint in Biological Sciences, and how Chekov moved from Navigation to Weapons Control. We can assume that Will Decker followed a similar path in his rise to starship command. We know that Jim Kirk did.

But in all of the aired episodes, we very, very seldom saw Kirk working along with Scotty—and never in a nonemergency situation. Although Kirk's duties required him to be familiar with Engineering operations and theory—and basic mechanics—it can readily be assumed that the mechanical side of things was not his primary interest or training.

Even though the need to get the *Enterprise* ready in jig time could be considered an emergency, the fact that Decker was so involved with the readying and testing of the engines tells us that he most certainly must have served as an engineer on board another ship previous to being given command. After all, when Kirk took over from Decker, you didn't see *him* down in the "boiler room" getting his hands dirty, did you?

Assuming that Decker did indeed come up through the ranks by a slightly different route than Kirk would indicate to us some of the reasons for the basic personality differences between the two men.

Kirk is the type who was literally "born to lead." Everything in his mental makeup forces him to assume and crave a position of power and responsibility. It was this psychological desire which led him to retake command from Decker in the first place . . . it was also this need which allowed him to succeed even with the handicap of almost three years away from deep-space experience.

Decker, however, was a person who accepted leadership as a logical step upward in what must have been a satisfying and rewarding career. But he lacked that one essential element that all successful starship captains *must* have: *ego*. Decker simply did not have enough faith in himself and confidence in his abilities to be another Garth of Izar, Matt

Decker, or Jim Kirk. Technical expertise aside, Decker was not top-flight command material.

(An aside: This is not to make light of Decker's skills. Our own beloved Scotty would most likely make only a fair captain himself! He, like Decker, aspires only to one level, and although Scotty would probably accept command if it were thrust upon him (especially if it were by Jim Kirk!) he would never be able to enter into it with the same wholehearted abandon that he gives to his "bairns." Even though we have seen instances in which Scotty is forced to assume temporary command of the ship, and he performs with skill and toughness, he never looks comfortable in the center seat. The difference between Scotty and Decker is that Scotty perhaps had the wisdom to realize his limitations, and never made the effort to gain a command of his own.)

We see several instances of Decker's reluctance in *STTMP*. He almost always opts for caution, and while this is ofttimes the most prudent course, events in the film usually prove him wrong. In the one case where he advocates the use of weaponry, it would be a mistake. One can chalk this up to inexperience, of course, but the fact remains that Decker did not arrive full-blown aboard the *Enterprise*—by the time he attained a captaincy, he *would* have had at least one other command (most likely two) and should have had enough deep-space experience to at least be able to concur with Kirk and Spock some of the time. It is obvious that Decker is one of those people who do not learn from history—even his own.

In the novelization of *Star Trek: The Motion Picture* we are given two very important facts about Decker, both of which reveal a great deal about why he would not have made a top-notch starship commander.

One: Roddenberry tells us that in the absence of his father, Matt Decker, young Will was greatly influenced by his mother and her involvement in the *New Human* movement. We are told that Will responded favorably to the philosophies of this group, and felt attracted to the special and unique rewards of group unity and consciousness. This alone should have disqualified him from Command, for if there is any one thing a starship commander needs, it is the ability to stand alone.

A captain must be able to adhere to the old adage "The buck stops here." Command is by definition a lonely job, and only a strong individualist can operate well within the framework of that loneliness. He must always be apart . . . and he must prefer it that way. His ego must be so strong that in the back of his mind the thoughts of "only *I* am able" and "*I* must decide" should be forever present. A captain is only human, however, so he needs close friends and advisers to help him reach his decisions, to gripe to, to relax with, and—occasionally—to provide a shoulder to cry on. But he must always remain a certain distance removed from those friends; for when push comes to shove, the captain makes the decision . . . and he makes it alone.

How in the world did Decker ever manage to survive the command or two he had previous to the *Enterprise*? Either he was very, very lucky, or else he was working on one of the all-time greatest ulcers! For a man who was drawn—by indoctrination and by personal desires—to a unity of minds, command must have been like being in hell . . . and being there all alone. It is an old joke among fans that starship captains seem to have a tendency to go nuts, but Decker was one of the best candidates for a nervous breakdown Starfleet has ever seen. It is very easy to imagine him breaking under pressure just as Captains Tracey, Garth, and Matthew Decker did.

If one assumes that the great incidence of mental breakdowns among starship commanders was due to the unbelievable isolation of command (and it is logical to assume so), then Starfleet Command was criminally negligent in allowing Will Decker, given his background, to ever command *anything*, much less the pride of the fleet. And Kirk must be considered negligent as well, for if he didn't know about Decker's background when he recommended him to take over the *Enterprise*, he damn well *should* have!

Two: We also know, both from the movie and the novelization, that Decker was very much tempted to remain on Delta with Ilia. And it is also obvious that his feelings were affected just as much by the Deltan life-style of unity through sex as they were by his love for the beautiful Ilia.

We have seen James Kirk tempted to give up everything—literally—for love . . . and we have seen him overcome that temptation. Will Decker also overcame his temptation to give up his career for love, but the difference lies in the style in which each man made his decision. Kirk not only allowed Edith Keeler to die, he actually prevented McCoy from saving her. Decker, on the other hand, slunk away from the planet Delta like a thief in the night, fearing that if he attempted to say goodbye to Ilia, he would not be able to force himself to leave.

There is the basic difference between the two men—and the basic difference between a successful starship commander and a run-of-the-mill (if not a total failure) starship commander. Kirk not only made his decision, he took an active part in making his decision a reality. Instead of meeting with Ilia one last time, and testing his determination to remain with Starfleet, Decker took the easy way out. It really wasn't a decision at all. It is a question of willpower . . . the ability to make an almost instantaneous decision and having the guts to stick to it. It also requires a strong ego, as one has to be able to convince oneself that the decision is right and proper, and that he is the only one who can make that decision. It is not bullheadedness or obstinacy, but the firm conviction born of training and experience that it is the *right* thing to do. We have seen James T. Kirk exhibit this talent time and time again. Had Will Decker lived, it is unlikely that we would ever have seen it in him.

Although no examples were quoted in either the movie or the novelization, Will Decker also seemed to be a bit too much of an aesthete to be a successful starship commander. In other words, he was just too sensitive. It was revealed in his choice of phrasings, and even in his demeanor. Decker would have seemed more at home in the ship's library than on the bridge. It is this quality that has earned Decker the appellation of "wimp" among many fans.

This is not to say that sensitivity is an undesirable trait in starship captains—to the contrary. A well-rounded commander must be quite sensitive to many factors . . . and he must, above all, be caring and compassionate. But there is a point where these qualities become a liability, and hinder a commander in the necessary dirty jobs that sometimes come his way. It is a delicate balance, and even the briefest glimpses into Decker's character showed he lacked that balance. He simply *never* came across as a strong and forceful personality, one who could command the admiration and respect of his crew and inspire them to follow him wherever he led.

The character of Willard Decker was specifically created for *Star Trek: The Motion Picture* to serve as a counterpoint to Kirk. He was supposed to be young and ambitious; foolhardy in his youth and inexperience; resentful of the usurpation of his powers and command by Kirk; and most of all, the very model of James T. Kirk at the same age. And if the character had been played like that, it would have made for a much more interesting contrast and confrontation. We would have been privileged to see Jim Kirk up against a mirror image of himself, one still starry-eyed and puffed-up, without the deadening years of toil, disappointments, and disillusionment.

Wow, wouldn't that have been fun?

But somewhere along the way, Will Decker went through a metamorphosis . . . and instead of a Young Turk Kirk, we had a character who served only as a device, good for giving Kirk a few dirty looks, moping around a lot, and "dying" at the end of the movie without a single qualm of regret from the audience. At no time during *STTMP* could we believe that Willard Decker was starship captain material; he was just too . . . well . . . wimpy. It is a shame, for not only would the film have been better served by having a stronger Decker character, our perceptions of the "Star Trek universe" and all the things we *know* go on in that universe would have been strengthened as well. If we cannot believe that Will Decker could command the *Enterprise*, then we cannot believe in the Jim Kirk that recommended him for that position nor in the Starfleet Command that allowed Decker to take over the ship. Our hold on the "'reality" of that universe is undermined, and it hurts. It hurts a lot.

But the Decker that was in *STTMP* is the Decker that we fans have to integrate into the Star Trek universe . . . a process which is most likely being taken care of by many fan writers at this very moment. Thankfully, fans are not required to go through so many mental convolutions to accept the "reality" of the Deltan Ilia.

Ilia, because she is an alien character, is not harmed nearly so much by a lack of character development as was Decker. We more or less expect aliens in any science fiction story or series to be somewhat mysterious and very different. This is especially true in Star Trek. It was one of the basic tenets of the series as stated by Gene Roddenberry that little or no time be used to "explain" things . . . you all remember the famous "policeman's pistol" illustration . . . and the same formula was used in the movie. Scotty didn't bother to explain to Kirk how the new engines worked, and likewise no one took the time to make a long speech about Deltans or Ilia in particular. (It would have also taken a disproportionate amount of screen time to delve into her background. We learned much about Spock during the course of the series, but almost all of the information came piecemeal, and in the context of conversation or data.)

So we could accept Ilia without too many reservations. True, we would have very much liked to know a lot more about the love affair she and Decker shared, but again there was not time (even in the novelization). The only thing that left most uninitiated audiences puzzled was the reference in the movie to an "oath of celibacy"; it is unfortunate that the references to Ilia's overt sexuality were cut from the movie in a quest for a G rating. (Why Paramount thought the movie had to rate a G will perhaps remain one of the all-time great Star Trek mysteries.)

Leslie Thompson here. I'm typing this article for Walter, and I had to interrupt to beg fans not to write in and ask me to explain that mystery. My imagination isn't genius enough to explain the corporate mind!

Ilia wasn't a bad character at all. In fact, if she had stayed around, we might have seen quite a bit of development in her relationship with the rest of the crew. It would have been quite amusing to see how Sulu reacted to her continual presence at his side, and the addition of another alien viewpoint besides Spock's would have made things more interesting.

The little we saw of the "real" Ilia, however, didn't give us much of an idea of how things would have proceeded if she had remained as a permanent member of the crew. Certainly, she was not emotionless, although it was evident that she was well able to hold her emotions in check. We are also told that Deltans are among the most skillful navigators in the fleet, and we see evidence of this when Ilia performs quite admirably during the wormhole incident. But we could expect no less, for even under a new captain, the *Enterprise* still remained the pride of the fleet, and only the most qualified people would be assigned to her. It was much easier for us to believe that Ilia could function as navigator than it was to believe that Decker could be captain.

Ilia would have no doubt become a valuable addition to the crew that Kirk has proudly called "the best in the fleet," and perhaps even Will Decker, who performed quite ably as first officer, would have eventually won our approval in that position. In fact, most fans would have welcomed them with open arms . . . for most of us realize that things *do* change, even in the world of Star Trek, and an occasional infusion of new blood is proper and healthy.

However, it would have been quite impossible for Will Decker to continue serving on the *Enterprise*. Although Decker became a bit more forgiving later, the initial conflict with Kirk would always have stood in the way of an effective working relationship between Decker and Kirk. An emergency is one thing, but we can assume that when Decker took command of the *Enterprise*, he used Captain's Privilege and brought some favored and special crewpersons with him (just as Kirk did when first taking command). These crewpersons would have quite understandably held some resentment for Kirk, and although we know they would have been loyal to him, the unspoken thought that Decker was the "real" captain would always have been there. Kirk would have had either to ignore it or have them transferred out— something he would not have wanted to do without justifiable cause.

Too, Kirk firmly believed that Decker merited command, and would not have wanted to deny him command of another ship just to keep him aboard the *Enterprise*, no matter how valuable a first officer he might be. But getting that new command for Decker might not have been so easy, for starship captaincies don't become available that often . . . it is probably safe to say that it is a once-in-a-lifetime opportunity. It would have been very unfair of Kirk to expect Decker to allow him to keep the *Enterprise* when the mission was concluded, and even more unfair of Kirk to expect Decker to accept a lesser command instead. (It would have seriously harmed Decker's career in any case, for whatever the reasons a commander is relieved, the fact that he *was* will forever cast doubts on his ability.) So even if things had worked out and Decker stayed on as Kirk's second in command, sooner or later there would have been trouble.

And you can't have two officers in charge of a starship who are constantly at odds with each other. Sure, it would have made for some doggone fascinating tales (and has, in a few other instances), but it is not realistic. And when you have a show such as Star Trek, where it is extremely important to have a number of firmly rooted and recognizably realistic elements to offset the science fiction and fantasy elements, such an ongoing conflict would be very harmful. Having Decker remain just would not have worked.

So we can see that it was impossible for the character of Decker to remain a permanent part of the crew from the moment of his creation . . . he was born to die. Ilia seems like more of a sacrificial lamb, first bumped off ignominiously by V'Ger and replaced by a shrill-voiced robot, then added to Decker's sacrifice as a throw-in.

It is appparent that both of these characters need to be replaced in new movies or episodes, for Star Trek cannot survive without some new faces and the necessary changes that time (both real time and Star Trek time) would bring. If we are to continue believing in Star Trek and the things it stands for, we must also be willing to accept the fact that over the course of the next few decades, things will change. Whether it be a new actor playing Spock or Kirk, or their eventual replacement by new captains and Vulcans within the series framework, some day Star Trek must look quite different. None of us looks forward to that time . . . but perhaps we should. For it is the idea and ideals of Star Trek which are important—more important than William Shatner or Gene Roddenberry or even those of us who watch—and if the things that Star Trek stands for continue, then we will have won.

And we will have won the future.

10.

ALTERNATE UNIVERSES IN STAR TREK FAN FICTION

by Rebecca Hoffman

To most fans, the allure of fan fiction is that anything *can happen! Freed from the restrictions of continuing-series format, fan writers have put the* Enterprise *crew through some oftimes strange, but always exciting, changes. In this article, Rebecca Hoffman looks at some of the more famous and interesting "alternate universes" that have sprung from the vivid imaginations of fan writers.*

While mainstream SF has been content with the theory of alternate universes for many years, Star Trek fans were first introduced to the concept on March 30, 1967, when the episode "The Alternative Factor" was aired. In this instance, the alternate universes were absolute opposites; on the one hand was the positive Lazarus who was matter, on the other was the negative Lazarus who was antimatter. Should the two meet anywhere except in the corridor between their universes, they would annihilate each other and all other existing universes as well.

The second season saw another example of alternate universes when, on October 6, 1967, "Mirror, Mirror" aired. In this episode, Kirk and others were actually transferred into this alternate universe. I prefer to use the word "alternate" to "parallel"; for while the mirror universe parallels the Starfleet universe in many respects, it is not a true parallel. There are many differences; and while the mirror universe is not a total opposite, many situations which occur in it are the opposite of the "real" Star Trek universe (such as ascending rank by assassinating one's superiors).

After this episode, the concept of alternate universes took off in fan fiction. Some were constructed consciously as alternate universes; others fall into the category by virtue of changes they make in the series format.

Alternate universes are created simply because each writer is looking at the worlds of Star Trek from his own unique point of view. Each writer sees it differently—if only to a small degree. Therefore, each writer has his own concept of Star Trek, and because of this, each writer's Star Trek universe is different from Gene Roddenberry's. Not even the professional writers have solved the problem of getting past their own views of Star Trek; and they don't always handle the prime universe well.

So what, then, is an alternate universe in Star Trek fiction? Strictly speaking, it is *anything* written by someone who is not part of the production staff of the show. This includes the professional novels. Though they must all be approved by Paramount, that is no guarantee of continuity, nor that the novels will even coordinate with the series. Unfortunately, many of them do not mesh well at all. Only Gene Roddenberry's filmed versions (whether live-action, animated, or movie) can be considered the canon, or prime universe. Even those have so many discrepancies between them that it makes one wonder. When we come to the fan fiction, however, *all* of it is alternate universe. But some examples are far more alternate than others.

There are many stories which can be considered "mainstream"—if there is such an animal in Star Trek fiction. They change nothing, add no new characters, and while many are stories which flesh out portions of episodes or tie up loose ends in episodes, other stories simply show the characters acting under different situations, but again make no changes in those characters or the series format.

These stories are the closest to Roddenberry's concept, and fans enjoy them. But the most intriguing stories are those which go beyond what was given us, those wherein—as in real life—people grow and learn and mature. And this is where the writers really jump head over heels into alternate universes.

I suspect the biggest reason alternate universes are so popular is that they totally free the writer's creativity, allowing him or her to work with the characters and plots on levels far more complex than television allows. At the same time, we sometimes wind up with stories disguised as Star Trek fiction which actually bear little resemblance to the original. In such cases, the reader has to totally suspend his disbelief—and yet a great number of these stories are well worth it.

In alternate universes, one finds many changes: A character dies; another falls in love and marries; galactic war occurs; the *Enterprise* is destroyed; Kirk is transferred to another command—there are many variables, and each leads to a different view of Star Trek. In this article, I wish to examine some of the main variations on the prime universe, all of which make major changes, some for the better and some for the worse.

Perhaps one of the earliest alternate universes was "Kraith," which was created by Jacqueline Lichtenberg. It was an entire panorama of Vulcan society, complex in the extreme, and thoroughly *alien*. The Kraith Vulcans really have little in common with those of the canon universe, but "Kraith" is well done, intriguing and ongoing. It is also interesting that there is now an alternate universe to an alternate-Kraith universe.

In one Kraith story, the Kraith Kirk is kidnapped into an alternate universe where a disconsolate Commodore Spock is searching universes to find a Kirk to replace his own. The situation so intrigued Scottish authors Sheila Clark and Valerie Piacentini that they took the idea further in "Variations on a Theme," and with Jackie Lichtenberg's permission, used the commodore and his dilemma to create a universe of their own. It is an alternate universe, yet it is definitely Star Trek, and is one very interesting saga.

Kraith is a Vulcan-oriented universe, but there are stories dealing with many other alien societies. Mattie Jones and Marilynn Ambos (*The Human Factor*) have created a series of stories dealing with the Romulans, delving deeply into their culture and history. The "Nu Ormenèl" tales by Fern Marder and Carol Walske comprise a voluminous compilation of stories about the Klingons and their civilization. Klingons are a popular subject in fandom, and are by no means limited to this one series. In four successive issues of *Southern Star*, M.A. Carson has been running installments of his "Klingon Dictionary," which includes not only vocabulary, but his concepts of the Klingon culture. Nor are the Tholians forgotten: Those crystalline creatures from "The Tholian Web" (live-action) have inspired Lisa Wahl, RAM, and Lynnalan to create "Intersect," a Tholian universe all their own—and their characters are not quite what the reader may expect.

Throughout the massive body of fan fiction, there are countless essays on most of the aliens presented in the series, and each one shows a view of an interesting alternate universe.

"Alternate Universe Four" by Shirley Maiewski, Virginia Tilley, Anna Mary Hall, and Daphne Hamilton next comes to mind. As is obvious from the title, this was intended to be an alternate universe. In this one, Kirk is court-martialed and cashiered out of the service. Afterward he is contacted by a secret organization known as Light Fleet. They are an advanced force trying to keep peace in the galaxy, and their personnel come from all races. Kirk then becomes a Light Fleet captain.

The next example is of stories set in the future, well past the time of the televised episodes. One such example is Jean Lorrah's "Epilogue," published in *Sol Plus*. It takes place some two decades past the televised episodes, when an aging Kirk goes to Vulcan one last time to bid his old friend Spock farewell. Kirk's mind is failing him, and he doesn't want to become helplessly senile. The Vulcans have perfected a method of stopping senility, but it involves regression into the past, and through the memories of Spock, his mother Amanda, and others, the reader learns about the devastating war between the Federation and a Klingon-Romulan coalition which ended Kirk's five-year mission early.

One of the most time-twisting, character-rending situations to come along in years has to be Leslie Fish's "The Weight" (published by T'Kuhtian Press). The *Enterprise* is back in time when an anarchist crewmember totally destroys the time scheme, leaving Kirk in an alternate universe controlled by anarchists—with counterpoints of himself and others of his crew on Earth. To get back to his own future and universe, Kirk literally must snap time back in on itself, and he, being the focal point, is himself snapped. The author uses the story to take Kirk apart and put him back together again in a fashion impossible in prime-universe Star Trek.

While the aforementioned examples are definite alternate universes, they take place either wholly or partially in a different time, another culture, or a place other than the *Enter-*

prise. But there are alternate universes which are totally *Enterprise*-oriented. Many of these stories feature new characters, and while these are legion, each stands out for its uniqueness.

Star Trek played with the concepts of the old gods such as Apollo ("Who Mourns for Adonais", live action) and Kukulkan ("How Sharper Than a Serpent's Tooth," animated), so it is not suprising that some fans write stories around legendary figures in human myth. But *Enterprise* crewmen who are vampires and werewolves? Indeed, yes. M.A. Carson's Dov Brian stories (published in *Southern Star*) center on a very old werewolf who is currently serving aboard the *Enterprise*. In *Berengaria*, Rebecca Ross has introduced Carmilla, a vampire born in the early twentieth century. In both cases, the authors have given their characters sound bases for their respective afflictions, and the explanations go well beyond old legend.

"Landing Party Six" (by various authors, published in *Warped Space*) is a bit more normal by comparison—but only because the characters in question aren't some form of supernatural creature. Instead, Landing Party Six consists of the wildest bunch of zanies to be found anywhere. They are caricatures of the authors, and while often played for laughs, occasionally they make some very serious points. Looking at the "Landing Party Six" characters from a totally dispassionate point of view, one wonders how some of them ever made it into Starfleet, much less onto the *Enterprise*. But this is the fun of alternate universes. The writer does not *have* to be limited to what would seem to be logical parameters—within reason, anyway. Even alternate universes can go too far—and without proper justification, they become simple wish-fulfillment fantasies.

Which brings me to another category—the love story. Romances range from gentle love stories to ones specializing in explicit sex. Admittedly many of these *are* fantasies, but in capable hands, they turn into intriguing alternate universes.

Two of the earliest of these concerned Spock. In D. T. Steiner's "Spock Enslaved," Kirk, Spock and others of the *Enterprise* crew are taken slaves on a planet where they are trying to negotiate a treaty. During his long captivity, Spock falls in love with a female slave. Although the story has an interesting plot, both Spock and Kirk are badly mischaracterized, and this is often the greatest problem in alternate universes. A certain amount of faulty characterization is due simply to the author looking at a character differently, but in this particular instance, it was necessary to the plot as set up that Kirk and Spock act in a manner which was completely out of character.

"The Daneswoman" by Laura Basta (published in *Suarian Brandy Digest*) is also a Spock romance, this time with a woman who is in every way his equal. Her background is nicely detailed, and the two characters mesh quite well. When one actually gets into the love scenes, Spock's actions could be considered a bit out of character. But Gene Roddenberry never told us how Vulcans make love, therefore it is very difficult to say what is in character and what is not. Given the *pon farr* ("Amok Time"), I suspect Vulcans are no less passionate in private than humans—but again, that area is total speculation.

Among the myriad romances are those that deal with characters introduced in various episodes. Kirk's romances with Edith Keeler, Ruth, Drusilla, Helen Johansen, Lenore Karidan, Marlena Moreau, Helen Noel, Shahna, Areel Shaw, Nona, Janice Wallace, Deela, Elaan, Reena Kapec, Janice Lester, Miramanee, and Odona have all been written about. Spock's liaisons with T'Pring, Droxine, and the Romulan commandress, as well as the romances between the Vulcan and Leila Kalomi and Zarabeth, have their fan stories. McCoy's various romances are good story subjects, for the women in his life include Tonia Barrows, Nancy Crater, Natira, and his ex-wife. There are stories about Scotty's women, Carolyn Palamas and Mira Romaine, as well as Lieutenant M'Ress, the Caitian from the animated episodes. Chekov wasn't left out either, for he enjoyed relationships with Martha Landon, Irini Galliulian, and Sylvia, the gunfighter's girl in "Spectre of the Gun." (Have I left out anyone? Probably.)

Stories about all these characters are pretty much "mainstream" and very close to the prime universe, as they rarely go further than the televised version, or keep the lovers together permanently. Most of these stories deal with the particular love affair in question and let it go at that. Still, it is speculation, and there are stories which take the same situation, the same two people, and end up with thoroughly different alternate universes. Nor do writers limit themselves to the

Enterprise crew. At least one writer, Charlotte Davis, is doing a series of stories about T'Pring and Stonn, the man she preferred to Spock in "Amok Time."

Writers also don't limit themselves to just the relationships established in the series. Some have jumped on the Kirk/Uhura bandwagon, most notably *Delta Triad*, which is based on a relationship between those two, and features a series of stories about their romance.

Spock/Christine stories are perhaps the most numerous. While no actual relationship developed between them in the series, Christine's love for Spock was of interest to many fans who have paired them in their stories. Some, like Juanita Salicrup's "Crossroads," have developed into a series.

Sulu is not forgotten. One author, Janice K. Hrubes, has done a good Sulu romance, "Swords and Sulu," and its sequel, "Murasaki." Romance did play a large role in Star Trek, and is forming a rather large portion of alternate universes, simply because of the changes it—by its nature—creates.

One romance in particular has gotten a lot of attention in fandom, and that is the one between Spock's parents, Sarek and Amanda. A whole host of permutations exist along this line: stories such as Ruth Berman's "It Seemed the Logical Thing" (published in *T'Negative*) or Jean Lorrah's "Night of the Twin Moons," which has a large number of stories spanning the time from Amanda and Sarek's first meeting through Spock's adulthood and career in Starfleet. Claire Gabriel's "Quartet Plus One" also traces Amanda and Sarek's relationship through a number of years. Johanna Cantor takes a different tack with this theme (*R&R*), for her Vulcans are far more alien than those created by either Lorrah or Gabriel, and the pairing between Sarek and Amanda is much more difficult.

Perhaps the most intriguing alternate universe romances deal with time travel. In Amy Falkowitz's "Rift Crossing" (published in *Rigel*), the heroine is brought forward from the twentieth century, and in the series, she marries Spock.

"The Displaced" by Lois Walling has the same theme, but with a twist, for her heroine, Sue, does not come forward to be thrust into the beautiful civilization the Federation offers. She's been taken from her time by slavers, and she's put in a slave camp, where later she finds Spock, who is in the final stages of *pon farr*.

"Echoes from the Past" by Rebecca Ross is a bit more gentle in the treatment of its time traveler, Aidan McLaren. Klingons bring her forward in time and eventually she winds up on Vulcan in the custody of Spock's parents. A romance does develop between Spock and Aidan.

"The Misfit" by Sharon Emily (published in *Star Trek Showcase*) sets the situation up a bit differently. In this universe, Amanda has died, and Sarek becomes involved with the *Enterprise*'s passenger Lorna Mitchell, who has been brought forward via the Guardian of Forever. Eventually the two do marry, and in succeeding issues of *Showcase*, their lives develop from that point.

Why this particular theme is so popular is unknown. Perhaps it is a way of bringing Star Trek closer to us twentieth-century humans. Though there are not an excessive number of these, most of them are novels with sequels, or else series of stories. These are alternate universes which strike a particularly sympathetic chord with many readers, and all of them are standouts because of their unique nature.

Perhaps the most basic alternate-universe stories are those which deal with the "Mirror, Mirror" episode universe. Laura Basta's series in *Babel* started with the return of Kirk to the *Enterprise*, his subsequent death at the hands of Spock, and Spock's decision to use the *Enterprise*'s resources to overthrow the Empire.

In *Human Factor*, Sapphira Cantrell has a series of ongoing stories wherein Spock confronts Kirk and eventually talks him into joining the conspiracy to overthrow the Empire.

Rebecca Ross' "Reverse" series (published in *Southern Star*) takes key televised episodes and presents them as they might have happened in the Mirror universe.

There are two Mirror universe tales which don't really fit this description, except on a tangent. "Echoes of the Empire" by Joyce Thompson takes place in a savage Star Trek universe, very much like the Mirror universe, but not quite. It starts with Sarek and Amanda, and traces their relationship—then later Spock's growth and development in a ruthless civilization.

Barbara Meek's novel *One Way Mirror* (published by Poison Pen Press) again concerns a twentieth-century girl, thrown into a Star Trek universe which parallels the Mirror universe in many ways, but which twists time and universes so that Star Trek's era is now—and is not at all idealistic.

The next alternate universe we come to is based upon the relationship which developed between Kirk, Spock, and McCoy. These are extremely emotional stories; in many, one (sometimes two) of the trio is killed, leaving the others to cope with the loss. There is also the hurt/comfort syndrome, which—like a soap opera—wrings emotion from the reader. A good example of this is the novel *Home Is the Hunter* by Bev Volker and Nancy Kippax (published in *Contact*), wherein Kirk is brought home after being held hostage by aliens for months. They were playing a game with the Federation similar to the one the Iranians played with us. Kirk and his men (none of his *Enterprise* crew) are captured by the aliens while on an espionage assignment. They are held and savagely tortured, both mentally and physically, and at long last, to save his men, Kirk breaks and confesses. He returns home a broken man, wallowing in guilt and self-loathing, and the road back to his old self is hellish.

Many of the hurt/comfort stories literally smother the reader in emotionalism. This one skillfully plays the reader's emotions to the limits, leaving the reader limp—and unable to read the novel in one sitting.

The most bizarre alternate universe (and often the least justified) could be considered an outgrowth of the above, simply because it concerns the relationship between Kirk and Spock. However, this carries the relationship to extremes. In Star Trek, we saw two men who have a close friendship. There is love, but it is the love of brothers, of comrades. The genre known as K/S—to my mind, and to the minds of many others, the most alternate of alternate universes—presents the two as participating in physical love with one another. This particular alternate universe has aroused a great deal of controversy these past few years, and while most of these stories fall into the category of sexual fantasies (of women, no less), there are some which are justified.

In "Game of Chance" by Frankie Jemison (published in *The Other Side of Paradise*), Kirk disappears during a routine survey of a supposedly uninhabited planet. The planet is inhabited by beings evolved far ahead of humans, who determine intelligence level based on telepathic ability, and since Kirk is pretty much a psi-null, they don't believe he's an intelligent being. He is, to them, a laboratory specimen, and they telepathically tamper with his mind, changing his sexual preferences from female to male, and making Spock the object of that preference.

The story is one of love—and just what Spock and McCoy will do to help Kirk return to normal. It is a story with definite justification behind it. Out there in space, we could find such beings as those who tampered with Kirk's mind. This story is plausible; it *could* happen.

Alternative 2 & 3, a novel by Gerry Downes (published in *Stardate: Unknown*), is less plausible in that Kirk and Spock *choose* one another—eventually they make it permanent. However, the story provides a long, slow buildup. It is no sudden relationship, and gives the reader a chance to orient himself and suspend his disbelief. It is also written with such skill that the reader willingly suspends that disbelief and enjoys the novel, even if he can't wholeheartedly endorse the premise.

There are other such stories which are fairly well written, but by and large, this genre is extremely unbelievable, simply due to what we saw in the series. Kirk was a skirt-chaser if ever there was one, and Spock's romantic encounters were all with women. It's hard to justify this alternate universe in most instances, and though there are some really good entries in the field, they seem to be few and far between. A fan once summed up the K/S stories as "Barbara Cartland heroes in drag." It's a very *strange* alternate universe, and is about as far from the prime universe as one can get.

The examples I have been presenting all take place strictly within the framework of Star Trek. But there is another segment of stories best known as Crossover Universes, which meld Star Trek with characters from other areas of fiction.

One fanzine, *Holmesian Federation*, edited by Signe Landon, contains stories which combine Star Trek with Sherlock Holmes. Many authors create for this zine, and the view is highly illuminating.

Southern Star glommed onto the crossover series early, and in its second issue ran a *Star Trek/Kolchak the Night Stalker* story, and have since presented a *Star Trek/Space: 1999* story and a *Star Trek/Kiss* story.

Showcase Presents the Alternate Universes of Star Wars is

mainly a *Star Wars* zine, but it carries a very believable *Star Wars/Star Trek* crossover story. A T'Kuhtian Press zine, *Dracula*, presented a story which melded *Dracula* and *Star Wars*. More of these stories are cropping up all the time, and I believe that in the future, more writers are going to work with the crossover stories, for they present even wider vistas for authors who enjoy taking diverse themes and creating something new.

Before ending, let me say that this introduction to alternate universes in fan fiction is just that—an introduction. The stories and fanzines discussed are but a small portion of a very large selection, and I have used them because they are the ones with which I am personally familiar. Many, many more exist, and doubtless in the years to come, there will be countless others. Star Trek fired the imagination of fans and spurred them to create their own personal variations, which took the writers and their readers far beyond the boundaries of a television program. There's a whole universe of intriguing stories at the fingertips of any fan, and the possibilities for multitudes of universes are endless. I only hope that this article has opened the portals to these universes for fans who—like all of us—want to go past the present and into the beckoning arms of tomorrow.

Author's Note: Many of the titles included are novels, published under their own titles rather than the auspices of another zine. In the cases of those which are published in a specific fanzine, I have noted the zine's title in italics. The same is true for short stories. As previously stated, all fanzines mentioned in this article are ones which I have read. I've been in fandom quite a while, and some of these zines are early ones, and are no longer in print. Also, some stories or series may by now be printed by a totally different fanzine. Anyone who is really interested in purchasing zines should contact the Star Trek Welcommittee. They produce a directory of clubs and fanzines which exist within fandom. Contact: Judy Segal, Editor, S.T. Welcommittee Directory, P.O. Box 414, Pawling, N.Y. 12564. Please enclose a self-addressed, stamped envelope with your query, as the Welcommittee is a nonprofit organization.

11.

SHE WALKS IN BEAUTY . . .

by G. B. Love

Trek editor G.B. Love may be the only person in Star Trek fandom who is reticent about putting his thoughts down on paper. It's only with much nudging that we are able to get an article or so out of him each year—and then only when the subject is one which really interests him. And, obviously, the chief communications officer of the Enterprise *is one of those rare subjects. . . .*

If you ever want a good, sharp look into the character of Communications Officer Penda Uhura, all you have to do is recall two brief lines of dialogue from one of Star Trek's most enjoyable episodes, "The Squire of Gothos." When the obnoxious Trelane pops aboard the bridge, he firmly grasps Uhura and says (in somewhat lascivious tones), "Ah ha, fair maiden!" To which Uhura replies with a solid shot to the ribs and a crisp, "Sorry; neither." It is a delicious moment.

And with only two words spoken, we find out all sorts of things about Lieutenant Uhura: She is proud of her heritage; she is not a virgin; she has—even in times of stress—a sense of humor; she is brave; she is stubborn; and she doesn't take *anything* off of *anyone* . . . not even a strangely powerful alien being. Not since Charles Foster Kane uttered the immortal "Rosebud" has so little told us so much!

But even that wealth of information does not cover all of the facets of the intriguing and fascinating Uhura. In following episodes, we discover that she is an accomplished singer, a skilled fighter, a skilled linguist, a highly trained and superbly competent technician, an accomplished actress, and one of the few humans who can play the Vulcan harp.

But all of that is common knowledge; it's in the episodes. What we must discover are the things we are *not* told—what Uhura's childhood was like, why she entered Starfleet, what her hopes, fears and most cherished beliefs are . . . in short, we must search for Uhura the *person* . . . and we have precious little to start from.

The episodes didn't even bother to give Uhura a first name. It was left to the fans to do so, and with almost Vulcan logic, they chose an excellent one: Penda . . . the Swahili word for love. Therefore, our favorite communications officer's name means in literal translation "she who loves freedom." What a beautiful and appropriate name for a character in Star Trek!

One of the few things we are told is that Uhura is a native of the United States of Africa. As such, we can assume that her childhood days were spent on that continent, and that she was raised in the traditions and customs of her people. The few glimpses of her relaxing off-duty in her colorful native garb would substantiate this (as well as leave us begging for more!), and the decorations and furnishings in her quarters show that she has attempted (as Mr. Spock has) to recreate as much of her native life-style as possible within the cramped and aseptic crew cabins.

Uhura's father was a teacher, her mother a diplomat. Both were natives of the USAfrica state of Kenya, and it was there Penda was born. As her mother had to do much traveling, it was left to her father, John Indakwa Uhura, to be responsible for the raising and education of Penda, her younger sister Lulua (pearl; "the pearl of freedom"), and her brothers Mweda (keeper; "the keeper of freedom") and Shukrani (thanks; "he who gives thanks for freedom").

Uhura's mother's maiden name was Majira Nafuu ("progression of the seasons"); her father was named after one of the most famous and revered African educators, Dr. John Indakwa. Majira, in her profession, uses the name Balozi (diplomat) Uhura Nafuu, which means "the progression of freedom by diplomacy," a very suitable name indeed!

John Uhura has since risen to a full professorship at the University of Kenya, but during Uhura's youth, he was repaying his debt to his tribe and family clan by serving as a grade-school teacher in the small village where he was born. So it was that Uhura and her siblings, unlike most youngsters on twenty-third-century Earth, enjoyed the unique life experience of living far in the undeveloped regions. It was this early exposure to the wilds and animal life that gave Uhura her unique love for freedom, unexplored areas, and small, furry animals (although many of the wild animals she grew

up with could hardly be described as "small and furry").
Grateful for the foresight of her ancestors who preserved the
wilderness and its animal life for her to enjoy, Uhura is
deeply committed to the Prime Directive and its stated aims
of protecting and preserving alien cultures and environments.

Most likely by the time Uhura had reached college age,
John had taken his position at U of K, and she would
naturally taken her undergraduate courses there. That is, until
she decided to join Starfleet and applied for admission to the
Academy. Her mother and father would not have objected,
but would probably have insisted that she first go back to her
home village and spend time in a worthwhile job there, as
they both had done before starting out on their careers. And
although Penda was brimming over with that wanderlust that
is common to all who join Starfleet, she would have agreed
without argument. For the African people suffered much
across the centuries, seeing entire nations destroyed by colo-
nialism or the theft of the youngest and strongest by slave
traders, and the ensuing loss of cultural values and histories.
So when peace and freedom was finally achieved on the African continent, the return to ancient and traditional tribal and
cultural practices was of the highest priority. The need and
desirability for continuing this practice was drilled into each
child, and each child could see for himself the value of it. It
is a simple yet infinitely beautiful system.

The time she spent teaching and working in the electronics
repair shop in her village served Uhura very well when she finally left to attend the Academy. Not only did she learn that
she had a definite gift for linguistics; she found she enjoyed
working with electronic equipment, something she would not
have even guessed about herself earlier.

Her time at the Academy must have been much like any
other student's there—hard work, long hours, and a growing
self-confidence as she continued onward when others had
failed or given up. But her great beauty and cheerful smile
would also have won her many admirers, and we can be sure
that she had to fight the boys off. Penda always sang, with
her family and fellow villagers, but during her years in the
Academy, she found that her voice had become lovely with
the fullness of maturity, and she was often asked to perform.
Singing was also an excellent way to stay among a crowd and

thereby protect herself from some of her more overzealous suitors.

Not that Penda needed protection. Her childhood was rough-and-tumble . . . she played daily in one of the wildest and most rugged regions in the world, and she also had two boisterous brothers who were always taunting their younger sisters to prove their "equality" and keep up in fighting, games, and tricks. Having killed her first lion at the age of twelve, Penda had no fear of the wolves at the Academy. Those who got too friendly quickly found themselves in a position where even vaunted Starfleet defense tactics did them no good!

(One of the more basic reasons for Uhura's popularity was the impressive figure she developed at about the same time she joined Starfleet. Penda, having been raised in a completely naturalistic world, was not in the least embarrassed by her somewhat late blossoming, but she did bemoan the loss of the sleek and slender form that had often led her father to call her "my little panther." As a result, she stepped up her physical conditioning, keeping herself as hard and as lean as possible.)

Although Uhura longed to continue her Academy studies and progress on to Command School, she was pragmatic enough to realize that, for women, Command was a dead end. Starfleet, for all its liberalism and good intentions, was still an institution run by men, and even the most skilled of women did not often advance beyond the rank of second officer. Uhura decided that she could achieve the same rank and duties in a shorter time by specializing in another field, and obtaining a choice position on a ship of the line. With her linguistic knack and her liking of electronics, it was natural that she chose Communications.

In Communications School, Penda soon discovered that her skill in languages extended to codes and ciphers as well. She breezed through her courses in these without effort, and was soon rivaling the knowledge and skills of her teachers. The added free time she applied to her classes in communications and shipboard electronics, and although she did not have a natural flair for the sciences, she enjoyed the work and excelled through application. All in all, her eighteen months in Communications School were among the happiest (and busiest) in Uhura's life.

Upon her graduation, she was faced with a difficult choice. She wanted very badly to get a berth on a deep-space mission, but Starfleet was in the process of scrapping older ships in favor of newer, faster models, and there was little room for rookies when experienced hands were constantly available. Starfleet promised more ships to come, but they had to be built. Until more ships were ready, Uhura and many other recent Academy and training-school graduates had to be content with having their names placed on a very long waiting list.

No one really knew how long it would be before the promised ships were ready, and the dean of the Communications School took advantage of this fact to talk the best of the recent graduates into signing on as instructors. Uhura was one of his top choices, and he spent many hours extolling the virtues of a teaching career to her.

Having taught in her village, Uhura knew that she really didn't want to make education her career. And, her dean's assurances aside, she had learned enough about the status of women in Starfleet to know that once she was "typed" in a position, it would be very difficult for her ever to transfer to another duty station. But as one delay in the new ships after another was announced, the prospects of a space assignment looked ever more glum, and Uhura was about to accept the teaching post when she heard about something else: Volunteers were being sought for the thankless task of manning skeleton crews on the ships which had been replaced. These crews would pick up the ship at a Starbase, ferry it to one of the Federation dockyards for dismantling, then repeat the process with another ship.

It was a risk, for such duty could lead to one being completely forgotten, but Penda decided to take it. If nothing else, she would at last be able to serve in space, and she was also shrewd enough to perceive that such duty would be both a challenge and an education.

As she reported to Starbase 9, and aboard the scout *Atlantica*, little did Uhura suspect how much of an education it was to be. In the course of their journey back to the dockyards on Altair 7, the *Atlantica* suffered every sort of breakdown, emergency, and foulup conceivable. Uhura, needless to say, was kept very busy, and in the process she gained a working knowledge of Starfleet communications and

its equipment that would have taken her years to learn any
other way.

Over the next eight months, she and her fellow crewmembers ferried half a dozen Starfleet ships of varying size and
purpose to Federation "boneyards," and with each trip,
Uhura learned more. Not only about her own duties, but
about everything, for she was often called upon to do double
duty wherever trouble sprang up in the worn-out ships. It was
the education of a lifetime, and Starfleet was quick to notice,
for when the new ships finally did become available, the first
crews for them were drawn from the veterans of the
"Junkyard Jockeys."

Uhura was promoted to full ensign, and assigned to the
spanking new destroyer *Adad*. It was, depending on how you
look at it, a fortunate time for her to get her first regular
duty assignment, for the troubles with the Klingon Empire
that had been the original impetus for the building of new
ships finally came to a head.

In a number of scattered engagements, none of which was
conclusive for either side, the *Adad* and other Federation
ships battled Klingon forces. In these engagements, the training in crisis situations that Uhura got on the rickety out-of-
service ships served her in good stead. When her superior
officer was injured in one of the battles, Uhura was promoted
to lieutenant and given command of Communications.

Uhura stayed at this post until the *Adad* was ordered back
to Earth to serve as part of the Planetary Defense Force.
Uhura, now having gotten a taste for space, decided to transfer. Several of her crewmates were amazed, as "Earthsitting"
was considered the cream of Starfleet duty: little danger, soft
hours, and lots of passes to the surface, which was home for
the majority of the crew. Her superior officers, however, were
pleased, and Uhura and those few others of the crew who decided to move on were quickly given berths on other ships.

Uhura was assigned to the Starship *Constellation*, commanded by then Captain Matt Decker, and she journeyed to
Starbase 3 to await the ship's arrival there. Shortly after arriving, however, Uhura badly injured some tendons in her leg
when a supporting strut collapsed while she was helping to
clear some rubble off trapped workmen. While she lay fum-
ing in sickbay, the *Constellation* came and went, with another
officer in the position that Uhura had so coveted.

Still on active duty, but without a post, Uhura was assigned once again to teaching duties. One day as she was jogging through the Starbase corridors to strengthen her legs, Uhura was joined by a handsome young man who introduced himself as Jim Kirk. They finished the jog, and made a date for drinks later in the evening.

When Uhura arrived at the bar, she was startled to see that Jim Kirk was wearing the greenish-gold of a captain. He explained that he had just been given command of the *Enterprise*, and was on his way to Earth to take over from Captain Pike and begin the several months of refitting the ship needed. He was also obviously very taken with her, and with a charming smile, asked her to tell him about herself.

Uhura, leaping at the chance to talk, poured out her frustrations to Kirk, in the process giving him a history of her entire Starfleet career. After a while she noticed that his charming, seductive manner had changed. He was still pleasant, but was treating her rather more formally. Thinking she was boring him, Uhura made her excuses and left early (and somewhat disappointed). By the next day, she was hard at work and had forgotten Kirk, as she assumed he had forgotten her.

She was wrong. About two months later, she was notified to report to Earth and the *Enterprise* as chief communications officer. It was then that she realized that Kirk, sensing an addition to his crew, hadn't become bored with her at all. He had already begun treating her as a fellow officer. It was not to be the first time she underestimated Kirk, as so many did, but it was the beginning of her immense respect and loyalty for him.

Uhura settled into her duties quickly and competently, and Kirk had no reason to regret his choice. Uhura was also pleased to see that an old friend of hers from Communications School, Lieutenant Lloyd Alden, was assigned as her assistant. They had dated in school, and in the course of being together so much on the *Enterprise*, they began their affair once again. Although they cared for each other, they were not actually in love, so Uhura was not brokenhearted when Lloyd was transferred after the shattering events at the edge of the galaxy. She was pleased for Alden, who got the post of chief on the *Constellation* that Uhura had missed; so it was that it was one of her lovers rather than she who died aboard the *Constellation* when it was devastated by the Planet Destroyer.

Uhura remained on the *Enterprise* throughout its original five-year mission, and when it returned to Earth, she and her friends, Sulu and Chekov, made a solemn pact to remain aboard, so that even in a small way, the wonderful spirit of that famous crew would remain alive. All received well-deserved promotions, and all refused more prestigious berths to stay with "their" ship. They were immensely pleased when Scotty, who had been planning to accept the post as head of Starfleet Engineering and Design, decided that he too could not leave his beloved *Enterprise*. So it was that none of them showed too much surprise when Jim Kirk pulled every string in the book to rejoin them once again.

So the beautiful Uhura, a few pounds heavier, and only a few lines on her dusky face to show the years of work, pain, excitement, and worry for her captain, remains at her station, opening hailing frequencies, calling Starfleet, and softly voicing the fears of them all. And she is happy.

12.

SHORT TREKS

Many of the articles we run in Trek *are considerably shorter in length than those included in this, and preceding, collections. But the majority of these shorter articles are so well written and interesting that we couldn't bear to deprive our paperback readers of them any longer. So we've put some of the best together in this section—entitled, appropriately enough, "Short Treks"—and we think you will find that they are just as well thought out and as well written as our longer articles.*

WHO (OR WHAT) IS "THE DEVIL IN THE DARK?"

by Isabel Real

For years I have admired the Star Trek episode that brought the silicon-based life form called horta to audiences throughout our Earth. That it was an excellent episode few will dispute, despite several technical errors that distracted from the contents. It was produced when Star Trek was still the quality program that made "addicts" of otherwise sane and healthy individuals.

The issue often discussed among devoted "Trekkers" is the *true meaning* of the story line; or if you wish to be less mundane, the *message* conveyed by the excellent "Devil in the Dark."

Obviously, the story shows us an alien of rather monstrous appearance who attacks humans in the tunnels of the mining planet Janus VI. This alien is proved intelligent through the Vulcan mind meld after she has been severely injured by phaser fire. Several other minor events are played out to reinforce the final argument of an alien being protecting her soon-to-be-hatched eggs from the thoughtless destruction caused by the miners. The ugly but lovable horta is the last of her kind, the mother of her race; she is attacking to defend everything she values, thus following one of the strongest-known instincts or motivations in all life forms: *to provide species continuity*.

The humans and even the logical Vulcan follow another instinct prevalent in life forms: *self-preservation*. Economic pressures are also present, in the oft-cited "per diem" that must be met by the mining colony. The miners, most affected by the unwanted presence of the alien, quickly develop an unreasoning hatred toward the horta, while we are allowed a glimpse into the sense of duty and discipline that causes the crewmembers of the *Enterprise* to begin the hunt. When both groups confront the alien face to face they react violently. Mr. Spock, the horta's defender, urges her destruction to avoid a fatal attack upon the captain of the starship, his friend Jim Kirk. At that point, his motivation is fear.

Then, if both sides have such driving, urgent, valid, and consuming reasons dictating their actions, who (or what) is the "devil" alluded to in the title? On the surface, we could assume that to the humans the answer is the horta, while to her the humans are far worse than the supreme evil.

But we, the audience, can observe more than the actions of either confronting force. Can't we see that neither the horta nor the humans are devils? Why, of course, the application of either set of standards proves that both foes are in the right—at least from their respective viewpoints, truth is, after all, a matter of perspective. And yet, *there is a hidden devil lurking in the dark*. In the dark, yes, but not in the dark of the tunnels of Janus VI.

It was the darkness of incomprehension and the devil of misunderstanding that I saw exemplified by my favorite Star Trek episode. It was impossible for the horta to communicate with the miners. She couldn't understand their reason for willfully causing such wanton havoc. It was just as impossible for the miners to realize the importance of "worthless" silicon nodules, to understand the horta's motives when she attacked and killed the humans. The events followed well-known patterns, the like of which we see often as a prelude to our Earthly conflicts and wars.

The message, then, is not so "hidden." It is the extremely basic premise: Understand others rather than fear and hate them. Strive to evaluate the reasons behind the actions of other beings whether horta or human. Communicate and the darkness will be dispelled. Comprehend and the devils shall cease to haunt mankind!

A THEORY OF RELATIVITY

by Paul Schwartz

Recently a large amount of information has come to light about the man Dr. John A. Watson called "the best and wisest man I have ever known." The reason for the occurrence of these revelations at this time is obvious. The facts, no matter how damaging, can do little harm now because all of the principals have passed away. Thus, we have speculation about the real identity of Jack the Ripper, for example, where no such speculation existed before. Because of all these revelations and speculations, I feel that it is time for me to put forth a theory of my own.

It is my considered opinion that Sherlock Holmes was not born on the planet Earth. He is, in fact, an alien from outer space. To take this one step further, I believe him to be a native of the planet Vulcan, and it is conceivable to me that he is either a relative or an ancestor of the science officer of the *U.S.S. Enterprise*, Mr. Spock.

Item: Both names begin with the letter *S* and end with *ock*.

Item: Both men are tall and slim, with an appearance that people describe as "hawklike."

Item: Both men are physically stronger than normal men.

Item: Both men respect and revere logic and use logic to run their lives and solve problems.

Item: Neither man was close to his parents for most of his life.

Item: Both men are talented musicians, and both men use stringed instruments.

I fully expect a theory as radical as this one would have its doubters, and I believe I am fully prepared for them. Let us assume that I am being questioned by one of these theory doubters and I am answering. I believe the conversation might go thusly:

Q: Sherlock Holmes had two brothers. Do you mean three Vulcans, all of the same family, came to Earth?

A: It is possible. However, I think the explanation is simpler. There is nothing to deny that young Sherlock Holmes might have been adopted.

Q: Since when do Vulcans abuse the use of drugs? Holmes' drug addiction was well known.

A: Considering the primitive times, I don't think there were many other ways for a Vulcan to survive the pain and agony of the *pon farr* (the Vulcan ritual mating time). However, some investigation into Holmes' relationship with one Irene Adler might prove interesting.

Q: What of Holmes' eating meat and doing violence?

A: A Vulcan would certainly understand the old axiom about "when in Rome . . ." It is recorded about Holmes that he never killed unless there was absolutely no choice left, and when food is discussed in the Holmes writings, meat is very rarely mentioned.

I could continue this for quite some time, proving or disproving the theory that Sherlock Holmes was a Vulcan and a relative of Spock's, but I'm not going to. After all, why should I spoil your fun? There must be dozens of people out there who could do this better than I . . . let them come up with their own explanations to either prove or disprove the theory.

"GENE, BABY, HAVE I GOT A STORY FOR YOU!"

by William Trigg

Everyone knows that television producers get many times more story ideas than they can ever use in the course of a season, and often script ideas submitted by one writer will bear an uncanny resemblance to those submitted by another writer. This was especially true of Star Trek, and thanks to an unnamed source within the Star Trek offices, we have a selection of story ideas that weren't *quite* what Gene Roddenberry had in mind. . . .

"The Squire of Levittown"—Investigating the appearance of a hitherto-unknown planet, the crew beams down to find a strange being who lives and dresses in the style of the late 1960s. Forcing the crew to remain in his split-level, ranch-style house, he nearly bores them to death with home movies, stories about "the guys at the office," and a point-by-point retelling of the 1967 Superbowl. Logic saves the day when Spock, posing as an insurance agent, convinces the alien that his homeowner's policy will be canceled if he does not let them go.

"Turnaround Intruder"—Dr. Janice Abzug, a renegade female scientist, exchanges bodies with Captain Kirk and assumes control of the *Enterprise*. After being ordered to rearrange the bridge furnishings half a dozen times, the crew mutinies, and the personality exchange is discovered. Complications arise, however, as Kirk (in Janice's body) has been seen skipping about the corridors singing "I Enjoy Being a Girl." Logic once again saves the day as Spock points out to Abzug that starship captains can have only one change of clothing, and informs Kirk that, as a woman, he would no longer be allowed to strip to the waist at least once per episode, thereby violating his contract. Both speedily agree to return to their own bodies, and all is well.

"Mudd's Chickies"—Intergalactic conman Harry Mudd beams aboard with three beautiful women who drive the crewmen up the walls. In reality, however, they are quite ugly, having used the illegal "Vesuvius drug" to transform themselves. Upon learning this, Kirk sentences Mudd to swab the decks, and orders a daily dose of the drug to be given to all female crewmembers.

"The Lights of Zorro"—After a violent ion storm, Lieutenant Mira Romanoff is possessed by alien life forms, and is forced to don a mask and cape and dash about the ship righting wrongs. . . .

"Blink of an Eye"—The *Enterprise* is plagued by the strange disappearance of crewmen, accompanied by strange buzzing noises. Several theories for this are postulated, but the disappearances continue, and the buzzing grows ever more annoying. Kirk and Spock make a last-ditch effort to find the cause, and logic saves the day as Spock points out that the crewmen have been falling out of an open hatch, and the buzzing is caused by a faulty head in Kirk's new tape deck. Everyone has a good laugh as the ship heads out to Starbase Eleven for crew replacements.

"Space Seeds for Prizes"—Mania grips the *Enterprise* crew as Harry Mudd returns with his most diabolical scheme yet: coercing the crew into selling packages of seeds. Hard feelings develop as all endeavor to sell the seeds to each other in the vain hope of winning a set of walkie-talkies, a bicycle, or even a pony! Logic once again saves the day when Spock points out that they would have no place to plant the seeds in space; and everyone shamefacedly writes home to his parents for money to pay for the seeds, and all agree that a valuable lesson has been learned.

"The Immune Syndrome"—After taking on a passenger who is discovered to be a carrier of the dread *ookaballakonga* disease, Dr. McCoy feverishly works to come up with an antidote before the entire crew can be affected. He manages to find it in ten minutes, and after everyone has been rendered immune, the crew spends the following forty minutes swapping gossip over coffee.

"Spock's Pancreas"—A beautiful female alien appears on the bridge, and after having knocked everyone unconscious, she steals Spock's pancreas to power the life-support systems of her race's starship. Kirk and McCoy are understandably upset until Spock awakens and informs them that a Vulcan's pancreas controls only his acting ability, and his was totally unnecessary to his function aboard the ship. McCoy, as usual, has the last word: "It didn't work anyway."

"Store Leave"—Everyone beams down to a strange world covered with shelves of merchandise and smiling natives who cheerfully give them whatever they ask for. Danger rears its ugly head, however, as Kirk's next Master Charge statement shows a debit of 14 million credits. . . .

STAR TREK AS EDUCATION

by Jacqueline Sullivan Gorski

Star Trek's importance to the evolution of man lies in its educational function. Star Trek teaches many things, such as the importance of camera angles in creating dramatic television, creativity in costuming, and the rudiments of astronomy. But most important among what Star Trek teaches are human values—values that are life-enhancing such as cooperation, reverence for all life, the beauty and uniqueness of the individual, and the need to respect and utilize each person's perspective during the decision-making process.

We have all felt the tension on the bridge as the *Enterprise* is surrounded in the neutral zone by Romulans. "Shoot, captain," cries Scotty, fearful lest the *Enterprise* fail to act and his "poor bairns" be blasted to nothingness. "Shouldn't we try to contact them once more, captain?" queries Mr. Spock, eyebrow raised perturbedly at the aliens' hostility but nonetheless willing to grant one final chance before firing. "Those damn Romulans," McCoy mutters, "haven't they sense enough not to meddle in Federation affairs?"

Star Trek teaches through its art. It is drama in which the audience participates directly, psychologically.* Star Trek's morals or values are not, at least in its better episodes, forced upon the viewer. Instead, by identifying with or rejecting various characters' actions, words, and values, the viewer comes to enlightenment concerning his own.

A real-life example of this concerns a close friend. White, college-educated, and recently moved from the Northeast to the South, this friend became increasingly troubled by what he perceived as unequal and preferential treatment granted minorities in his new geographical location. Though by no means a Star Trek fan (as witnessed by his habitual falling asleep during the opening strains of "Where No Man Has

---

*David Gerrold, in *The World of Star Trek*, called Star Trek a "morality play." It certainly is, although it differs from the medieval plays in that its guiding values are more sophisticated, are secular as opposed to religious, and are not set in a visibly Christian framework.

Gone Before"), he one day watched with me the entire episode "May This Be Your Last Battlefield." Never before verbal on the themes of Star Trek, he suddenly began openly and enthusiastically discussing the "point" of the episode, that of the stupidity, ugliness, stagnation, and destruction caused by the hatred between the two races. This hatred, you will remember, was generated by the sole fact that while one race was white on the left side and black on the right, the other was black on the left and white on the right.

It was obvious through the friend's comments that he was actively relating this Star Trek episode to events in his own life. Psychological participation in the Star Trek drama had led to an intense physical reaction against the horror and sterility of prejudice. This, one assumes, will function toward helping him remain more open-minded and tolerant in the future.

Someone new or indifferent to the Star Trek world may ask, "What makes Star Trek special? Other television shows have taught us human values before. Think of *The Defenders*, which showed us man's continuous struggle for justice, or *Gunsmoke*, which proved that the good guys must always shoot down the bad."

Star Trek serves as a unique educative vehicle for man's spiritual evolution in at least three ways. First, it has a cosmic setting. The "we," the "good guys," in Star Trek include not only all Terran races, sexes, and nationalities, but also every species throughout the universe that believes in peace and the continued intellectual and artistic exploration of life. Second, Star Trek teaches that cooperation between beings is essential both for mutual survival and the accomplishment of sophisticated tasks, be they technologically or ethically complex. Just as each person on the bridge recognizes that his survival depends upon the interfunctioning of all crewmen, so, too, do the Organians, Klingons, Romulans, and Federation members know that continued existence demands mutual cooperation.

Finally, Star Trek teaches the value of *each* individual and the need for recognition of his life perspective in the total design and functioning of the group. During that perilous moment on the bridge, Captain Kirk listens to Scotty's cry for attack as well as Spock's plea for a last attempt at communication. He looks around the bridge mentally registering the various crewmembers' suggestions, whether verbal or merely etched on their tense faces. Like a giant computer, recording and processing each individual's view, Kirk arrives at a synthesis of all views and incorporates them into one life-sustaining action. "Lieutenant Uhura," he begins, tongue in cheek, "send this message to Starfleet Command: 'Unless this area clears of Romulans within fifteen minutes, Earth time, the *Enterprise* will self-destruct contaminating this sector for three years.' "

The value of each individual viewpoint has been preserved, yet transformed into the functioning of the whole. The *Enterprise* sails on its way and Star Trek, once again, has taught us something.

GET ME SECURITY

by Martin Rand

Let's take a look at some of the most maligned people in the Star Trek universe. No, not the Klingons, nor the Romulans—these are good guys, members of the *Enterprise* crew. They are the Security forces.

How many times, in how many episodes, have you seen a landing party beam down to a planet, and among their number were one or two red-shirted Security officers? And you know before the action even starts that if anybody is going to get it, it will be one of the guys in the red shirts. In episode after episode, Security men seemed to be nothing more than phaser fodder.

Joking aside, Security is probably the most high-risk assignment aboard the *Enterprise* or any other spacegoing vessel. But what sort of man or woman would volunteer for such dangerous work?

None of the televised episodes nor any of the "official" works of fiction has ever laid out exactly how many people serve in each department aboard a ship such as the *Enterprise*. (In many cases, we can assume that crewmembers "double up" on certain duties; after all, we've seen Helmsman Sulu working in the astrobiology department.) But we can also assume Security personnel have a full-time job, for there are relatively few of them on board.

A reasonable guess would be about fifty per starship. This number is not as large as it would first seem to be; fifty people is less than one-eighth of the *Enterprise* complement of 430-odd. Also, the *Enterprise* works by eight-hour shifts, so only about sixteen Security officers would be on duty at any given time. (All would, of course, be on twenty-four-hour call for Red Alerts or emergencies.) And a large number of those on duty would be assigned specific duty stations, requiring a reserve to be available for a call from Kirk or for special duties.

In "The Trouble with Tribbles," Kirk ordered Security personnel to accompany each group of Klingons on shore leave, and in "BEM," the *Enterprise* is called on to provide several Security teams at one time. In these cases, all (or almost all) of the Security forces would have to be mobilized or on call, so it is not hard to visualize a situation where members of other ship departments would have to be called in to double up as Security forces.

If we assume that the fifty-member Security complement is correct, that means that in the twelve heavy cruisers that make up the main line of Federation fleet forces, there would be a standing complement of only about 600 Security personnel. Starship duty is the crème de la crème, so it is easy to see that competition for these posts would be quite fierce. Who doesn't want to be the best of the best? Obviously, the Federation can pick and choose out of its entire armed forces for these 600 people, not to mention the several thousand more who are Security personnel on destroyers, scouts, etc, and are, they hope, working their way up to starship status. Those Security members serving aboard starships would be the Best Starfleet had to offer; and knowing Kirk, those aboard the *Enterprise* would be the best among those.

Obviously, extra training above and beyond standard Starfleet training would be required of Security officers. Strategy and tactics, armament and arms, and hand-to-hand combat would be requisite; as well as ship operations, a smattering of diplomacy, and a strong foundation in first aid and trauma therapy. This would just be the beginning, and by the time the training was finished, each aspirant to Security would have to be an expert in all of these . . . or wash out. So each would have to live and breathe his occupation, for only the most dedicated would be chosen to fill the posts. And it is this dedication which allows them to face the many and ever-present dangers that come with the job.

So in the Security complement serving aboard starships, we have what could be considered the top 600 fighting personnel in Starfleet. (They could be considered as the Federation's equivalent to Gordon R. Dickson's *Dorsai*.)

But the main objective of Security is protection. Their job is to prevent trouble, not to instigate it. They would be trained, and superbly trained, to fight, but the brunt of that training would be for defense, not attack.

So perhaps the Security men weren't just a convenient scriptwriter's device when someone needed to be killed off. It is only logical to assume that the majority of ship fatalities would be among Security personnel. After all, they are usually among the first to land on any planet, they are required to protect the rest of the crew, and they are the first to go in when there is any imagined or actual danger or fighting.

But this does not explain away the fact that in Star Trek, Security never seemed quite able to manage for itself. Captain Kirk always had to direct their efforts. Each of the other members of the crew were able to—and did—act on their own initiative to help Kirk or to protect the ship; and often the result was the same as if Kirk had been there personally directing their efforts. Security was never given this chance— at least, not onscreen where we could see the results. Perhaps part of the problem was that Kirk had no regular security chief to depend on; if this was the case, then the lack of such a chief was a great failing of either the show's premise, Starfleet, or Kirk.

There is a two-sided problem in the presentation of Security on the screen. On one hand, the Security people always seemed to be the ones getting killed; on the other hand, the forces were never used to their full potential. It seems that there should have been a happy medium in there somewhere. Perhaps in future episodes (especially now that the Security forces have been given much-needed functional armor) they will be given an independence of action that will make them a wonder to behold in action, and a credit and a comfort to Captain Kirk.

We can always hope, can't we?

COMMANDER SCOTT ON ENTERPRISE
UPRATED ENGINE DESIGN

by Joe Rudich

Stardate 7486.2, U.S.S. Enterprise

I am dictating this from my office aboard the *Enterprise*, Constitution II Class Starship. By now almost everyone has seen films of this craft, which has been vastly improved since the end of our original five-year mission. Of course, the greatest improvement, in my view, is the new warp drive system. After the *Enterprise* was put into drydock, its refitting began, and was hastily completed for a mission of supreme importance. That was a wee bit over one month ago, and afterward, we began complete testing of the new ship and its engines. Now those tests are finally over, and our hopes have been borne out.

The most notable structural difference between the older version of the ship and the new is the engine nacelles. By sight, anyone can see the difference; the Constitution I Class nacelles were cylindrical (as the warp drive housings on all our starships have been), whereas the Constitution II Class nacelles are flattened, higher than they are wide. It may seem inconsequential, but in fact it is the real secret to the *Enterprise*'s success. To illustrate this, consider two of our early warp drive starships, the United Nations Starship *Messier* and the USS *Horizon*.

The *Messier* was a first-generation warp-drive starship, and had a maximum acceleration of Warp 2.9. The *Horizon* was a second-generation warp-drive starship with a maximum acceleration of Warp 3.25. Both used cylindrical drive nacelles, remember. The total speed increase, from *Messier* to *Horizon*, from first-generation warp drive to second-generation warp drive was only 12 percent.

With cylindrical nacelles, the old *Enterprise*'s greatest speed was Warp 8. While its drive is only a slight improvement over the old ship's fourth-generation warp drive (known as advanced fourth generation), the newer *Enterprise*, with contour nacelles, can go as fast as Warp 12—a 50 percent improvement.

Ironically, the Federation gained this advance through Klingon Empire technology. When the Klingon warship *Korezima* was disabled and abandoned (its self-destruct failed to operate), the USS *Moscow* recovered it for Federation study. (It was this capture which speeded Klingon development of the *K't'inga* class warship.) Engineers had long suspected the Klingons held some secret which enabled their ships to slightly outperform our ships of equal energy output.

The secret found in the *Korezima* was the contour nacelle. Long ago, it was learned that two cylindrical nacelles produced the proper harmonies for warp drive. However, looking at a forward view of the *Enterprise* shows that the starship is bilaterally symmetrical, meaning that it can be cut in half only one way if the plane, or for that matter the mass, is to be equal on both halves. The ship cannot be cut through the center of the interconnecting dorsal between primary and secondary hulls without upsetting the symmetry. Theoretically, a spherical starship would be perfect for cylindrical nacelles. However, past experience has demonstrated the value of the dual hulls.

The Klingon Empire must have known this from the outset of their warp-drive excursions. Also, they too must have found usefulness in dual hulls. Their solution was to match nacelles exactly to the ship; thus, since a ship is bilaterally symmetrical, the nacelle should be also, in a pattern which would offset a vessel's symmetry pattern.

In a starship with less-controllable drive reaction, bilaterally symmetrical nacelles could be highly dangerous. No doubt Klingons have a long history of spacecraft mishaps. For the *Enterprise*, though, it is an ideal system . . . especially with the new intermix formula.

Whatever your convictions, you've got to admit those Klingons have some engineers . . . so they can't be all bad.

—*Commander Montgomery Scott*

WHATEVER HAPPENED TO FINNEGAN?

by Linda Lee

The last time we saw the obnoxious Finnegan, he was out cold from a well-deserved right cross from Jim Kirk. But that Finnegan, as we learned later, was only an android duplicate constructed from Kirk's memories (what a disappointment that must have been for the captain!). At no time are we given any information about what happened to the real Finnegan. If Kirk had any personal knowledge of Finnegan's whereabouts, he would certainly have said something when the android first appeared. ·

So we can assume that somewhere along the way Kirk lost track of Finnegan—not that he would especially want to stay in touch with his old nemesis, but you never know about Kirk . . . someday he just might feel like looking up Finnegan and *really* whaling the tar out of him.

It could be, however, that Finnegan is either dead or out of the service entirely. We really don't like to think that he is dead, for although he is boorish and loudmouthed, he's still pretty darn *likable*! And if he was willing to put up with the many years required at the Starfleet Academy, it is unlikely that he would leave the service. (Unless, of course, he pulled one of his tricks on the wrong person . . . say, for instance, an admiral.) It is much more likely that Finnegan settled into his routine in Starfleet, making the usual advances of an average officer, and is currently assigned to some out-of-the-way post where he neither can nor wants to do anything spectacular enough to catch the notice of Jim Kirk half a galaxy away.

Or would he? The Finnegan we saw in "Shore Leave" (as much as his android duplicate may have been colored by Kirk's painful memories) was hardly shy, and it is hard to think of him willingly taking second place. He is loud, boisterous, and energetic—and if he is also intelligent and courageous, then he has the makings of a starship captain. But does he have the necessary compassion?

Events as related by Kirk would say no. But we must remember that the young Jim Kirk at Starfleet Academy was a very determined, even grim, student, and any sort of horseplay or hijinks would not have been his style—at least not while actually within the Academy walls. Most likely he blew off his steam while on leave.

Such a person would be an easy target for a fun-loving upperclassman, and we can be sure that Finnegan zeroed in on Kirk from Day One. It has long been a custom of military academies (and apparently will remain one) to allow upperclassmen to "haze" freshmen, and Finnegan was only indulging in that time-honored sport. It is entirely possible that his attentions to Kirk were hardly the persecution that Kirk imagined (or remembers) it to be. And however much it was, it would have eventually helped to strengthen Kirk in several ways—obeying orders, controlling his temper, doing a job despite distractions. Which, of course, is the purpose of hazing, and the reason why it is not only allowed but encouraged at military academies.

So, however gleefully and overzealously, Finnegan was only doing his job when he hazed Kirk. Therefore, we really can't take his actions into account when we think about what may have happened to him in the ensuing years, for even if he was boorish, he very well could have outgrown it. You must remember that he was only about twenty-one or twenty-two at the time he and Kirk served at the Academy together.

So where is Finnegan today? Well, I would suspect that he is serving as a second officer or a security chief on one of the starships. Such duties would seem to fit his personality, and if he was a captain, Kirk would certainly know of it, for even in a large fleet, the "club" of captains is somewhat limited.

We know Finnegan was at least a competent student, for he was allowed to teach and order about underclassmen at the Academy, and such duties are assigned by instructors to students who show signs of leadership ability. You will remember that Kirk held a teaching position at the Academy for a short while—and one wonders just how rough he was on *his* students.

So we can assume that good old Finnegan is still out there in space somewhere, doing his job and having a good time at it. And if he is, then he is a fine Starfleet officer and a credit to his ship and the Academy. Perhaps one day we will be privileged to witness the scene when he and Kirk finally run across each other—and sit down, have a few drinks, and talk over the "good old days."

GAFLOOEY

by Mary Jo Lawrence

I didn't feel the least bit foolish sailing down the highway with a bowl of potato salad perched precariously on the seat next to me. It never occurred to me that normal people don't drive around in a battered old station wagon with a huge bowl of potato salad for company. Then again, I have claimed to be many things in my life, but "normal" isn't one of them. Actually, if the truth be known, I was so high that I probably even talked to the humble bowl of potatoes and mayonnaise as we drove along. The salad, being a quiet sort, just listened to me in amiable silence.

At this point, you might justifiably ask, "What has this woman been smoking (or drinking, or sniffing)?" The answer is, "Nothing!" You see, I get high on Star Trek!

Star Trek addicts are no different from any other junkies. They need their regular "fix" just like all the rest. For some, this entails privately reading at least a dozen pages of Star Trek fiction (affectionally called "treklit") before they retire for the night. Others require a more formalized prescription. They have joined one of the hundreds of Star Trek fan clubs that exist throughout the world. Still others come together in great and small numbers to attend the many Star Trek conventions. Some Star Trek addicts are up to one con a month!

But no matter how severe your addiction—whether you are FIAWOL (*F*andom *I*s *A W*ay *O*f *L*ife) or FIJAGDH (*F*andom *I*s *J*ust *A G*od *D*amned *H*obby)—Star Trek is a powerfully seductive narcotic.

Within our local ST mafia we have people at many stages of addiction, but once in a while we all get a case of the trekkie-jeebies and nothing will quiet them but an injection of pure, unadulterated Star Trek! This has led to a series of bimonthly (or whenever-we-feel-like-it) Star Trek parties. We call them "zine reads."

Since we are simply a bunch of friends who are mutually

interested in Star Trek and are not involved in any type of organized fan club, zine reads are very informal get-togethers to which everyone brings his or her newest zines or projects (perhaps a story manuscript or a piece of art, slides, photos, videotapes) to share with the group. A bag of food and a sleeping bag are optional accessories. Zine reads can last anywhere from six to forty-eight hours, and they never seem long enough.

So it was that my potato salad and I headed down Highway 19 for an all-night trekathon zine read. There hadn't been a get-together for about two months, and I was really ready for an intense session of trek-talk and general gossip and camaraderie. The sun was peeking through a silver-lined hole in the otherwise gray sky—the weatherman had predicted rain, but this was a good omen! God is on the side of Trekkers!

This feeling of euphoria was only slightly diminished a moment later when, as I stopped for a red light about two miles from my home, my rear bumper was rudely jarred by a hot-rodding teenager. My car wasn't damaged, but the teenager's front end was sort of crumpled. He didn't want to file an accident report and I was in a hurry to be going, so I agreed, silently offering my thanks that the holdup had been minimal. I was especially anxious to see a friend who was coming in from out of town.

Star Trek addiction has the singular effect of getting me to look at things through rose-colored glasses—like a terminal case of Pollyannaitis. For example, the auto accident was good luck because it didn't hold me up too long.

Arriving at the site of the zine read (cleverly disguised as a normal suburban ranch-style home), I tucked the potato salad under one arm and my latest manuscript under the other, clenched the drawstring of my sleeping bag between my teeth, and dove into the middle of a back-thumping, greeting-shouting, merry-making gang of fellow Trekkers. The zine read was well underway.

After depositing my faithful companion in the refrigerator for a well-deserved rest, and finding a comfortable corner for my sleeping bag, I glanced around for my out-of-town friend. After a moment of searching in vain and a couple of concerned questions, I found out that she had arrived about an hour before me, only to receive an emergency phone call and have to turn around immediately and drive two and a half hours home.

My initial disappointment was only momentary, for I figured it was really better this way as I could now spend more time getting to know the several new faces I'd spotted about the place. Trekstasy strikes again!

I grabbed a soft drink and was about to introduce myself to one of the new faces when there was a hair-curling shriek from somewhere in the rear of the house. Fifteen people ran in the general direction of the scream and found our hostess standing ankle-deep in water in her laundry room, her hands wrapped hopelessly around a broken water main which was sprewing gallons of water through her tightly clenched fingers. It took a good ten minutes of frantic scurrying before fifteen women decided that they couldn't find the shut-off valve. The hostess, by this time soaked and miserable, muttered something about a neighbor's husband knowing where it would be. Someone ran off to find him. It took about five minutes for him to shut the water off—four and a half minutes of hysterical laughter and thirty seconds to twist the valve (which was located somewhere in the backyard!).

Everyone worked at sopping up water while the hostess changed clothes and contemplated her husband's reaction when he returned from his fishing trip. The neighbor somehow fixed the leak so we could use the necessary plumbing facilities, and the zine read was back on the trek. There was a murmur of uneasiness, though, when the hostess' sister-in-law remarked that her water heater had sprung a leak at home just as she was about to leave to come to the party. First there was my auto accident, then the emergency phone call, then the water main, and now this piece of news . . . another catastrophe to come? Surely nothing else would go wrong. And nothing else did . . .

. . . for a couple of hours. The zine read progressed normally as Star Trek wove its spell and we all succumbed to the lure of escapism and clambered aboard the Starship *Enterprise* for a magical mystery tour. We had a dramatic reading from someone's manuscript, some photos were flashed around, and there was even some high-level zine trading and slide selling going on.

Soon it was dinnertime and we began to prepare for a barbecue supper. The hostess went out in the back yard to prepare the grill. Two and a half minutes later she was back in the house gasping for breath, slamming the door behind her. It seems a colony of wasps had decided that her old grill was the perfect place to build their nest, and they were highly incensed when she dared disturb them by lifting the grill cover. Trekkers that we are, we believe in the principles of IDIC, but we were hungry! The wasps could live, but not in the grill! A task force of hardy volunteers set out to roust the wasps from their home. Since I suffer from congenital cowardice, I wasn't one of them and didn't watch the mission from the window, so I don't know how it was accomplished. But soon the grill was ready to be fired up.

The hostess, after being assured that *all* the wasps were gone, ventured forth once more to start the fire. A half hour later she went out to put on the hot dogs, only to find that the fire had never started properly and the grill was colder than Sarpeidon. Everyone was ravenous by this time, so there was a group effort to get the fire going. Another thirty minutes passed with no luck. My poor potato salad was wilting fast out on the picnic table under the majestic spreading willow tree. Besides, I was ready to eat the hot dogs *cold*! I shooed everyone away from the grill and got the fire started on my own. Just to make sure, I watched it until it was ready.

Once the word got out that the fire was hot, someone volunteered to cook the hot dogs, declaring herself to be a "tube steak gourmet." We all sat around under the willow tree, trying to be patient, waiting for the epicurean delight of these much-touted wursts. The rest of the pot luck was already spread out, making our collective mouths water.

It wasn't really that long before the chef came hesitantly toward us bearing a covered tray. As she set it down and pulled off the cover we sat agape, staring at forty skinny, wrinkled, black sticks. "What's that?" we all chorused. "I wasn't used to the grill," she apologized.

Dinner was delicious anyway. Everyone had brought a dish to pass, and each one was wonderful and more scrumptious than the last. The pièce de résistance was when I carefully unfolded two delicate, pointed green ears on the sides of my bowl of potato salad. Everyone howled!

We had just heaped on the goodies and were trying to balance plates, hot dogs, and bottles of cola on our laps when the rain that had been threatening all day suddenly arrived! There was a mad dash for the house, with everyone trying to salvage something of dinner and at the same time bring in all the assorted picnic paraphernalia. We scrambled for the door clutching soggy, charred hot dogs and giggling insanely at the run of luck. True to form, the psychology of a trekoholic is to laugh in the face of adversity. As long as we were all together, the good times far outweighed the bad.

We did manage to salvage our supper, and everything was delicious. The rest of the evening was nervously uneventful. We kept waiting for the other shoe to drop. Something else was bound to happen. But it didn't.

The next day dawned clear and sunny. It was like a vindication of the previous night's disastrophe. We took full advantage of the weather and had our breakfast al fresco out under the willow. Somehow orange juice and coffee cake never tasted so good! But then, I always eat well after I've tied one on.

THE STAR TREK FAMILY TREE

by Jaclyn J. Murphy

In his article "A Theory of Relativity," Paul Schwartz makes the point that the immortal Sherlock Holmes is in actuality a native of the planet Vulcan. In this, I am afraid, he is mistaken, for Holmes' background and antecedents are too well documented for such a theory to be applicable. However, he *was* on the right track, especially in the title for his article. Sherlock and Spock *are* related: Spock is Holmes' great-great-etc. *grandson.*

In his "biographies" of Tarzan and Doc Savage, the famous science fiction writer Philip José Farmer postulates the existence of the Wold-Newton family, the descendants of two groups of people who were exposed to radiation from a meteorite several hundred years ago. These descendants are all mutants to one extent or another, and as the effects of their mutations proved to be mutually beneficial, they intermarried to an amazing degree, producing a large number of astounding offspring.

Among the Wold-Newton family members have been

Tarzan, Sherlock, and Mycroft Holmes, Fu Manchu, Doc Savage, the Shadow, James Bond, and many, many others who have gained fame through their exploits or intelligence. Among the major traits found in this family are great strength, great intelligence, and (above all) great strength of will and the ability to *use logic.*

Members of this family exist today, still utilizing these powers (Lew Archer, Nero Wolfe, Travis McGee, Modesty Blaise), so it is quite logical to assume the Wold-Newton family will continue to flourish and prosper over the next three centuries, to the time of Star Trek.

And it is just as easy to assume that Spock's mother, Amanda Grayson, is a linear descendant of that family, through one branch or another. She is strong, has great powers of will and intelligence, and showed a remarkable facility to grasp and utilize Vulcan methods of logic. And with the superior genetic structure of the Vulcan Sarek added to the unique Wold-Newton mutation, it is little wonder that their offspring, Mr. Spock, is such a remarkable being. He truly has the best of both worlds!

But Mr. Spock is not the only member of the Wold-Newton family to be currently serving aboard the *Enterprise!* Mr. Farmer tells us that one of the most recurring and distinctive features of such mutants is their piercing gray, green, or *hazel* (a combination of the two) eyes. And who on the *Enterprise* has hazel eyes? Why, Captain James T. Kirk, of course.

Even if the distinctive eye color were not a clue (many people who are not members of the Wold-Newton family have gray, green, or hazel eyes), we could easily assume that Kirk belonged to the family by the character traits he has displayed. He is immensely courageous, tenacious (another strong Wold-Newton trait), cunning, strong for a human of his size, adaptable, and, when he has to be or wants to be, coldly and professionally logical. Kirk also has the lust for life commonly associated with the family, and in many instances shows the somewhat quirky sense of humor that has marked the family across the centuries.

It seems as if the Kirk family was also infiltrated by the Wold-Newton influence at some time in the past as well. Therefore, it is not so strange that he and Spock should seem to be related at times: They *are!*

And if we look hard enough, perhaps we can find some other members of the Wold-Newton family in Star Trek: Zefrem Cochrane, with his super-scientific knowledge, seems to be a good candidate; as does Garth of Izar (several notable members of the family were quite insane too!). And what of Uhura—she who can speak many languages, has great technical skills and courage, and is strangely light-skinned for a native African?

These are only a few examples of the influence of the Wold-Newton mutation spreading through the human race, strengthening and improving it, and most assuredly, by the time of Star Trek, there are hundreds, perhaps thousands, of others. We do not know who they were, but we know what they did. They were the first to reach into deep space and open the galaxy, they were among the first colonists on new and unexplored worlds, they were the first to dare go where no man had gone before!

But, as they say, blood will *always* tell!

EMOTION VS. LOGIC—NO CONTEST

by E. R. Gow

In *Star Trek: The Motion Picture*, it was implied that as a result of his mind meld with V'Ger, Spock finally came to accept and appreciate his emotions as a vital part of his psychological makeup. He was no longer concerned with the achievement of *Kolinahr*, the Vulcan training which is intended to eliminate all emotion. However, in spite of Spock's big breakthrough, there was something about it which seemed somehow incomplete. The problem is this: In both the television episodes and the movie, logic and emotion are treated as two entirely unrelated thought processes. Even when Spock realized that he needed both logic and emotion, he still did not establish the real connection between the two.

We know that Spock is no stranger to emotion. His behavior often revealed his feelings of love, loyalty, compassion, etc, and although he resisted any outward display, we know that he did, in fact, understand the emotions of the humans around him, even though they were sometimes illogical.

What he never did seem to comprehend, however, was the

phenomenon of intuition—the long shots that Kirk often played, the hunches that turned out to be correct, even though there were insufficient data available to arrive at those conclusions logically. Yet, intuition works! After the fact, one can usually work backward to trace the casual connection leading up to the end result—a *logical* chain of events, once all the pieces are in place. But how is it that a human can often reach an accurate conclusion from seemingly insufficient data, while a Vulcan, with all his impressive mental capabilities, cannot? Even Kirk doesn't understand it—he just knows it works.

I suspect that Vulcans once had the faculty of intuition, but lost the use of it when they adopted their repressive mental disciplines. It has been stated in the television series that Vulcans are by nature a highly emotional race, and that logic had been held in high esteem by them for only a relatively short time. The violent passions to which Vulcans are naturally prone are brought under control by rigorous training, beginning in early childhood. In their attempt to prevent a recurrence of their violent past, Vulcans teach their children to repress not only their destructive emotions, but all of their emotions. Once they have accepted the premise that all emotions are undesirable, it becomes logically obvious that the most desirable state is *Kolinahr*, where all thought is impersonal, sterile; no concern, no caring, no needing. However, this basic premise (that all emotions are undesirable) is false, and the explanation which follows is one which even a Vulcan can understand.

I submit that the Vulcan desire to eliminate emotion through the discipline of *Kolinahr* is illogical, since it is emotion which makes possible the most efficient form of logic— that which we call *intuition*.

When there exists an emotional involvement, a *need* for an answer, not merely intellectual curiosity, the mind often ceases to function in the usual mode of conscious logic. Unfettered by the conscious mind's relatively slow, deliberate process of deduction, the subconscious mind is capable of producing an answer in moments.

Consider a starship traveling on impulse power, then jumping to warp speed, then returning to impulse power again. To an observer, the starship seems to disappear at the point at which it enters hyperspace, then reappearing out of nowhere at a distant point. Based on its speed before and after the journey through hyperspace, it would seem that the ship could not have traversed the intervening miles in the relatively short elapsed time. Yet we know that the ship has indeed passed through every inch of that distance, but its passage was too swift for the eye to perceive it.

The logical process can operate in much the same way. When the mind shifts into "hyperthought," the speed of logic increases so dramatically that when the conclusion is reached, it seems to have appeared out of nowhere, and we call it *intuition*. Since the conscious mind cannot perceive the journey through "hyperthought," we assume that it is impossible for the necessary deductive process to have occurred in the short elapsed time. Although it appears that the mind has "jumped" to the conclusion, the subconscious mind has indeed passed through every step of the deductive process before producing its answer.

The subconscious mind not only operates at a faster rate than the conscious mind, it also draws on information of which the conscious mind is unaware. There are innumerable bits of information which we receive subliminally, information which may never reach the conscious level. It has been demonstrated that a person under hypnosis is capable of recounting events or repeating information which could not be remembered in the state of normal waking consciousness.

It is quite possible that our subliminal perceptions also include sounds outside the normal auditory range, light waves beyond the visible spectrum, and other electromagnetic impulses too subtle to be consciously perceived. The analysis of such information by the subconscious mind can produce a conclusion which seems to have no basis in logic—the *intuitive* feeling, or *hunch*, which most frequently occurs when there exists a *need* for an answer.

The coolly disinterested method of logical deduction so highly regarded by the Vulcan race can actually be counterproductive. The mental discipline which enables them to control their thought processes also limits them to the use of the conscious mind. They can only analyze information of which they are consciously aware, and although their memory and the speed of their deductive process may be greater than that of humans operating at a conscious level, it still does not approach the efficiency of intuition. Only by releasing control of their thoughts, if only for a moment, can they utilize the extraordinary capabilities of the subconscious mind.

A Vulcan who achieves *Kolinahr* feels no emotion, and therefore no *need*. He has eliminated the means of achieving what he desires most. In a world of starships, he has gone to great lengths in an attempt to perfect the internal combustion engine. The Vulcan race would make a giant leap forward if, in addition to their other mental abilities, they could master the use of intuition. It would be a natural step for them to take, since they already hold logic in such high regard. And intuition is simply logic traveling at warp speed—powered by emotion.

13.

THE VILLAINS OF STAR TREK

by Leslie Thompson

*Readers who have been wondering why Leslie hasn't ap-
peared in the pages of* Trek *as often lately will be advised
that she has been devoting most of her time to completing
her college studies. But now Les has graduated (with honors,
of course!) and makes a return to* Trek *at a running start
with this article. And don't be fooled by the title . . . it's* not
what you think. . . .

When Star Trek made its debut on national television in
1966, it took a programming tack which was quite different
from that of most series airing at that time: Star Trek explored and developed adult themes, examining Man's relation
to his own technology, his inner self, and to the alien beings
he would encounter as he explored the far reaches of space.
Couched as they were in terms of science fiction, Star Trek's
stories often escaped the cutting knives of network censors,
but just as often, the points they attempted to make escaped
critical reaction and approval.

Like any other continuing series, Star Trek had its share of
villains. There were Bad Guys; the kind you hate, the kind
you love, and, of course, the kind you love to hate. And
many of these were aliens, allowing the series to examine human interrelations in the guise of alien encounter.

Not all of these "villains" were evil in the traditional sense.
Most were acting correctly or patriotically or rightly by their
own lights, and they saw the *Enterprise* crew as the villains.
It is to Star Trek's credit that we were so often allowed to see
both sides of an issue, even if the "other" side's viewpoint
was given only briefly through the discussions of the *Enterprise* crew members.

Star Trek also broke new ground by combining many of
the "villains" used by other types of programming: rare diseases, berserk technology, injustice and/or discrimination,

172

mental illness, etc. Such themes were quite common on doctor shows or lawyer shows and such, but Star Trek managed the leap that made such evils serve as the "monster of the week." And easily so, for do not all of us see cancer or anti-Semitism to be at least as horrifying as the Salt Monster?

The Salt Monster was the first villain to confront the *Enterprise* crew, and from the very beginning, Star Trek made a statement about what sort of television show it intended to be.

(Of course, "The Man Trap" was not the first episode to be filmed, but it was chosen to be the first episode aired. The viewing public only knows what it sees on the screen, and this program—little matter that it was chosen by network executives for action, monsters, and violence—beautifully stated Star Trek's aims.)

The Salt Monster was not really a monster at all . . . except in the eye of the beholder. And even that did not always count, for the creature could appear to be anyone or anything. It was only when the true form of the Salt Monster was finally revealed that the audience perceived it as "monstrous"; until that time it had only been an enigma. But the rub was this: The true villain of the program was not the monster, nor Professor Robert Crater, who allowed humans to die to protect it—the villain was the circumstances which forced McCoy to kill the last of a race.

Think of it. The very first villain, the very first monster to be presented on the spanking new space show, was a *very* endangered species! And, more important, *no one was wrong!* Not the Salt Monster, not Crater, not Kirk, not McCoy . . . no one. Each was acting according to his own beliefs about what best served the creature or the ship or science; there was no intentional evil.

It was quite an unusual and stunning concept for the time. Here was a television program which presented stalwart heroes, rampaging monsters, sneaky and somewhat underhanded "mad scientists," and a number of horrifying deaths —and yet, no one was to blame. And, in the end, everyone lost. There were no winners.

It was a theme which Star Trek was to develop over the following seasons: There can be small triumphs, battles won or lost, decisions made, living or dying—but in the long run, there are no winners.

It was quite a change from the run-of-the-mill television programming of the time, quite different from the Us vs. Them, Good vs. Evil problems and simplistic solutions presented on most other shows. (And, except for the excellent anthology program *The Outer Limits*, the first time such themes had been presented on a science fiction/fantasy show.) As if to prove to those in the viewing audience that such values were no fluke, the theme was reiterated in the next episode, "Charlie X."

Charlie Evans used the great mental powers given him by the Thasians in a manner which was quite natural to him. Raised in a totally hostile environment, he protected and supplied himself as easily and as unthinkingly as we would breathe.

Charlie was not evil, of course, merely immature and undisciplined. Based on his own experience, he was acting correctly when he used his powers for his own gratification. And it was not until the boy became obsessed with the control he had over others and insisted that Kirk take him to an inhabited planet so he could widen that control (and the growing pleasure that it brought him) that Kirk was forced to consider him a villain and act against him. Kirk sympathized with the boy's awkwardness and anguish, but acted to protect his own interests and those of his ship and crew. It was not pleasant for Kirk, by any means. It was a battle he did not want to fight; but had to fight, and had to win.

Even more so than in "The Man Trap," the true villain in this episode is a "force" acting upon each person concerned. Charlie was driven by his growing lust for power and his overriding need for approval from others. Kirk and the others only sought to protect themselves, and, to a lesser extent, to protect Charlie. Again, in the end, everyone failed, and there were no winners.

In "Where No Man Has Gone Before," we see a similar situation. When the latent psychic powers of Gary Mitchell are unbelievably enhanced by the force field at the edge of the galaxy, he also becomes obsessed with power and his ability to control others. And it is not until the last avenue of possible treatment or avoidance of the problem has been tried that Kirk is forced to consider Mitchell as a true villain.

There are, however, several major differences in the two stories. Mitchell has a past history of using people and is a somewhat self-centered and vain man, while Charlie Evans is merely immature and unused to operating in a social situation. Mitchell styles himself as a "god," which Charlie did not do; and Mitchell also seems to be drawn to evil actions and ultimate aims, whereas Charlie was only "showing them all." In the balance, we can see that Mitchell was much more of a classical "villain." He did what he did because he *liked* doing it—Charlie was only acting as he always had. It is the old question of free will: Gary Mitchell chose to be evil; Charlie Evans really had no choice.

In both instances, however, the old adage that "power corrupts" was borne out, and it is a theme to which the show returns in many other episodes.

In "The Naked Time," we see the first example of a disease being the villain—and ultimately responsible for the villainy of some crew members, as the loss of inhibitions and uncontrolled emotions brought about as an effect of the virus almost cause the destruction of the *Enterprise*.

It is interesting to note that this is the first episode of Star Trek which ends on a happy, triumphant, and successful note. The disease is *evil* and the ability of the crew to overcome its effects is *good*; when they do, they win.

And the moral of the story? No moral; just a variation on the Star Trek theme: No *being* was hurt in the victory, so the victory was total. But this episode was the first to present the Star Trek Rule: *Stay in Control!* It is a rule we see embodied in Spock's Vulcanism, in the Prime Directive, in IDIC—an individual, especially one encountering new beings and new technologies, must keep himself in control, or he loses his essential veneer of civilization and becomes less human.

The Rule is to play an ever-increasing role in future episodes, although the instances of loss of control will be much more subtle and individualistic. As we saw in "Where No Man" and "Charlie X," Mitchell and Charlie could not control the powers bestowed upon them; in "Man Trap," none of the participants had control over events, although all had a modicum of control over themselves; and in "Naked Time," the loss of control was total.

The Rule popped up again in the very next episode, "The Enemy Within." Kirk, split into a "good" half and a "bad" half, becomes an enemy to his ship. The good half is too indecisive and overly compassionate to be an effective leader;

the bad half is too emotional and inner-directed to be trust-worthy. Both are villains; both are a threat to the *Enterprise*. There is a loss of very necessary control by both halves.

We see that with the first five episodes, Star Trek began hitting its psychological stride, and that all but one of the major themes (see below) had been introduced. Each of the episodes concerned themselves in some way with the failure of people to control their egos and emotions; and in four of the episodes, there was no clear-cut victory and no winner. It was already becoming apparent that the focus of the series would not be on space, or aliens, or the future, but on *man*: his relations with others, his successes and failures, his inner self. It is not your typical sci-fi show by any means!

In "Mudd's Women" we see the first true villain to appear in Star Trek, although Harry Mudd is that ever-popular variation of the "roguish and lovable" villain. But Mudd is also the first human corruptive force to appear on the series, and one of the very few that will appear during the course of the series (unlike many other programs, where almost all of the evil or misery is caused by one or two villainous types).

Although the conclusion of the story does give us a victory of sorts, and offer us a few winners, the twist is that during the course of the story everyone involved is used in some way by Harry Mudd: Eve, who only wants love; Magda and Ruth, who want to remain beautiful and snare rich husbands; the miners, who are lonely; and Kirk and crew, who only want to repair their ship and stay alive. The Venus drug, un-like the virus in "Naked Time," is not evil in itself, nor are its effects.

The upshot is that everyone concerned needed to exercise a little more control over their actions, desires, and responses. But, as we saw in "Where No Man," "Charlie X," and the conniving of Harry Mudd, there is a danger in being con-trolled by others as well.

There is a hint of this in "What Are Little Girls Made Of?" when Kirk fears that Dr. Roger Korby, in his android body, plans to assume control of all humans once he has suc-cessfully transferred them to similar android bodies. Korby, although acting in a very villainous fashion, is not truly evil; he has instead lost an essential part of his humanity.

In "Miri," the villains are again disease and immaturity. And both are conquered by the participants' gaining self-control, i.e., maturity and humanity. Again, when the *disease* is conquered, we have a happy ending and everyone wins.

"Dagger of the Mind" again presents the threat of outside control of one person by another. And in Dr. Tristan Adams, Star Trek finally gets around to presenting its first truly evil villain. And, lo and behold, Adams *is* in control of himself— he merely uses that control for his own ends. Thus we see that in Star Trek, one is not considered a true villain unless he *chooses* to do evil . . . circumstance is not enough. And it is also interesting to note that it was not until the basic themes of Star Trek had been presented and explored that such a villain was featured.

The next episode, "The Corbomite Maneuver," was the first to present an alien villain—although we were soon to discover that he really wasn't a villain at all, but a friendly (if overly suspicious) representative of a great federation. But it is only through the innate goodness and humanity of the *Enterprise* crew that the encounter comes to a happy conclusion. Had the crew lost their heads, their self-control, they could have been destroyed (or, at the very least, lost the opportunity to meet with a superior and "more human" race). And here, for the first time, we see a happy ending to an episode which did not feature an outside force or disease as the cause of the problem. And why? Because this is also the first episode in which *everyone* stayed in control, thereby reiterating the Rule.

"The Menagerie" makes a very strong statement for free will and individualism, the strongest that Star Trek had yet made. The Talosians, in their desperate search for beings to repopulate their dying planet, use mind control and illusion to test assorted races.

Their search, however, is doomed to failure, since any race with enough will and adaptability to succeed will also rebel at slavery, no matter how pleasant and beneficial it may be. This episode is the strongest protest yet against outside control of people, and yet another instance where villainous actions are caused by good intentions.

The road to hell was well paved in the next episode, "The Conscience of the King." Kodos/Karidian massacred thousands in an attempt to save thousands more; his daughter Lenore killed to protect him; Kevin Riley almost committed murder to avenge the dead. Again, each acted in a manner which he or she thought best, and although we may not agree with their motives, still there were no winners. Everyone lost something or was diminished in some way by the events of this episode.

"Balance of Terror" was the first episode in which the *Enterprise* fought an actual battle in space, and also the first in which much screen time was given to the villains and an examination of their motives and drives. Here, events once again forced the participants to lose control—the Romulan commander had to test his cloaking device and follow the orders of his superiors; Kirk had to keep the Romulans from returning home with valuable information and avenge the deaths of Starfleet personnel.

And, again, no one really won, for the Romulans were killed, and although the *Enterprise* won the battle, Kirk found no enjoyment in it, and the events would only lead to a resumption of such skirmishes in the future.

In "Shore Leave" and "The Galileo Seven," members of the crew are threatened because they lose control when forces beyond their understanding confront them. The giant humanoids are not true villains, as they act only out of fear and the need to protect their territory; the androids conjured up on the shore-leave planet are only as villainous as the subconscious desires of the crewmembers make them.

"The Squire of Gothos," the ineffable Trelane, is not a villain either. He is a child misusing great powers; and, again, the true villain of the piece is the lack of humanity caused by immaturity.

In "Arena," the Gorn captain is a pretty reprehensible fellow, quite unwilling to treat with Kirk and dedicated to Kirk's destruction. However, the Gorn has been told (as has Kirk) that if he loses the battle, his ship will be destroyed. So he is only acting to protect his interests, and we can imagine several members of Starfleet who would have been just as unwilling to bargain as was the Gorn.

This episode has a fairly happy ending thanks to Kirk's humanitarian refusal to kill the Gorn. So now we see that Star Trek is taking another step: It is no longer necessary for the participants to remain in control at all times, it is only necessary for humanitarian values to win out in the end. This is, of course, a much more positive and realistic view, but it could only have been presented after the Rule was firmly established.

Ben Finney is a tried-and-true villain whose tampering with computer record tapes forces Kirk to endure a "court-martial" for Finney's "death." Finney's motive is a classic one: revenge for a long-ago failure which Kirk reported. In this episode we see the first glimmerings of what is to be the last major theme of Star Trek: man's overreliance on, and ultimate betrayal by, machines. This theme was further developed in the next episode, "The Return of the Archons."

The computer-spirit Landru is the first computer/machine villain to be presented in Star Trek. In keeping with the thematic devices, Landru controls to too great an extent; the people absorbed into the "Body" are without free will and lose their individuality; their culture is static and stagnant. Of course, Landru was built by man and given power by man, and—ultimately—betrayed man. It is only through the intervention of the *Enterprise* crew that Landru's stultifying influence is destroyed, thereby affirming the value of individualism and humanity.

Now we have all of Star Trek's thematic villains: the man out of control (either by outside influence, disease, etc.); the man who has lost his humanity; and the man who has allowed his humanity and self-control to be usurped by machines. In each case, individual freedom and free will are lost, and the usual upshot is that everyone loses something.

Khan, in "Space Seed," is another classic villain. He is intelligent, egotistical, strong, and charismatic. And he performs one of the classical functions of the villain as well: coercing another person to betrayal. There is nothing in Khan that we do not see in ourselves; yet he is all the more evil for that. Khan and his followers feel themselves to be superior in every way to the rest of humanity, and therefore deserving to rule, but they are in reality less than human, for they have lost compassion and the belief in equality. This is an episode with no winners—but then, there are really no losers either. Each side has to be satisfied with half a loaf. Kirk loses his battle to have Khan and his followers join with the Federation for the mutual benefit of each group; Khan decides to follow the advice of Milton. But we have a glimmer of hope—Khan has found love with Marla McGivers, so perhaps he will become a little more human one of these days.

"A Taste of Armageddon" again takes up the theme of the loss of human values when men surrender their freedom to machines. The war fought by computer between Eminiar and Vendikar has stagnated both societies, even though the peoples of both planets feel the reverse is true. It is only when Kirk and Spock destroy the computers and force the people of both planets to face real warfare that the leaders decide to take matters into their own hands again and talk peace. They have regained their humanity and individualism (and their freedom). Again, when the machines are removed from the picture, a happy and optimistic ending results. We can clearly see that in the philosophy of Star Trek, the influence of computers and machines has now become equated with disease and madness.

"The Devil in the Dark" returns to the theme of misunderstanding between different beings. This episode elaborates on the statement that the essential "human values" may be shared by aliens as well as humans, and that it is necessary to try to understand the motives of the villain before trying to destroy it.

"Errand of Mercy." My, was it really so long before the Klingons first appeared on Star Trek? But then, perhaps the ultimate Star Trek villains could not be presented until the basic themes were developed. If the Klingons had been the enemy and the aggressor from the first episode, Star Trek could easily have become just another war show set in space.

There are no bones made about the Klingons. They are out-and-out villains; lusting for combat and conquest, evil by choice and custom, and taking great pleasure in their evil. They are the antithesis of all the Federation and Kirk and his crew stand for, and as such, the most classical villainous types of all. Finally, after half a season, Star Trek presented Good vs. Evil; Right vs. Wrong.

But, even in this episode, we have no clear-cut winners. Sure, the end of the threatened war is desired by the Federation, but things are ended on the Organians' terms, and that seems to rankle Kirk as much as it does Kor. The "war" is not ended, it is merely changed into nonaggressive competition—of the kind quite unsatisfying to warriors.

And here we see a twist to the theme: Events and people are controlled by an outside influence, the Organians; and although they are benign, still a great amount of free will and freedom of action has been taken away from both the Federation and the Klingons. With "Errand of Mercy," we see that outside control, even though it may occasionally be the best thing, is not always easy to swallow.

Lazarus A, in "The Alternative Factor," is quite mad, desiring the destruction of two universes because he cannot stand the thought of his exact duplicate living in a parallel universe. In his madness, he has lost both self-control and his humanity, and his double, Lazarus B, loses his freedom when he sacrifices himself to eternal battle with Lazarus A in the time corridor. Again, no winners.

The Parasites in "Operation: Annihilate!" are in the same league as any other disease-organism villain, and they are quickly and soundly defeated. This cannot be considered too much of a happy ending, however, as thousands of people (including Kirk's brother and sister-in-law) are killed.

T'Pring is also a classical villain: the conniving female. Due to her machinations, Spock is forced to battle Kirk, Vulcan custom is disrupted, and poor Stonn seems to be destined to fight a lifelong battle to tame his shrew. And, in the happy conclusion to this episode, Spock and Kirk both lose—and win!

In "Who Mourns For Adonais?" the "god" Apollo only wants the adoration and worship from humans that he enjoyed long ago on Earth. Kirk points out that if they acceded to his demands, they would become less than human, and such a situation would be intolerable to them. Apollo can never understand this attitude but is forced to accept it. He is a tragic villain, and to be pitied more than despised.

Machines once again serve as the villain in "The Changeling" when the amalgam of the Nomad probe and the alien probe, *Tan Ru*, threatens the *Enterprise*. For a change, the machine is not attempting to control human behavior but to eliminate "defects"—including defective humans. In a scene which points up the major failings of machines—their inability to adapt—Nomad causes itself to blow up. Once again, a malfunctioning machine has been treated as a "disease" by the *Enterprise* crew, and all is well after it is eliminated.

Everybody gets a chance to be a villain in "Mirror, Mirror," an episode that postulates a universe wherein the Feder-

ation is the Empire; it and all of the crew are totally dedicated to evil. This episode tells us that even the best of
men and women can go wrong somewhere along the line,
and points up in a dramatic and graphic fashion the value of
a humane attitude in our own *Enterprise* crew.

Another computer god is the villain in "The Apple," stag-
nating a civilization and threatening our heroes. And, in now
typical fashion, Kirk and Company give it a quick fix, just as
they do "The Doomsday Machine," although in that episode,
the defeat of the villain costs the lives of an entire starship
crew.

A curious twist is presented in the next episode, "Catspaw," when Sylvia becomes even *more* evil as she adapts to
human form. Obviously, this episode by Robert Bloch speaks
of the barrenness of having human emotions and desires
without the will and compassion to control them.

Computerized androids are the villains in "I, Mudd," although they are aided and abetted in fine fashion by Har-
court Fenton himself. Backward logic saves the day again,
and Harry Mudd ends up with his just deserts.

The Orion disguised as an Andorian in "Journey to Babel"
is your run-of-the-mill villain, attempting to disrupt the peace
talks in order to gain an open field for his comrade's piracy.

The Klingons show up again in "Friday's Child," this time
fostering rebellion among the people of Capella IV to gain
mining rights—a particularly underhanded way to skirt the
Organian Peace Treaty. Thanks to McCoy's ability as a mid-
wife, Krass is killed and the Federation gains a new ally . . .
and the mining rights. The Klingons, as usual, end up gnash-
ing their teeth.

Another mysterious disease is the villain in "The Deadly
Years," and this time its effects are to rob some of the crew
of their "freedom" and humanity by causing them to age rap-
idly and lose physical and mental agility. The Romulans also
make an appearance, but they are little more than a device to
heighten the suspense.

In "Obsession," the Cloud Creature is treated as another
disease, completely malevolent and evil, with no attempt at
communication made with it (unusual for Star Trek). It is
defeated quickly and efficiently, and life goes on.

With these last few episodes we see a change from the sort

of episodes which characterized Star Trek in the beginning. Most of the villains featured in the last of the first-season episodes and in the majority of the second-season episodes have been clear-cut, evil villains—usually of the machine or disease sort (or Klingons, Romulans, etc.). So the "everyone loses" type of ending has just about disappeared, for machines or diseases are defeated, and with a quick dusting of hands, the *Enterprise* crew flies away. However good or bad these individual episodes may be, and however well they reiterate the themes, they are not satisfying, for they are not as realistic and involving as the early shows. No important decision is required of Kirk; no compromises have to be made. By this time, the Theme has stultified into Formula, and only on a few occasions will an episode be able to break out of that formula.

The "Wolf in the Fold" was a very ancient, very evil psychic manifestation which preyed on strong emotions, and was able to control others to do its bidding. In this episode, the terror was played up a bit more, and the "infestation" angle played down (it was not until the end of the episode that we learned the entity existed). But because the entity was so omnipresent, it was much more convincing and horrifying than the Cloud Creature from "Obsession," which we were only told was evil and sentient.

"The Trouble with Tribbles" again featured the Klingons, this time almost as comedy relief! The awkward Organian Peace Treaty, which served its purpose in keeping Star Trek from becoming a space-war show, was also responsible for the relegation of the Klingons to the status of Resident Meddlers, and consequently downgraded them from Villains to Nuisances. The troublesome Tribbles were considered as just another infestation—a lot cuter than the Parasites but no less deadly, and just as easily disposed of.

Another statement about slavery was made in "The Gamesters of Triskelion," but to much less effect than in "The Menagerie." The Providers acted evil out of boredom, and once Kirk had convinced them that teaching their captives how to live as free men was more exciting than the games, they performed a quick turnabout. So nothing was stated about the need of man for freedom, or the rights of sentient creatures. The moral of this tale seemed to be "idle hands,

etc." Quite a comedown from the powerful statements of
"Menagerie."

"A Piece of the Action" featured villains galore—except
they weren't *really* villains, just fun-loving copycats making
use of a lot of old *Untouchables* sets and props. The formula
was sidestepped a bit here, as the misuse of technology was
the danger for a change, and not the technology itself.

"The Immunity Syndrome" was a particularly mindless
show. Having encountered and conquered all sorts of disease
microbes, the crew now encounters and conquers a disease
"macrobe." A perfect example of the time and talent wasted
when the formula is followed to the extreme.

"A Private Little War" again had the Klingons meddling in
the affairs of an underdeveloped world (at least they were
not clowns this time). However, this episode marked a return
to the type of story that Star Trek had done so successfully
during the first season: Kirk was forced to make a tough decision, one which could perhaps only worsen the situation,
and probably did. And, for the first time in quite a while, we
had an episode without a happy ending . . . and no winners.

The Arretian Henoch was a villain of the old school—
charming, reveling in his evil acts, seductive and conniving.
"Return to Tomorrow" worked within the formula very well,
utilizing as it did the evils of mind control (actually, in this
case, it was more like possession), an individual who chose to
be evil, and the loss of humanity when confronted by great
power and/or overwhelming technology.

Not so successful was "Patterns of Force," the first of the
"what if?" stories which were to pop up on Star Trek with increasing frequency from this point onward. It did feature,
however, two villainous types: John Gill, who lost control
and interfered in a world's development; and Melakon, who
warped Gill's works to gain power for himself. Any point to
the episode was rendered incoherent, thanks to the heavy-
handed symbolism.

The villains in "By Any Other Name," the Kelvans, followed in the footsteps of Sylvia when their evil was increased
due to taking on human form. And, as in her case, it was the
same reason that they were defeated.

The "mad starship commander" showed up once more in
"The Omega Glory," and we were again treated to a man

who was villainous because he was misguided. This was another nothing show, and another "what if?"

A computer is again the villain in "The Ultimate Computer," and in this case, we are told that it acts evilly because it has been programmed with the paranoid engrams of its creator, Dr. Richard Daystrom. As in most machine/villain episodes, the computer is tricked into destroying itself by applying twisted logic.

The ultimate "what if?" episode marked the end of such foolishness (at least as a major plot device). "Bread and Circuses" had only two so-so villains: the renegade Captain Merik, and the Roman Claudius Marcus. Among many other flaws, this episode also featured a particularly reprehensible ending.

"Spock's Brain" is notable only for the fact that Mara and her followers needed the Vulcan's brain to power their computer (called the "Controller," naturally), and that the apple of knowledge that allowed Mara to do the evil deed was given by a machine.

"The Enterprise Incident" again harked back to the early days of the series, presenting as it did no true villains and no real winners, although the ending is not nearly as dark in tone as some of the early episodes.

But "The Paradise Syndrome" does have just such a solemn and sad ending. It follows the formula in that the danger and eventual deaths are not caused by any overt villainy or misunderstanding, but instead by the damage done to Kirk's mind by the obelisk computer and its original failure to operate to deflect the asteroid.

"And the Children Shall Lead" gives us the first truly evil villain in quite a while. Gorgan is not only seemingly good and friendly, but he also uses the most reprehensible sort of mind control—against children. It is interesting to note the return to the Rule in this episode, since once the children regain control of their own minds and perceptions of reality, Gorgan fades away.

Again, there are no real villains in "Is There in Truth No Beauty?" unless, of course, you consider the madness (and subsequent loss of control) of Larry Marvick as villainy. Again, a restatement of the Rule, although much more subtle in this instance.

The Melkots of "Spectre of the Gun" could be considered villains, but one could also consider their actions to be proper as well. They *did* warn the *Enterprise* away, after all. And when Kirk and Company did not react with violence to the attack of the Earps, the Melkots agreed to treat with them. This episode made a strong statement for the value of control, as well as the need to keep a firm grip on reality.

Another malevolent force shows up in "Day of the Dove," but this time the Klingons as well as the *Enterprise* crew fall under its spell. It is overcome without too much difficulty, and another happy ending ensues.

In "For the World Is Hollow and I Have Touched the Sky," a computer is again the villain, but for a change it is not defeated by logic. The disease affecting McCoy is also a minor irritation. The only thing notable about this episode is the fact that our good Dr. Leonard McCoy takes on the role of villain when he deserts his new wife without a second glance. . . .

The Tholians are the aggressors in "The Tholian Web," but can hardly be considered villains, since they are only protecting their own space. It was a refreshing change to see an "alien encounter" episode which did not end with the aliens being so impressed by the courage, control, etc. of the *Enterprise* crew that they made an immediate turnaround and opened peaceful negotiations. No winners, no losers; but a more realistic result.

"Plato's Stepchildren" are a lazy and vain bunch who are corrupted by great powers, and they are defeated when Kirk and Spock gain the same powers and use them humanely. Again, the virtue of control over self-indulgence is touted.

The real villain of "Wink of an Eye" is the radiation which has speeded up the Scalosians, and not the Scalosians themselves. Another infestation episode; strictly formula.

The Vians in "The Empath" have a benign aim, but in the loss of humanity of their sterile, intellectual existence, resort to villainous means to achieve those aims. A happy ending results when the Vians decide Gem's race is to be saved, but they don't seem to have learned anything themselves about the true values of humanity.

"Ellan of Tryoius" has several villains: the unseen Klingons, the jealous Kryton who conspires with them, and the spoiled and willful Ellan herself. This episode harks slightly back to the first season, as a series of compromises which are not quite acceptable to all have to be made.

"Whom Gods Destroy" presents yet another "mad starship captain," the shape-changing Garth of Izar. None of the unfortunate madmen in this show can be considered as true villains.

No winners in "Let That Be Your Last Battlefield," but like "Patterns of Force," the program was so badly overwritten and blatant with symbolism that any message was lost in the overkill. It is interesting to note, however, that Kirk was more concerned with eliminating a disease bacterium on Ariannus than with the problems of either Lokai or Bele.

The absence of a disease is the problem in "The Mark of Gideon," and for a change, Kirk is called upon to supply the illness rather than the cure. It could hardly be called a happy ending when millions more are doomed to die because of the disease.

Another malfunctioning computer is the villain in "That Which Survives." This episode is scarcely more than a vignette, serving merely as an opportunity for the *Enterprise* crew to rid the galaxy of one more malevolent machine.

Alien beings infesting the mind of Mira Romaine serve as the villains in "The Lights of Zetar," and they are quite evil in intent and action. This episode is one of the few in Star Trek in which adaptability is seen as a handicap and not as an asset.

The millennia-old Flint in "Requiem for Methuselah" is quite villainous in his single-minded desire to have the android Reena gain human emotions. But the Rule comes into play, and when Reena finally gains real emotions, she does not have the experience to control them, and so dies. A subtle comment (again) on the essential inhumanity and lack of adaptability of machines.

Dr. Sevrin, in "The Way To Eden," is another classic villain: the zealot. Like all fanatics, he considers any action justified in achieving his ends. He is also a carrier of disease, and uses machinery malevolently. A perfect formula villain!

Heavy-handed symbolism again surfaces in "The Cloud Minders"; and, also again, there are no true villains. The simpleminded solution to the problems of the two opposing forces hardly seems enough to cause a radical change in their society—it is much more likely that civil war will result.

Four extremely evil villains from Star Trek's history show up in "The Savage Curtain," and again, they are created by a superior race to test the *Enterprise* crew. Aside from a look at the fascinating Surak, nothing special.

Janet Lester, the "Turnabout Intruder," is quite mad, and her accomplice, Dr. Arthur Coleman, only slightly less so. Neither qualifies as a true villain.

The animated Star Trek series also followed the formulas developed by the live-action series, as well as using the same thematic villains: man (or beings) out of control; loss of humanity; the threat of machinery.

But in *Star Trek: The Motion Picture*, the ultimate Star Trek villain finally appears: V'Ger, an immense, unimaginably powerful *machine* originally created by man that has lost control of itself in its desperate search for the meaning of existence, i.e., *humanity*. And it was given such power by alien technicians expanding upon the original design and programming of a Voyager spacecraft.

So we can clearly see that in *STTMP*, Roddenberry gave us all of the villains we have seen in the live-action and animated episodes wrapped up in one not-quite-so-nice package.

And how is V'Ger defeated? In a manner which was always implicit, always suggested in the series, but never quite taken to that extreme: A *man* sacrificed his life (or at least his temporal existence and individuality) to give a *machine* the humanity which it could not discover for itself.

The Rule (Stay in control!) is in effect again. With the faith gained by its merging with Decker and Ilia, V'Ger can now move on to another plane of existence. It has finally adapted; it is in *control* of its own destiny for the very first time and thus no longer searching. It is no longer a threat, no longer a villain.

Star Trek, through all of the live-action, animated episodes and the movie, has shown us that although men (and alien beings) may be evil, and outside influences and diseases and infestations may be evil, and injustice and bigotry may be evil, still each of these may be overcome if all parties concerned keep their heads and remain in control.

By IDIC, by the Prime Directive, by saying, "I will not kill . . . today!" we gain and reaffirm our basic and essential hu-

manity. And humanity, humanitarianism, human rights is
what Star Trek is all about. So how very true was the ad slo-
gan of *Star Trek: The Motion Picture:*

The Human Adventure Is Just Beginning.

14.

EMPIRES, GODS, AND OTHER INTERESTED PARTIES—An Examination of Advanced Aliens In Star Trek

by Walter Irwin

This article was frankly inspired by Steven Satterfield's fine article "The Preservers," which you have already encountered in this collection. Walter felt that the subject deserved a closer, overall look, and the following article is the result. And he naturally hopes his article will inspire others. . . .

The United Federation of Planets is a far-reaching organization of worlds which have banded together in the interest of mutual defense, commerce, and the advancement of knowledge. But the member planets of the UFP make up only a very small percentage of the inhabited planets in Star Trek's galaxy. Many other planets are members of other groups or are captive members of opposing empires. And, aside from these federations and empires, there are a number of alien races who have immense powers and space-spanning capabilities which would easily allow them to join together to control many of these same planets. Indeed, in the past, a few of these races had formed such associations, but have since abandoned them for one reason or another.

Add to this the extremely great number of planets in the galaxy which have yet to be explored—much of the galaxy itself is a question mark—and you can get a general idea of just how vast a number of possible federations, empires, etc. may yet be discovered, as well as the yet unknown superior races which may or may not desire their presence to be discovered.

Of continuing concern to the UFP are the Romulan and Klingon empires. These were apparently the first opposing groups met by the Federation as its ships began to explore the galaxy. (We are given a hint that Earth and the Romulans fought a devastating war some time in the past, but it is unclear whether or not Earth was affiliated with the UFP at the time.)

The Klingons are by far the more aggressive and warlike of the two, even though the Romulans consider themselves to be a warrior race. Perhaps the fact that the Romulans developed warp flight much later than either the Federation or the Klingons explains why their empire is smaller and less spread out.

Thanks to the earlier treaty ending the war with the Romulans and establishing the neutral zone, and the opposed Organian Peace Treaty, the Federation has been technically at peace with both empires for some while. However, skirmishes and confrontations occur occasionally, and all-out war is possible with either at any time. So it is no mystery that the UFP keeps a sharp eye on both empires, and is very concerned by the current alliance between the two.

The *Enterprise* encountered the *Fesarius*, a ship of the First Federation, early in its five-year mission. The commander of the ship, Balok, proved to be friendly, as was his federation, and a cultural exchange was arranged between the two federations. We can assume that they continued on good terms, but as nothing has been seen of any representatives of the First Federation since, there has been little in the way of plans to consolidate the federations or to form a joint defense. It could be that the First Federation feels no need for this (as may the UFP), for the *Fesarius* was an enormous vessel of great power and range. If they have an entire fleet of such ships, then they have little to fear from the Klingons or the Romulans. But wouldn't it be something to see Commander Kor's face if Jim Kirk popped up commanding a mile-wide *Enterprise?*

The first of the very powerful races encountered by the *Enterprise* were the Thasians. These noncorporeal beings can perform seeming miracles through mental power alone; and that power is of a type that can be taught to humans, although they have done so in only one case, that of Charlie Evans, and because it turned out so badly, they are unlikely to do so again. Little more is known about the Thasians. We know that their powers are not limited to their own world; nor are they dependent upon machinery. When one of the Thasians appeared to Captain Kirk, he took the form of a human face, but whether this was his true appearance or one taken only for convenience of communication is not known. It is likely that beings with such powers would have ventured out into the galaxy at some time in the past, but they now seem content to remain on their home planet.

The first of the known races to venture out into space are the Vendala. They are a very ancient race and have acquired great powers over the course of time, although these powers are limited in scope when compared to those of the Organians or Thasians. As they seem only to show themselves one at a time, we can assume that they are either a very shy race, or else have some sort of ethical or religious taboo against appearing to outsiders in groups. The large, terraformed asteroids in which they live probably also serve as their spaceships, but we are given the impression that the Vendala have lost much of the curiosity and wanderlust that is a necessity for exploring space. As a dignified and peace-loving race, and the pioneers of galactic exploration, the Vendala are much respected and highly honored among UFP members—and, we would expect, among the other spacegoing races as well.

Another race which spent much time exploring the galaxy in the far past is the Arretians. The surviving Arretians, Sargon, Thalassa, and Henoch, tell Kirk that their race was responsible for "seeding" much of the galaxy, taking sentient beings from one planet and transporting them to an alien, but inhabitable, planet to ensure the survival and future success of humanity. (Sargon refers to them as his "children.")

The Arretians have limited mental powers, and are extremely intelligent. Even so, they still have humanlike emotions and desires, and it is perhaps due to their failure to overcome or eliminate their emotions that their world and civilization were destroyed. Unlike other advanced races, they were unable to make the next step of evolution, and so disappeared.

The Preservers may or may not have been the Arretians, but the available evidence says they were not. The only trace of the Preservers which has been found is the obelisk on the Indian Planet, which gives a few examples of their musical-tone language and a very graphic example of their superadvanced technology in the asteroid deflector system. Their mission seems to be a bit different from the Arretians' as well—the Preservers rescued endangered races and reseeded them only to preserve as many examples of human culture as possible. It is likely that they were more interested in observing these races than in facilitating their development. But the actions of these two advanced races in the dim past could well be the reason why so many similar humanoid races exist throughout the galaxy.

Two other races, both very ancient, both considering themselves "gods," had taken an interest in helping along the development of primitive cultures—particularly those on Earth. They are the peoples of Apollo and Kukulkan. We are told that Apollo and his fellow gods visited ancient Greece on Earth, there to teach man and in turn to be worshiped by him. Kukulkan most likely visited Earth alone, concentrating his efforts mainly on the Mayans, but apparently visiting many other parts of Earth as well, giving rise to legends of dragons and winged serpents. Of the two, Kukulkan seems more altruistic, giving knowledge for its own sake; the "Greek gods" seem primarily interested in being worshiped. The sources of the powers of each is unknown: Kukulkan needs his ship to travel in space, and is quite defenseless against the attack of the powercat; Apollo depends on the devices inside his "temple" to perform his magics. Both must be credited with a fair measure of mental powers, however, for they are able to make themselves understood by primitive Earth peoples, and such powers seem to be gained over the course of time by all ancient races.

The Megans of the alternate Magick Universe also visited Earth many centuries ago, but they seemed to act primarily as observers and took little overt action in human affairs. Their appearance led to the legends of devils as magical beings with reddish skin, horns, and cloven hooves. We can assume that if the Megans eventually found their way to Earth, they had also done quite a bit of exploring in their own galaxy via their magical powers.

The Arretians also inhabit an alternate universe, the Counter Clock Universe. (They may or may not be the alternate counterpoint to the Arretians of our universe. They could well be, however, as time runs "backward" there, and the race which has long since been destroyed in our galaxy could just now be regressing to its origins in the Counter Clock galaxy.) The Arretians technology is quite advanced—

Karla 5's ship is capable of Warp 36—but as time passes, and the race regresses, their knowledge is being lost.

The most fascinating race to be found in an alternate universe is the Galactic Empire of the mirror universe. It is indeed a mirror of the Star Trek universe; everyone on board the *Enterprise* has an evil counterpart on the ESS *Enterprise*. Most of the planets that make up the Federation in this universe are apparently members (or captives) of the Empire; the mirror Spock is very much present. It seems probable that the mirror universe diverged from our own fairly recently, for if the divergence had taken place too far in the past, it would be highly unlikely that physical counterparts of the crew would even have been born let alone being assigned to the *Enterprise*. What happened in the mirror universe to cause the creation of an Empire rather than a Federation (and what *will* happen when Spock 2 attempts to overthrow the Empire?) is a matter of speculation, as is the status of the Romulans, Klingons, etc. in the mirror universe. Perhaps *all* of the races there are reversed, and *they* are the Good Guys!

It would be scary indeed to live in a galaxy in which the Organians were evil! Luckily for the Federation, in our Star Trek universe, the Organians are totally dedicated to peace and goodwill. They are, however, quite adamant about preserving their privacy and autonomy. It is not until the ships of Kirk and Kor are about to engage in battle (and consequently, the Federation and the Empire as well) that the Organians drop their pose of being primitive people and reveal themselves to be the incorporeal and immensely powerful beings they truly are.

That is about all that is known about the Organians, save that their present form is a final step in their evolutionary process, from matter to pure energy. As advanced beings, they value peace, but have also demonstrated that they will act as "aggressors" to prevent other races, particularly the Federation and the Klingons, from warring, and will enforce peace upon them, even if neither side actually desires it. Such an attitude would give us an idea that the Organians spent much time journeying throughout the galaxy in the dim past, and perhaps they did their share of "seeding" as well.

The Metrons don't seem to be quite as patient (or as meddlesome, depends on your viewpoint) as the Organians, but they are no more forgiving of inferior races' making a battleground of their space. They are also apparently extremely powerful, transporting Kirk and the Gorn captain instantly to the battle planet, halting the starships in midspace, and disabling weapons. The Metron who appears to Kirk is in human form (a young boy), and we have no reason to assume that this is not their natural appearance, so apparently they have not yet advanced evolutionarily as far as the Organians, but are well on the road.

(Speaking of the Gorn, they seem to have starflight capability, but we only learn that they consider the base on Cestus to be infringing on their territory. So we do not know if they control only a system or two, or if there actually is a Gorn Empire. If there is not, then it is likely that they are doing their best to acquire one, for if the Gorn captain is any example, they are a very belligerent and warlike race.)

The Melkots are another highly advanced race, but unlike the Organians and Metrons, they still seem to be interested in preserving their empire. They warn off the *Enterprise* in no uncertain terms, and when the order is ignored, they take immediate action. That action shows them to be in command of great mental powers—powers strong enough to force the *Enterprise* crew to believe they are actually on a planet, in Tombstone, and that they can be killed by the Earps' bullets. It is unlikely that the Melkots have explored much of the galaxy or are interested in expanding their territories, for once they are convinced of the peaceful intentions of the crew, they are quite willing to negotiate. And we do know that the Federation has never encountered them before (although they do know of them).

The only encounter with the energy beings of Trelane's race does not lead to any sort of intercourse, and consequently we learn little about them. We can assume, however, that they are on an evolutionary par with the Thasians, for Trelane performed many of the same sort of tricks that Charlie X did. Trelane did require a power source, however, although it was not made quite clear if it was the true power or merely a focus for it. (It is also possible that the immature Trelane needed the power source as a "booster" to his immature mental abilities.) These beings are quite secretive about themselves, and feel that it is either not necessary or not prudent to make contact with humans at this time.

Great mental abilities are also exhibited by the Talosians,

although we are told that in their case these abilities led to their downfall. They are also limited to telepathy and illu- sion-casting; we have seen no evidence that the Talosians can change or create matter as many of the other races encoun- tered can easily do. The Talosians are desirous of repopulat- ing their barren world with beings from another planet, but they resort to capture and virtual slavery to achieve their aim, which is an indication that their knowledge, while great, is far from omniscient.

The same applies to the Vians. They do not seem to possess any special abilities beyond advanced knowledge; and they too went about their altruistic aims in a clumsy and callous fashion. The Vians are probably not quite so advanced as they *think* they are. . . .

Sylvia and Korob exhibit great powers of mental control, illusion, transmutation, and the like, but that power is ap- parently created or greatly augmented by mechanical devices; for once the devices are removed, they revert to their natural forms and quickly die. Again, as in the case of the Megans, we can assume that they scoured their own universe before resort- ing to ours for new living space. Such powers as they exhibit would make starflight ridiculously easy.

The Kelvans, in their natural forms, are beings with hundreds of tentaclelike limbs. They exhibit great mental control (but not telepathy) and are devoid of emotion and physical sensation. They are also extremely warlike in a cold and logical fashion. They possess the capability of starflight fast enough to make the trip from the Andromeda Galaxy to our own (even though it still takes years), and their tech- nology is sophisticated enough for them to modify the *Enter- prise* so that it can achieve great speeds, although not nearly as fast as the Kelvans' own ships. We can assume that their weaponry and defense capabilities are as great, so it is well that the exploration party chose not to return to Kelva and report on our galaxy's defenses. Having apparently already conquered *all* of their own galaxy, they probably wouldn't have too much trouble with ours.

The Kzin are a catlike race of great belligerency, and were at one time in the past possessors of quite a large empire. Having been defeated by the Federation and stripped of all but their own home systems and a few ships for defensive purposes, they have turned to piracy, and are quite proficient at it. The overriding desire of the Kzin is to regain their empire and exact vengeance on the Federation, and they are constantly seeking a method of doing just that. It is fortunate that the Kzin are apparently so untrustworthy that even the Klingons will not help them in their goals.

Very little is known about the Tholians. It is likely that they control some sort of empire, for they are quite insistent that the *Enterprise* leave their territory, and will not even consider talking. It is possible that the Tholians are not native to this galaxy, for they are quite unlike any other being yet encountered, as is their technology. It is very possible that they are from an alternate universe, as their territory includes the area in which interphase with other universes occurs quite often. They may also have highly developed mental powers, for they apparently possess no limbs as we know them, and may operate their ships and machinery by telekinesis.

The Orions are also pirates, but they are such by choice and tradition. They maintain a careful neutrality to allow themselves to all the more successfully operate their piracy operations, and most of their technology is stolen or copied from any available source. They will deal with anyone for anything, hiring themselves out as spies, saboteurs, etc.; and they do a brisk trade in illegal goods, including the much-desired green Orion slave girls.

The Medusans are a race so hideous that any human who looks upon them immediately goes mad; but they are also highly intelligent beings with spaceflight capability and are renowned as the best navigators in the galaxy. It is not made clear if Kollos—the Medusan ambassador in "Is There in Truth No Beauty?"—is a representative of a single planet or of an empire. We can assume that whatever size the Medusans' sphere of influence, it is not limited to one world or system, for they could only have earned their reputation as navigators by traveling great distances through space.

The rock creature encountered in "The Savage Curtain" is obviously possessed of extremely great mental powers, for he is able to create replicas of heroes and villains from the thoughts of Kirk and Spock, create a hospitable environment in the midst of a lava-covered planet, and interfere with the operations of the *Enterprise*. There are obviously more of his race on the planet, but they are never seen. The rock creature seems to be satisfied to discuss philosophies, and from his general demeanor, it is unlikely that his race has ever been interested in exploring beyond their own world.

The only things we know about the beings who created the shore-leave world is that they are humanoid in form, quite intelligent, and still have the desire and need to play. The Caretaker tells Kirk that he feels humans are not ready to learn any more about his race as yet; however, in "Once upon a Planet," the Caretaker's grave is marked "The Last of His Race." This could be true, for if the beings still existed and visited the world, they would have known the Caretaker was dead and that the computer running the planet was malfunctioning. It could be, however, that his race has simply evolved beyond the need for the planet, and the Caretaker has chosen to remain behind to cut off any inquiry into his people's origins and eventual fate.

The most intriguing race encountered in Star Trek was never seen at all—their presence was felt only in the 1960s—and they used an Earthman as their agent. The unnamed race which raised Gary Seven and sent him to twentieth-century Earth is obviously a very powerful and far-reaching one. They are also benign, desiring that Earth make it successfully through this difficult period—with a little help from Seven, Isis, and Roberta Lincoln. They are most likely the beings who, when first visiting and examining Earth, started the many "flying-saucer" sightings, and were responsible for the disappearance of a great number of persons (including, we can be sure, either Gary Seven as an infant or his parents or ancestors). They will most likely still be around in Star Trek's time, Seven feels, but he also refuses to reveal anything about them, for if they want to be known to the Federation, they will reveal themselves. It is quite possible that agents such as Gary Seven are still operating within the Federation. The most interesting character introduced in this episode is Isis: Is she actually one of the mysterious beings sent to oversee Seven, the beautiful female her true form? Or is she another human raised by the beings, taking the form of a cat to be less noticeable? Or is she actually a cat, able to take human form at various times?

It is one of the great losses to Star Trek fans that this "pilot" did not become a series, or that Gary Seven and his helpers did not appear again in Star Trek.

We have seen that there are many, many races and planetary affiliations within the Star Trek galaxy (and sometimes outside or parallel to it) beyond the United Federation of Planets. And, within the vast, unexplored regions of the Milky Way Galaxy—our galaxy—there are undoubtedly many, many more. Some are friendly, some are not. But that is why the USSS *Enterprise* makes her journeys—to seek out those new life forms and new civilizations. And as long as we have our imaginations and our dreams, the Starship *Enterprise* will continue to go where no man has gone before.

15.

REQUIEM FOR A HACK

by Kiel Stuart

In The Best of Trek #3, *we presented an example of Star Trek fan fiction parody. This time, Kiel Stuart presents a different kind of parody: a satiric reworking of one of Star Trek's most famous episodes. We laughed our heads off when we first read it, and we think you will too. . . .*

"Captain's Log: Stardate 63754.001. Dear Diary (yawn), uhhhh . . . zzzzzzz. . . ."

That dread disease known to Fodderation officials as the Blahs struck the crew of the Starboat *Enteritis* with a vengeance. Seventy-five percent of the crew—twice the usual number—were asleep at the wheel. A drowsy Captain Jerk decided their only recourse was to find a planet with a supply of quadrowheatiecale—the breakfast of champions . . . or at least people who were awake.

On the fifth day of their search, Jerk dragged himself listlessly to the bridge in the dwindling hope that his sleeping crew (not known for lightning efficiency in the best of times) might have found a suitable planet. Booting his comatose science officer in the kidney, Jerk demanded a report.

Stifling a yawn, Mr. Schmuck mumbled, "My Feeler Gauges indicate that, fortunately for us, we are at this exact moment in the space-time continuum hovering over a planet that is totally lacking in quadrowheatiecale, but which is, however, a rich natural source of the element commonly known as Ritalin, which has a similar effect on the human body."

By the time Schmuck had finished his dissertation, Jerk was asleep.

Naturally, instead of beaming down a couple of expendable Security goons, Jerk, Schmuck, and "Bozo" McClown went themselves. No use, thought Jerk, in wasting my dramatic talent. Without checking who—or what—inhabited the planet, they took picks and shovels, and were busily squabbling over key lights when Jerk cried out.

"Bozo, I hear something!"

"Oh, do y'all mean that canned music that wafts forth whenevah we-all are about t' encountah new life an' new civilization?"

"Nay, doctor," said Schmuck. "I believe that the captain is referring to that 5,000-cycle-per-second vibration coming from behind yon papier-mâché boulder."

The creature that approached them resembled a Mr. Microphone with a pituitary condition. Christmas-tree lights festooning the apparition blinked menacingly. Open-mouthed, they allowed it within touching distance before whipping out their fizzlers, which—what else?—had gone dead.

"Naughty, naughty," said a human voice. From behind the phony rock stepped a man of about forty, his bearing suggesting immense boredom and digestive troubles. Nevertheless, the robot ceased to blink.

"I'm Arman Flint," said the robotmaster, "the richest person in the galaxy. You cheap souvenir hunters will kindly remove yourselves from my private property, or Robby the Robot will french-fry you." For emphasis, Robby's store-window lights disgorged a spark that ignited the underbrush.

Nonplussed, Jerk threw out his chest. "We are in need of your Ritalin. I have a sick crew up there."

McClown put his own two cents in. "Have y'all evah seen a victim of the Blahs? In jess a few short hours he is rendered totally worthless. The effect is like watching an entire hour of *Charlie's Space Angels*."

Arman grew reflective. "The seventies . . . *The Gong Show* . . . disco . . . est . . . people saying, "Have a nice day" . . . happy faces . . . people nodding out in the streets . . . sounds of their snores filling the night . . ."

"You are a student of Earth history, then?" asked Schmuck, dissatisfied with his only line in the scene.

Arman shrugged. "Anything you say."

"Well? What about it? Hah?" prompted Jerk, preparing to rave about philosophy and human need.

"All right. Anything to keep you from foaming at the mouth."

Somewhat disappointed that Flint had given in so easily, Jerk considered raving anyway, but the others were already digging, and he was loath to pass up an opportunity to flex his muscles.

Laughing silently, Flint watched them toil. "Never mind the picks and shovels. Robby will do the work. Meanwhile, you can come relax at my bachelor pad; here, hop in the Maserati."

Arman's little "bachelor pad" was vast and overdecorated, and had obviously cost a dictator's ransom in Intersellar Beans. The spacemen craned their necks, gawking at the many wonders, nearly crashing into several fragile-looking Santa Claus mugs on a simulated woodgrain stand.

"Make yourselves at home," sneered Arman, backing out of the room, lowering a huge bar across the door, activating an electrically charged wire fence, and posting an armed guard at the window.

"Should we'all trust 'im?" wondered McClown.

Jerk looked up from a Naugahyde-bound volume of *True Confessions*. "I don't see why not, Bozo. If he doesn't show up with the Ritalin by the time we've killed this case of brandy, we'll go get it ourselves."

Recognizing an opportunity to steal a scene, Schmuck left the paintings he had been studying and hurried over to his companions. "This is without a doubt and beyond all possible shred of incrimination one of the most unusual and least expected collections of the art form known to you as 'painting' that I, in my travels throughout the galaxy, have ever had the immense privilege of scrutinizing at close range." Shaking the sleeping McClown, he continued, "Most of the work seems to be that of three men: Fakerino of the sixteenth century, Anonymous of the twentieth, and Swipo, of Marcuswelby II."

"Big deal," growled McClown. "This heah is Serium brandy an' Ah aim t' make it an integral part of my ecosystem. Jimbo, y'all want some? I know Schmuck doan' drink."

The Vulgarian snatched up a bottle, uncorked it, and drained the entire contents at a gulp.

"Lordy," groaned the doctor, "kin the two of us handle a Vulgarian with a snootful?"

"I hardly think that this minuscule amount constitutes a snootful, as you so archaically put it. However, I am forced by the circumstances at hand to admit that I am very close to feeling a totally unaccustomed emotion."

"Ah'll drink to that," said McClown. "Which emotion?"

"Greed, doctor. None of these Anonymousi have been cat-alogued, yet according to my vast and thoroughly superior knowledge of the subject of art, all are quite authentic, down to the last fluffy dachshund. If they are indeed undiscovered Anonymousi, they are worth a very large bundle."

"Maybe they're fakes," mused Jerk, gazing at a particularly bizarre rendering of a doggy poker game.

"Why would a man as filthy rich as Flint hang fakes?" de-manded the doctor.

"The real ones are in the vault?" suggested Jerk.

At that moment Flint entered with Robby, who dumped an armload of Ritalin ampules on the table and stood blinking industriously.

"I regret my earlier haste in diagnosing you as souvenir hunters. Allow me to extend my hospitality." Flint gestured toward an ostentatious flight of stairs. Jerk's jaw flew open.

At the top of the steps appeared a rather overstuffed speci-men of feminine pulchritude, who jiggled and bounced de-lightfully as she descended. Jerk made a move toward her, but Schmuck deftly applied a half-nelson to his overeager captain. "But you heard what Flint said," whined Jerk.

"Ah thought y'all lived alone," beamed McClown.

"This is Raining Kopeks, my legal ward. I found her on my doorstep in a basket when she was but a baby."

"And seeing that she has since grown to such admirable proportions, all in all not a bad deal," muttered Schmuck.

Hearing him mumble, the girl undulated forward. "Mr. Schmuck, I do hope we will find the time to discuss the chronosynclastic infandibulum and its relationship to the tur-boincabulator ingatron phenomenon."

"If you have the dime, I have the time," answered the alien, valiantly struggling against the elbow Jerk was shoving into his ribs.

Flint sighed. "Yes, it certainly is a shame that she was or-phaned at the age of twelve when her parents were killed in a roller derby."

"Tell me, Raining," said Jerk, breaking one or two bones in Schmuck's left foot, "what else interests you besides the ingatron ignition phenomenon?" He winked broadly.

"All knowledge," she said. "Anything less is betrayal of in-tellect."

"There's more to life than knowledge," said Jerk with a wiggle of an eyebrow.

Flint squeezed between Jerk and the girl. "Raining possesses the equivalent of eighty-seven university degrees." He looked Jerk in the eye. "She is aware that although the intellect is not all, knowledge often prevents one from *making a fool of oneself*, if you catch my meaning."

"Flint taught me," simpered Raining. "You are the first other humans I have ever seen."

"Yes, it is indeed a sad story how I found her in the woods at the age of five, running with a wolfpack," said Flint, crossing his fingers. "Now, doctor, if you care to accompany my loyal albeit not too bright robot, you can finish collecting the Ritalin." As McClown followed the beeping Robby, Flint turned back to Jerk. "And you, sir? What will be your pleasure? Chess? Backgammon? Parcheesi?"

Schmuck's elbow snapped Jerk back to reality. With a challenging look at Raining, he said, "How about checkers?"

Checkers had always been difficult for him, and Raining was a grand master. Jerk had just crowned her for the fifth time when Flint came over to gloat.

Seeing that all this nonsense was drawing attention away from him, Schmuck looked about for a diversion. In one corner of the room was a rhinestone-encrusted piano, upon which rested a candelabra. Schmuck walked to the piano and idly leafed through some sheet music on its music stand.

Jerk, seeing through this ruse, embarked on some scenery-chewing. He rose slowly, pacing the room. "Greed is everywhere. It exists in all places, from the basement up to the stars . . . those tiny points of light up there . . . to be human is to be avaricious. We were never meant to live in paradise. We would then cease to exist. What is reality but dogs eating dogs across the sands of time?"

As Flint and Raining exchanged puzzled glances, Schmuck began playing the piano *fortissimo*.

"I haven't the slightest idea what you're talking about, captain, but it sounds depressing," shouted Flint. "But as long as Mr. Schmuck seems intent on making a racket, you should see that Raining is an accomplished dancer as well."

Just as things were getting interesting, McClown barged gracelessly in. Schmuck left the piano at once, but Jerk continued to drag Raining about until the doctor tripped him.

"Th' Ritalin's no darn good," he whined. "It's got large amounts of vitamin C in it, which is nice, but which renders it totally useless fo' owah purpose."

"Stupid robot," hissed Flint. He kicked the blinking tin can toward the lab, a muttering McClown in tow.

"Funny that Robby should have made such a 'mistake," said Jerk.

"Something else could also be described as 'humorous,' sir. The fox-trot I have just played is by Liberace. It is also unknown. But it is in Liberace's own hand, which my undeniable genius of course had no difficulty recognizing. It is unquestionably the work of Liberace, but it is totally unknown. Also, the ink is still wet."

"Meaningless," snapped Jerk. Where had Raining disappeared to? "See you later," he said to Schmuck, and set off to find her, delicious visions dancing in his head.

The halls of Flint's abode were decorated with many strange and wonderful things—paintings on black velvet, plaster statues of saints and sports heroes, crowded knickknack shelves—and Jerk was craning his neck to get a better view of these when he collided with Raining.

Alas, she appeared troubled, her eyes slightly crossed. Jerk looked deep into her nose and said, "You went away and I became a television show dying for lack of Neilsons." Hoping that this mumbo-jumbo would catch her unaware, he tried for a quick kiss. Failing, he pointed to a door. "What lies beyond there?"

As she looked, he took advantage of her concentration to nibble her ear. "I do not know," she said, unaware of his lips on her ear. "Flint has said I must not enter that room."

Probably keeps all his money there, thought Jerk. "Then why have you come here?"

"I . . . I am not sure. I come here when I am troubled in mind."

"Are you troubled now, Raining?"

"Yes," she answered, foggy-eyed.

"By what, Raining?"

She looked at Jerk's hands, which had somehow become entwined about her waist, and frowned, searching for an answer. Encouraged, Jerk pressed his luck (also his attack) and asked, "Are you happy here with Flint?"

"He is very kind and wise," she said slowly.

Also very rich, thought Jerk. "Yet you are upset," he continued aloud, trying desperately to come up with a good line. "Come with me, Raining. Come to a place where there is hope and life. Come with me to the stars . . . those tiny points of light up there. . . . Do you know love?" He wound to a stop, out of clichés for the moment, and cunningly reached for her.

"Oh, dear!" she gasped, looking over his shoulder in wide-eyed horror.

Jerk turned reluctantly, coming face to face with an angry Robby, its Christmas-tree lights working overtime. It moved swiftly, but Jerk was even quicker, ducking behind the girl like lightning. Robby ignored her, singlemindedly pursuing Jerk. He ran, but it clung to him like a bad grade of peanut butter.

Wait! He still had his fizzler! Hurredly whipping it out, he fired at the enraged tin goon. Nothing. Rats, he thought, why do we even bother with these duds?

Robby had him cornered now. Sparks shot ominously at his feet.

It was at this precise moment that Schmuck, more concerned with building dramatic tension than with his captain's life, leaped from behind a plaster statue and fired his own fizzler. Robby disintegrated gracefully. Jerk contemplated apoplexy.

"Fortunately, the writer was too concerned with your rather harrowing situation to deactivate my fizzler too," said the smug Vulgarian.

Before Jerk could throttle his first officer, Raining jiggled away, leaving them to follow a trail of Evening in Paris back to the central room.

Pacing, snarling, cross-eyed, his lower teeth showing in a painful grimace, Jerk confronted Flint. "That overgrown Tinker Toy of yours nearly wasted me! If Mr. Schmuck (who if he waits that long next time will be demoted to janitor second class) hadn't destroyed Robby, he would have been wearing my uniform!" He threw the alien a dismembering glare.

"Now, captain, I'm sure you're overreacting. I programmed Robby to repel all invaders. Apparently, it thought you were attacking Raining."

How right it was, thought Schmuck.

Advancing on the obviously much-older Flint with intent

to do damage, Jerk spat, "Your mechanized flunky isn't here to save you this time."

In return, Flint made a casual gesture, and through the door floated another Robby, an exact duplicate of the first, right down to the huge key protruding from its back. Jerk veered off, hemming and hawing. "I was only testing you, anyway," he sulked.

"It is well that you did not choose to fight, for I could beat you up with one hand tied behind my back." Flint turned to Raining. "You see what a chicken he is?"

Raining appeared to be trying to solve an immensely complex equation. "I am glad that he was not offed," she said at length.

Flint looked disappointed. "Oh well," he said, "at any rate your Ritalin is ready. This time it is without vitamin C, and all of you had best keep your hands in your pockets, lest Robby misinterpret your motives." Flinging a raspberry at Jerk, he left, dragging Raining behind him. Schmuck was once again forced to apply a wrestling hold to the captain, ere he grabbed the passing girl.

"Let me go, Schmuck! Can't you see it's me she wants, not that dried-out, desiccated, wrinkled . . ."

"Rich . . ."

". . . dirty old man . . ." He halted with a sob.

"Captain, since we are once again helpless and dependent on Flint to come through with the desperately needed Ritalin, I respectfully suggest that you refrain from pawing the young lady should your paths cross again. It seems that despite his outwardly decrepit appearance, our friend is not solely interested in Raining's mind."

"Schmuck, you mean . . .?"

"That you are not the only one around here who has to take cold showers? Precisely."

For lack of something better to do, Jerk drew out his Tom Corbett walkie-talkie and hailed the ship. He heard snores and a muffled yawn as Engineer Spot answered his call.

"Spot? Here, Spot. C'mon, boy."

"Noch, brouch, mckennough, schenectady," came Spot's voice from the speaker.

"My God," said Jerk. "Practically everyone on board asleep? What about that pocket calculator check on Flint?"

"Loch murch grech vas deferens."

"Hmmm, no record of his past, eh? Spotty, run a check on Raining Kopeks and report back to me. Jerk out."

"If I might be permitted to speak," ventured Schmuck.

"You will anyway, so go ahead."

"Well, I am certain that what I am about to say has nothing whatever to do with our dilemma . . ."

"Then why say it?"

". . . nonetheless, I feel the information might be useful to store in our memory banks for future reference. I, in my infinite genius, was able to obtain a quadcorder reading of Flint while you were engaged in linguistic battle. Since I never make an error, we must assume that the following is true: Arman Flint is a great deal older than he appears."

"I knew it!" crowed Jerk. "Plastic surgery? Health spas? Vitamin E?"

"As I was about to say, and in the event that certain people unsatisfied with the amount of their fan mail will allow me to continue, the age indicated by my readings is far greater than what you are undoubtedly mistakenly imagining. I would say, as a rough estimate, that our host has lived somewhere between 6000.2375 and 6000.3047 years. However, I would not consider that pertinent data, any more than the fact that he has no past that could be considered as such."

"I suppose not, Schmuck." The walkie-talkie quacked tiredly. "Jerk here. What is it, Spotty?"

"Doohan nocher richter a wulla sochus."

"I see. No record of her either." He snapped the device off. "Raining and Flint . . . people without a past . . . held together by what sinister and dark design, and to what evil end? Something very strange is going on here."

"Perhaps for tax purposes . . ." suggested Schmuck.

"That's it," agreed Jerk, not feeling up to dramatics anyway. He rose and paced a few steps. Much to his delight, he again collided with Raining. Bodily removing the protesting Schmuck from the premises, he turned to her.

"I have come to bid you farewell," she said hazily.

"I don't want to say farewell."

"I am glad that Robby did not charcoal-grill you."

So am I, thought Jerk. He grasped her by the waist. "Now I know what it is I have lived for," he lied, hoping to maneuver her to the couch. She seemed innocent, unsure, but there was an underlying sense of urgency in her actions, as if she had eaten something that did not agree with her, and could not locate the Alka-Seltzer.

"My place . . ." she began.

"Or yours?" he was quick to interject.

"My place is . . ." she continued.

"Where I am," countered Jerk, switching hands.

". . . here . . ." she said.

"Where?" said Jerk, always willing to be helpful.

"There."

"Who?"

"What?"

"Hah?"

She was silent for a long time. Then, slowly coming to the realization that she was confused, she broke free of his hands and ran off.

Jerk started after her, soon becoming hopelessly lost. He wound up at the lab, where Schmuck and McClown stood throwing Petri dishes at one another.

Seeing him, McClown began to pale. "Flint hid the Ritalin! If we doan' get it soon, we'll all be in a lot of trouble, 'cause everyone on board is gonna be asleep, and there'll be no one t' beam us up!"

"*However*," said Schmuck above the screaming doctor, "If the chief surgeon will cease his incredibly voluble hysterics, I will endeavor to uncover the hidden substance by tracking it with my quadcorder." He made an expansive hand gesture. "Nothing up my sleeve . . . no mirrors . . . the hand is quicker than the eye . . ."

"Get on with it," snapped Jerk, a bit crankily.

Miffed, Schmuck moved his device about. The little green light on top blinked: COLD . . . COLDER . . . GETTING WARM . . . HOT . . . TILT!

They had come to a door in the corridor.

"The very same door that Raining is forbidden to enter," mused Jerk. "We may not have found the Ritalin, but we've probably stumbled onto a big hoard of cash." He was nearly trampled by Schmuck and McClown in their rush to get some of the pickings.

To their surprise, the Ritalin was there, on a table labeled "Bait." But, alas, there was no gold, silver, Confederate notes, trading stamps, or anything else remotely suggesting a new

Ferrari each year and a condo on the Riviera. Abruptly for-
getting the plague aboard ship, they wandered about the
room in case there was some gold dust they had managed to
overlook. In his concentration, Jerk nearly fell over a draped
figure on a table, labeled "Raining #17."

Probably some plaster statue, he thought, still intent on the
hoped-for cash stash. It was Schmuck who drew his attention
to it, and the sixteen other draped figures around the room.
Pulling back the sheet, Jerk exposed a figure that bore a remarkable resemblance to the Raining they knew. Thinking it
was she, defenselessly asleep, he lunged, but Flint's voice
stopped him dead.

"Oh no, you don't, you pervert. Ownership rights and all
that." He strode over and drew the sheet back over Raining
#17.

McClown waved one of his salt shakers over the form.
"Physically human . . . yet not human. Jes' like some others
I could name," he said, sticking his tongue out at Schmuck,
who responded with the ancient Vulgarian thumb-on-nose-
and-waggling-fingers salute.

"Oh, I get it," said Jerk suddenly. "She's a robot."

"Yeah, and all mine, too," snapped Flint. "So kindly keep
your hands to yourself the next time she jiggles onto the horizon."

"But I don't understand," Jerk (being even more dense
than usual) said.

"I created her out of a pile of army surplus nuts and bolts.
The centuries of loneliness and my own cooking were to end
with her."

"Centuries?" asked McClown.

Bored with the incredible stupidity of his companions,
Schmuck, who had himself only just now caught on, said,
"Your collection of Fakerinos . . . your Liberace manu-
scripts . . ."

"Yes," said Flint, cutting short Schmuck's long-sought
dramatic revelations. "I am both Fakerino and Liberace."

"And who else, might I ask?" asked Schmuck, trying to regain lost ground.

"Let me see . . . do the names Shakespeare, Da Vinci,
Beethoven, and Lincoln mean anything to you?"

"Indeed they do."

"Well, I was none of them. However, I was Primo Carnera, P. T. Barnum, and Colonel Sanders. And I did meet Albert Shanker's housekeeper once."

"Then you were born . . ."

"In Secaucus, New Jersey. I was a loan shark. One day I ran afoul of the local syndicate. I fell to the ground, decapitated, but I soon grew a new head. I also grew to realize that I had a good deal going there."

"A freak," said McClown, drawing on his vast knowledge of interplanetary medicine. "You weren't Tod Browning too, by any chance?"

"You learned you were immortal," said Jerk enviously.

"Yes, and able to sell the public a defective bill of goods many times over, which is how I built up my vast empire. I knew the greatest hacks in history: gossip columnists, press agents, politicians. But I grew weary of groupies, and retired to this planet and built Raining—after a few false starts. She is the perfect woman, captain—no wonder you drooled all over yourself when you saw her. Well, all I can say is tough darts, she belongs to me."

"Does she know she's merely the reincarnation of a World War II radio set?" asked Jerk.

"Does she look as if she knows that two and two are four?"

"I imagine not." Visions of connubial bliss with Raining sprouted wings and flew the coop of Jerk's mind. "Let's get out of here, Schmuck. I suddenly remembered there's a crisis aboard the *Enteritis*."

"And just where do you think you're going?" sneered Flint.

"Back to the ship. Who wants to know?"

"You must be more stupid than you look to think I'd let you go now. The minute you get back you'd set up a tourist trap with me as the main attraction."

"We could give you a cut," suggested Schmuck.

"Two can play at this game," cried the recluse. "Behold! A little trick I learned from a wizard at King Arthur's court." He produced a battered wand and waved it in the air, muttering, "Hocus, pocus, who's got the crocus?" Miraculously, a copy of the *Enteritis* appeared from nowhere, suspended by kitchen twine. Flint took a vial labeled "Magic Powder" and sprinkled some on the effigy.

As the spacemen watched in horror, the *Enteritis* became a

plastic model kit, complete with easy-to-follow instructions, colorful enamel, and paste-on decals!

Flint thumbed his nose at them. "Yes, captain. Once I sell this to some avid Trekkie, your fate is sealed!"

"No!" lisped a familiar voice. They turned to face Raining, who had wandered aimlessly in because Flint had carelessly left the door open.

"Whoops!" he said.

"This is very naughty of you," she reprimanded, as Flint tried to position himself in front of the dummy on the slab.

"I must do it," he said.

"I'll never play checkers with you again," she threatened. Recognizing an ideal time to add to the confusion, Jerk began one of his long-winded speeches.

"She loves me, not you, Flint! Come away from all this, Raining, and we shall be as two Forsythium crystals shining brilliantly into the darkness that always lies just before the dawn. Every cloud has its silver lining, and we shall walk through the storm with our heads held high. We're not afraid of the dark, are we? Do you not know Love? The time has come for man to reach out to the tree of knowledge and pluck the fruit of a victory! Too long have we been living a lie! We will wander through eternity, happy together, no matter what the weather! Give me back my ship, Flint!"

"Anything to shut you up. Here."

Grasping the girl firmly by the shoulders, Jerk looked deep into her slightly crossed eyes and said, "You do love me, Raining, even though you are only a robot?"

Flint cast his gaze helplessly upward and gave forth a mighty sigh.

"I . . . only . . . a robot?" faltered the hopelessly confused Raining, as Flint snatched her from Jerk's grasp.

"*No*! You love me!" roared the wealthy old hack.

Not to be outdone, Jerk yanked her away. Breathing into her left eye, he intoned, "Those stars . . . those tiny points of light out there . . ."

Enraged, Flint shoved Raining onto the floor and dealt Jerk a vicious Indian burn. "She's mine, you little git!"

"No she isn't! She loves me, you old fake! I'm younger and prettier!"

Raining hauled herself upright with the aid of a table. Schmuck and McClown were oblivious to her plight, having already made bets on the outcome of the fight, and watching it intently.

"You *twit!*" yelled Flint.

"*Pinhead!*" retaliated Jerk.

Raining watched with increasing consternation. "No!" she cried. "I . . . was not . . . human . . . now, I think . . . therefore, I . . ."

"*She's human!*" roared Jerk, so deafeningly that Schmuck and the others fell to the floor. He leaped into the air, capering about like a demented baboon, and dropped to one knee in yet another tirade. "Since the dawn of time, man has struggled to be human . . . to think, to hope, *to feel*! We are not cabbages to be sent to market! We must all strive to be human, lest we cease to exist! And the essence of humanity is love! Do you not know love, Raining? You love me, not Flint, don't you, toots?"

"Raining, I'm richer than he is," countered Flint. "Could he buy you a mobile home, a water bed, and a solid gold statue of Alfred E. Neuman?"

In the heat of battle, neither man noticed that her eyes were crossing and uncrossing with alarming regularity. She took a hesitant step toward one, then the other. "I think . . . therefore, therefore . . ."

She collapsed in a heap. Schmuck pointed his quadcorder at her and shook his head.

"The excitement was too much for her. She blew a capacitor."

Flint shrugged. "Oh, well, back to the drafting table."

Witnessing the cruel fate of his beloved severed the last of Jerk's self-control. His subsequent overacting fit forced the others to stuff him in a large refuse container in order to carry him back to the ship.

Much later, the Ritalin had taken effect and things were back to normal: Fully one-third of the crew was awake and on the job.

In his lonely cabin, Jerk was morosely fondling a regulation NFL football when Schmuck entered with some useless data. The captain looked up. "Schmuck . . . if only I could forget her."

"Sir, may I suggest any one of the following: a course in self-hypnosis, taught by a fully qualified instructor, designed for easy assimilation by the amateur; a slight overindulgence of some of the more exotic liqueurs in that secret cabinet under your bunk that you think nobody knows about; or three rounds with . . ." He was interrupted by loud snores from Jerk.

McClown burst in, babbling as was his wont. "Jimbo, Ah've made a discovery. Flint is headed fo' th' last roundup soon. . . . Oh, he's asleep. Ah mighta know'd y'all could do that in a minute flat," he said to Schmuck.

"What was that about Flint, doctor?"

"Lak Ah said, he's finally dyin'."

"I see. You mean that in leaving the Earth's complex magnetic fields, in which he was formed and with which he lived in perfect balance, he sacrificed his immortality?"

"No, Ah mean Ah poisoned his brandy." He looked at Jerk, who had begun drooling onto his sleeve. "He's dreamin' of her again. Ah shoah do wish he could fergit her. Ah realize that y'all will nevah know th' agony an' ecstasy of love, 'cause your glands is funny. But jess th' same, Ah wish he'd fergit." With a final disgusted look at the alien, McClown turned and left.

Schmuck studied the sleeping captain. Should he? Could he do this noble deed? Yes. He would.

He tiptoed to the door, locking it. Rubbing his hands together, he turned back to Jerk. Long, sensitive alien fingers eased up the captain's nose, and a look of intense concentration formed on Schmuck's face as he began the ancient Vulgarian mind-sync.

"Forget, captain," he whispered. "Forget . . . forget that fiver I owe you. Forget that slight mistake I made plotting the course last month, which nearly resulted in all our deaths. Forget those holograms you have of me in that cheap motel on Donalduckus IV. . . . Forget . . ."

About the Editors

Although largely unknown to readers not involved in Star Trek fandom before the publication of *The Best of Trek #1*, WALTER IRWIN and G. B. LOVE have been actively editing and publishing magazines for many years. Before they teamed up to create TREK® in 1975, Irwin worked in newspapers, advertising, and free-lance writing, while Love published *The Rocket's Blast—Comiccollector* from 1960 to 1974, as well as hundreds of other magazines, books, and collectables. Both together and separately, they are currently planning several new books and magazines, as well as continuing to publish TREK.